THE ART OF SURRENDER

'Now I'm going to whip you. You can scream and struggle as much as you like because I've had the foresight to ensure that my playroom is thoroughly soundproofed. So feel free to express yourself. To tell you the truth, I find the sound of a man in pain rather arousing. Sooner or later, I'll want to come. The more I hurt you the hornier I'll get. Eventually, my cunt will be so wet that it drips down my thighs.' She stroked his bollocks with a fingernail, making him wriggle and buck.

'Once or twice I've almost reached orgasm while whipping someone; all it took was a little touch from a willing tongue to tip me over the edge. I bet you'd like to do that, wouldn't you, Michael? You'd like to press your tongue against my crack, suck on my clit and make me come in your mouth?' Her fingernail traced up the length of his crack and circled his hole.

'Yes!'

D1638807

THE ART OF SURRENDER

Madeline Bastinado

This book is a work of fiction.
In real life, make sure you practise safe, sane and
consensual sex.

First published in 2005 by
Nexus
Thames Wharf Studios
Rainville Road
London W6 9HA

Copyright © Madeline Bastinado 2005

The right of Madeline Bastinado to be identified as the
Author of this Work has been asserted by her in
accordance with the Copyright, Designs and Patents Act
1988.

www.nexus-books.co.uk

Typeset by TW Typesetting, Plymouth, Devon

Printed and bound by
CPI Antony Rowe, Chippenham, Wiltshire

ISBN 978 0 352 34013 9

*All characters in this publication are fictitious and any
resemblance to real persons, living or dead, is purely
coincidental.*

This book is sold subject to the condition that it shall not,
by way of trade or otherwise, be lent, resold, hired out or
otherwise circulated without the publisher's prior written
consent in any form of binding or cover other than that in
which it is published and without a similar condition
including this condition being imposed on the subsequent
purchaser.

To David Read
For loving me

You'll notice that we have introduced a set of symbols onto our book jackets, so that you can tell at a glance what fetishes each of our brand new novels contains. Here's the key – enjoy!

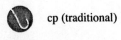 cp (traditional)

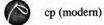 cp (modern)

 spanking

 restraint/bondage

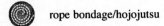 rope bondage/hojojutsu

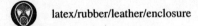 latex/rubber/leather/enclosure

 fem dom

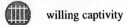 willing captivity

 medical

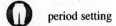 period setting

 uniforms

 sex rituals

One

Jude walked into the darkroom and stood still to get her bearings. It was pitch-black. She could sense other people but she couldn't see them. The sound of a woman's excited breathing seemed the only tangible presence in the small space. It made her shiver.

Gradually, her eyes grew accustomed to the darkness. She'd expected seats, like in a cinema, but the room was empty of furniture, the walls blank. A couple kissed in a corner. Other than them, she was alone with the soundtrack filling the space. She found the recording arousing. It seemed to get under her skin.

She could hear a young woman's breathing. It was ragged and loud. Every so often she moaned and the hair on the back of Jude's neck stood up.

'Doesn't that feel good? You want more?' The man's voice was barely a whisper. It was the sexiest sound she had ever heard.

'I said, do you want more?' This time the voice was loud and demanding. It was immediately followed by a loud cracking sound like the impact of a cane or crop. A bright flash and an image appeared on the blank wall.

Jude held her breath. There were five more cracks, each accompanied by a brief image on the wall. A close-up of a female arse, hands cuffed behind, creamy thighs and black stocking tops. A plump pussy. A riding crop whipped her upturned buttocks in rhythm with the sound. Each time the image appeared there was a new crimson stripe.

The woman's breathing grew more frantic. It filled the room, invading Jude's senses. Her armpits prickled with sweat.

'Please! Please!' Her voice was quiet and imploring. Jude could hear the hunger in it.

'Please what? Tell me what you want.'

'You know what I want. Please!'

'I said, tell me what you want. Make me believe you want it.'

The woman started sobbing quietly. Jude knew she was struggling to accept her need, her shame and his power over her. She'd give in; it was inevitable. She'd obey him, then she'd understand the meaning of submission.

'Please, Master. I want you to hurt me.'

'And I will.'

The breathing grew louder and she began to moan. The moan became a roar and an image flashed onto the wall of a woman's torso. Ropes circled her breasts. Metal clamps were attached to each nipple, connected by a chain. A man's hand tugged hard on the chain.

The roaring stopped and the picture vanished. There was a moment of silence before the woman on the soundtrack began panting hard, sobbing and whimpering. When these cries became moans the image reappeared. This time the nipple chain was wound round the man's hand and he was pulling so hard it bit into his flesh. The clamps gripped her nipples mercilessly, stretching them.

She howled and Jude could imagine the tears staining her cheeks, the sweat-dampened hair clinging to her face and the taste of salt in her mouth. The couple in the corner were fondling each other now, hands groping inside clothes, totally absorbed in their own lust. Jude's own nipples ached.

2

She let herself out of the room. The light hurt her eyes and she leaned for a moment against the wall until they adjusted. She looked around the gallery. People clustered around each exhibit. A drunken man she recognised as a famous critic stood looking up at a huge marble sculpture of an erect phallus.

Jude got a glass of champagne and walked over to the buffet. She felt a tap on her shoulder.

'You've obviously just come out of the darkroom. What did you think?' Jude turned round to look at her friend, Dee Kane.

'Hello, Dee. Great opening night. I can tell you've worked really hard. How did you know I'd been in there?'

'Because you're breathing like a steam train and you've got that cute little flush on your throat you always get when you're turned on.'

'Shit, do you think anyone else has noticed?' Her eyes scanned the room.

'Only if they've been to bed with you and know the signs as intimately as I do.' She leaned close and blew on Jude's neck. 'Are there many people here who qualify?' She checked nobody was looking then nibbled Jude's earlobe.

'Probably less than you'd imagine but more than you'd think.'

Dee laughed. 'But what did you think of the darkroom? I mean, I know it turned you on, but . . .'

'Is it art?'

'Exactly. You know I always try to showcase controversial artists. What do you think of Michael Read's work?'

'It's a fabulous show, Dee, and I notice you've made quite a few sales. It's interesting. I love the way he uses mixed media, even embellishing photographic images with pigment and texture. And some of the sculptures are wonderfully tactile.'

'And what do you think of the subject matter?' Dee took a sip of her champagne. 'I'd have thought that was right up your street.'

'As I said, interesting. An entire show composed of images of bondage and sadism is certainly very provocative. It's dark and edgy and atmospheric. I like the one where a loop of film showing a woman's face twisted in pain is projected onto the sculpture of a man's torso.'

'Is she in pain? I thought she looked as though she was on the point of orgasm?'

'Maybe she was. Maybe both. That's part of the point, I think. But some of it – the darkroom for example – well, I think it's just designed to shock. Or worse, to arouse.'

'What have you got against being aroused?' asked a masculine voice.

Jude looked round at a tall, handsome man with chestnut hair and deep, brown eyes that seemed to stare into her soul.

'Jude, this is Michael Read. Michael, this is my friend –'

'Jude Ryan, of course,' he interrupted. 'I'm a great fan of your work. I'm anxious to know whether you might become a fan of mine.'

They shook hands.

'Well, as I was just telling Dee, it's certainly provocative.'

'And arousing, I think I heard you say. I hope you aren't one of those people who believe that art has to be dry and worthy. After all, isn't it the duty of the artist to stimulate the senses as well as the intellect?'

'Well, yours certainly succeeds on that score. There were a couple in the darkroom who appreciated your work so much they felt compelled to put on a little exhibition of their own.'

'I assure you, I take that as a compliment. But let me refill your glass. Ten minutes in the darkroom has obviously made you very . . . thirsty.' He took her glass. 'Dee? Another for you?'

Dee shook her head. 'No thank you, Michael, I've got to circulate and supervise, I'm afraid. There are more than a few guests who might scratch each other's eyes out if I don't keep them apart. I'm glad you were able to come, Jude. See you soon.' She kissed her friend on the cheek. 'Bye, Michael.'

They watched Dee walk away, her tight, short, black dress straining across her ample rear as she moved.

'She is gorgeous, isn't she,' said Michael. 'I can't tell you what a bonus it is dealing with a gallery owner who's such a work of art herself. It makes the whole thing so much more interesting, don't you think?'

'Yes, she's quite lovely. Dee and I are old friends.'

'Yes, I did notice that you appeared to be on . . . intimate terms. And it's common knowledge that Dee Kane prefers girls.'

'What are you implying?'

'I don't know.' Michael leaned close and whispered, 'Is there anything to imply?'

'Perhaps. But I never kiss and tell. It's your voice on the tape, isn't it? In the darkroom. I recognised it when you spoke really quietly just now.'

'Yes, it is me. Some people have been kind enough to tell me that I have quite a sexy voice. What do you think?'

She looked at him for a long moment. 'Well, it certainly seems to have an effect.'

'Really? I am flattered – honoured even.' He gave an exaggerated bow.

'Tell me something, Michael, I'm curious. Why are there no images of submissive men in your work? Why is it only women on the receiving end?'

'Well, you know what they say. Art reflects life.'

Jude leaned in confidentially. She could smell Michael's aftershave and, behind it, another more

5

natural, masculine note. 'So, in other words, you enjoy dominating women so you use their images in your art?'

'Do you find that a problem? I wouldn't have thought you'd object to a little kink. You are famous for your sexually explicit paintings and sculptures, after all.'

'No, I certainly don't object to a little healthy kink. In fact, my heart always quickens a little when I meet a kindred soul. It's just that, well, you seem like a man who enjoys exploring the dark side. I just wondered if you'd ever . . .' she rotated her finger in mid-air, 'turned the tables.'

'What do you mean? Have I been on the receiving end of the crop instead of wielding it?'

'Yes. So, have you?'

He shook his head. 'No, never. I haven't.'

'But would you?' She took a step closer and placed her mouth millimetres from his ear. 'Have you fantasised about it? Ever wondered what it's like to completely let go, to totally relinquish control to a truly powerful woman? Ever wanted to taste the lash? Are you telling me that you've never wanted to experience total surrender?'

'It's never even crossed my mind. I really don't think it's my thing.'

'You might be surprised what you can learn to enjoy if you just give it a try.'

He shook his head. 'I'm afraid I've never even been tempted. Sorry if that disappoints you.'

'Not at all. But perhaps you're just not certain that you're man enough?' She looked into his eyes.

'Or alternatively, I've just never met anyone who was woman enough. And I've certainly never met a woman who wasn't prepared to obey me. Eventually.' He spoke quietly, using the same tone as Jude had heard in the darkroom. She felt her nipples hardening.

'Is that a challenge, Mr Read?'

'Perhaps. Are you saying you think you'd be able to resist me?'

6

'Well, if you ever want to find out, give me a call.' She found a pen in her handbag, scribbled her phone number on her copy of the catalogue and handed it to him.

She walked away.

'Thanks for helping me clear up, Jude. It's times like this that I miss Sadie. She's such an efficient manager, I've had to work twice as hard since she went to help out at the New York office.' Dee turned out the lights in the gallery and they stepped into the street. 'I swear the critic from the *Clarion* would have stayed all night if you hadn't announced the bar was closed.' She locked the door.

'No problem. I'm always glad to help. Especially if my assistance puts you in a generous mood.'

'Aren't I always generous where you're concerned?'

'You are, but I just wondered if you might feel in the mood for a little reciprocation. After all, you must be missing Sadie pretty badly by now.' She smiled.

'You need to ask?' Dee's voice was low and throaty.

'You might have a naked man strapped to the dining-room table desperate for a good rogering for all I know.'

Dee shook her head. 'Not on Fridays, the cleaner comes. She'd be scandalised to discover how reckless I am with her lovingly polished surfaces.'

'Reckless; I like that in a woman. Your place, I assume? It's much closer than mine. I could have you naked in five minutes' time.'

'If we walk quickly, we can make it three.'

Dee's house was a few streets away from the gallery. It was a tall, narrow building with high ceilings and neoclassical mouldings. It was furnished in an elegant uncluttered style and decorated with pieces from the gallery.

Jude took off her coat in the living room and draped it over the back of a chair.

'Is that piece new? The sculpture in the fireplace?' she called to Dee, who'd gone into the kitchen for some champagne.

'Yes.' Dee briefly stuck her head around the door. 'It's from the show I did last month. It's lovely, isn't it?'

'It is. Lovely lines.' She knelt by the sculpture and touched it. 'It's marble. If you close your eyes it almost feels like skin.'

Dee came out of the kitchen carrying a bottle of champagne and two glasses. 'You look lovely on your knees. Shall we go upstairs?'

Jude followed Dee up the staircase. The bedroom was dominated by a huge female nude over the bed. It was Jude's work and it had always been one of her particular favourites. Dee had bought it at Jude's first big exhibition and the two of them had become friends.

Dee sat on the edge of the bed and Jude went over to the window to close the curtains. She took off her shoes.

'I bet you even wear those "fuck-me" shoes in the supermarket, don't you?' Dee was smiling at her.

'Absolutely. My feet are so used to them that they ache like mad if I wear flatties. Anyway, I like being able to tower over men. It gives me a sense of power.' She unzipped her dress.

'You're five foot ten, you'd tower over most people in your stockinged feet.'

'That might be true. But there's something about stiletto heels that make men go quite weak at the knees.'

'And weak at the knees is just how you prefer your men . . .'

'It's always a good start.' She stepped out of her dress and stood in front of Dee in a black silk thong and fishnet stockings. She walked over to the bed and picked up a glass of champagne. She took a sip. 'Mmm, I adore champagne. You know what they say about good bubbly, don't you?'

Dee shook her head. Jude leaned forward and whispered in her ear. 'It's like drinking stars.' She took a mouthful of champagne, then lifted Dee's chin. Dee parted her lips, ready to be kissed and Jude slowly dripped the champagne into her mouth.

'One of us is a bit overdressed, don't you think?' Jude pulled her friend to her feet and began to undress her. She unzipped Dee's tight black dress and slid it down. Underneath she was wearing a boned satin corset the colour of an aubergine. Frothy lace panties peeked out at the bottom and her ample breasts almost spilled over the top. A band of plump thigh was visible above black lace stocking tops.

'Well, you're a dark horse, darling. You look like a Christmas present waiting to be unwrapped.' Jude began unhooking the corset. When she reached the bottom she tossed it aside and slid her fingers under the top of Dee's tiny panties. She pulled them down and Dee lifted her bottom off the bed. Jude removed them and lifted them to her face. She inhaled.

'Nectar,' she said, 'I can tell Mr Read's work affected you too.'

'Guilty as charged. But the question is, what are you going to do about it?' Dee cupped the back of Jude's head. She stroked her cheek with one finger then kissed her. Dee's mouth was hot and wet and silky and reminded Jude of something else she desperately longed to kiss.

She sat back on her heels and slowly removed one of Dee's stockings. 'Get on the bed. Raise your hands above your head. Yes, that's it.' She tied one end of the stocking around Dee's wrists and the other to the rails of the brass bed. She spread Dee's legs apart and quickly removed the other stocking and tied her left ankle to the bottom of the bed. She took off her own stockings and secured Dee's other leg.

'One stocking left,' she said, 'what shall I do with it?' She picked up Dee's discarded panties and pushed them into her mouth. She tied the last stocking round her face, holding the panties in place.

Dee was small and blonde and her breasts were disproportionately large. Her nipples were already erect. They stood out like ripe raspberries against the pale mounds of her breasts. Her plump pussy was completely shaved and Jude could see that she was wet.

'Do you still keep the toys in the same place?' Jude ran one manicured finger along the length of her friend's slit. Dee nodded.

Jude retrieved a large wooden box from under the bed. She selected a short riding crop with a moulded rubber handle in the shape of a phallus. She drew the tip of the whip slowly along Dee's moist pussy then bought it down hard against her inner thigh. Dee gasped through her gag.

Jude whipped the tender inside of each thigh, hard. Then she gave Dee's pussy half a dozen lashes. Her body trembled.

She raised the crop in the air above Dee's right breast. Dee flinched and closed her eyes. Jude cut her across the meat of her breast several times. The crop swished through the air and each stroke left a livid, red mark against Dee's pale flesh. Then she aimed three swats directly at the nipple, bringing the crop down in exactly the same spot every time. Dee struggled and her breathing became ragged.

Glancing at Dee's pussy, Jude noticed that moisture was running down between her buttocks.

'Slut,' she said, 'I'm whipping you and you're getting off on it. I bet you want me to climb between your legs and make you come, don't you?'

Dee nodded, eagerly.

'Well, I'm not going to, not yet. I've got to finish whipping you first.' She traced the edge of Dee's nipple

10

with the tip of the crop. 'Is that what you want?' She leaned forward and put her mouth right next to Dee's ear. 'Do you want me to whip you – to hurt you – before I let you come?' She pinched the erect nipple.

Dee nodded and Jude could see the entreaty in her eyes. The crop sliced through the air – one, two, three, four – on Dee's left breast. Angry stripes appeared and Jude leaned forward and kissed them. Dee started to moan. Jude sucked the nipple, drawing it into her mouth. Gradually, she began to nibble, increasing the pressure of her teeth until Dee's moans became a roar. She sat up and placed three perfectly aimed swipes of the crop at the sensitive nub.

Dee's breathing was loud and rasping. Her body was filmed with sweat and her usually neat hair was tousled and messy. Jude dropped the crop and kissed each of the weals on Dee's body in turn. She took her time, slowly anointing each mark with her tongue, soothing it.

Finally, she reached Dee's crotch and nestled between the spread legs. She blew softly on the marks that slashed across her mound. She put out her tongue and ran it slowly along the length of her swollen pussy.

Dee moaned softly through her gag. Jude's mouth found Dee's clit and she tickled it with the tip of her tongue. She used her thumbs to spread the swollen labia. She lapped at her friend's clit. Dee's pussy felt soft and wet and velvety against her face. She loved the salty-sweet taste of it and the musky aroma that was so familiar.

Jude sucked hard on the tender button. She took it between her teeth and nibbled on it. Dee pulled against the restraints, making the bed creak. She rocked her hips, rubbing her crotch against Jude's face.

Jude knew Dee was close to orgasm but she wasn't ready to let her come. She stopped licking and blew softly on her engorged flesh. Dee let out a high-pitched wail and Jude knew she was feeling unbelievably frustrated. She picked up the riding crop and slid its cock-shaped handle into Dee's dripping cunt. Dee wriggled and twisted her body, raising her bottom off the bed.

Jude fucked her slowly with the whip handle. Dee groaned and bucked her hips. Jude removed the whip and Dee whimpered in protest. She pressed the tip of the lubricated crop handle up against her rear hole. Feeling it there, Dee thrashed her legs, fighting against the stockings tying her to the bed-frame.

Jude slid the crop handle home and Dee's whole body quivered. She parted her friend's engorged labia with one hand and began to lick her clit. Her other hand slowly and rhythmically fucked Dee's nether hole with the thick rubber handle.

She sucked hard on the sensitive bud, flicked it with her tongue. Jude knew Dee was on the edge now and she kept up the pace, licking her pussy rhythmically.

Dee began to writhe and buck. The bed creaked. The muscles in her thighs were taut and trembling. Her clit twitched in Jude's mouth. She gave one final, frantic, thrust with her hips, grinding her crotch against Jude's face. She screamed through her gag, a long continuous note of urgency and passion. She was coming.

Jude's mouth worked its magic on Dee's cunt. She licked her friend's spasming clit, sucking the orgasm out of her.

Finally, Dee's muscles relaxed and the wailing stopped. She lay still, her rapid breathing the only sound in the room. The air smelled of sex. Jude climbed up the bed and undid Dee's gag. She kissed her, exploring and probing her mouth with her darting tongue.

Dee was covered in sweat. Her hair was matted and messy. A single tear shone at the corner of one eye. Jude broke the kiss and Dee gasped in protest.

'Don't worry,' Jude said, 'I've got something else for you to kiss.'

Two

Jude stood in front of her easel. Winter sun saturated the studio. The CD player was turned down low. Music helped Jude work, got her in the right mood. Today she felt in need of something uplifting and tranquil so she'd chosen Mozart's *Ave Verum*. She was dressed in loose cotton trousers and an old T-shirt. Both were spotted and smeared with oil paint.

She looked at her model, eyes half closed so that she could see the shadows better.

'Can I take a break in a minute? Only I'm busting for the loo.' He smiled at her sweetly and somehow managed to look wholesome and innocent in spite of the fact that he was completely naked.

Jude put her brush down. 'Sure, Chris. I could do with a break too. It's nearly lunchtime anyway. I'll brew a fresh pot of coffee and buzz down for Alma to bring us up a sandwich.'

He broke his pose. He extended his arms above his head and stretched his spine, then wandered off to the bathroom.

Chris was her favourite model. He was tall with a sculpted, yet natural-looking body and tousled chestnut hair that had a habit of falling over his face. His lips were soft and full and their slightly feminine quality had the effect of softening his face. Without them he might have looked harsh and macho. His eyes were a shade of blue you rarely saw in adults. It made him look vulnerable and innocent. Yet he was all man. He had an animal quality, instinctively sensual and abandoned in his movements. She loved the challenge of trying to capture his contradictory qualities on canvas.

Jude took a step back and looked at her painting. Not bad. It needed some work but it would work out. In spite of her years of experience, every time Jude started a new project she worried it would be a failure. It wasn't until the painting or sculpture began to take shape that her confidence returned.

She walked over to the phone, on a table at the edge of the room, and pressed the button that would connect her to her housekeeper in the kitchen. 'Hi, Alma. Chris and I are ready for lunch. Thank you.'

Jude fetched some water from the sink and put on a pot of fresh coffee. She got milk out of the fridge, sugar, mugs and spoons from the shelf and put them on a tray. Chris came back into the room and sat down on an old sofa. The walls of the studio were lined with an assortment of furniture and props she used in her paintings. It gave the room a temporary, cluttered air. It was Jude's favourite room in the house and it was here that she felt most at home.

'Do you want to put something on? Alma's coming up in a second with our lunch.'

Chris shrugged. 'She's seen it before and the whole world's going to see it too when your painting's finished. Why bother?'

'Exhibitionist.' Jude smiled.

'Of course. An ideal qualification for an artist's model, don't you think?' As if to prove his point he spread his legs wide, displaying his crotch.

'Your manhood's looking impressive today. Did you give it a little stroke while you were in the loo?'

'Can you blame me, if I did? It isn't easy being naked when you're in the room. You look at me so hard I feel

14

as if you can see right into my soul. Sometimes I feel your eyes on my body like fingers, exploring every curve.'

'I suppose all artists must have a little of the voyeur in them.'

'It's a bit more than voyeurism, isn't it? You like to touch as well as look.' Chris took his penis in his hand and began to stroke. He gazed at Jude.

There was a tap at the door and Alma came in carrying a tray. She walked over to the dining table where Jude usually ate lunch and set it down. On her way out she paused briefly and watched as Chris pleasured himself, shook her head slowly and walked on.

Jude laughed. She carried the coffee things over to the table and poured herself some coffee. Chris lay back against the sofa, eyes closed, stroking his cock.

'Aren't you hungry, Chris?'

'Not at the moment, I'm horny. Can't you help me out?'

'You know the rules, Chris. During working hours I'm your boss. Whatever arrangement we may have in our own time is completely separate.'

'But I really need to come, and it's my lunch hour.'

'Then come,' she said, and bit into her sandwich. 'And you're very lucky that your boss has such a lax attitude towards masturbation on company time.'

'If you'd help me out, I wouldn't need to masturbate.' He looked at her, his eyes pleading.

'If you can't wait until later that's your problem. Play with yourself, if you have to, but don't expect me to help. And I'll be very angry if you get your filthy mess on my sofa. Remember what happened last time?'

'How could I forget? I had so many stripes on my arse I couldn't go to the gym for a fortnight.'

Jude stirred sugar into her coffee.

'Can't you give me a little inspiration? Please?' He smiled, using the sulky-little-boy face that he always put on when he wanted a favour.

Jude stood up and took off her top. She threw it on the floor and put her hands on her hips. 'Will this do? Or do you need more?'

'I want you naked. After all, I sit here all day naked for you, it's only fair.'

Jude slipped out of her trousers and panties.

'That's a lot better, but will you put the boots on, please? You know how much I like them.' He used the sulky face again, sticking his lower lip out for emphasis.

Jude laughed. She walked slowly over to the wardrobe where she kept costumes and props. She found the boots; a shiny patent-leather pair with laces up the front. They were so tall they almost reached her pussy. The six-inch heels were made of a shiny silver metal and were as thin and vicious as nails. She carried them to the sofa and sat down beside Chris to lace herself into them.

Jude took her time with the boots, as she knew Chris loved watching her put them on almost as much as he loved her wearing them. He watched with rapt attention as she straightened the long tongue, pulling it flat and laying it neatly between the flaps. She threaded the laces carefully through the eyelet holes and pulled them hard, maintaining the correct tension. Out of the corner of her eye, she could see Chris was drinking in every detail. He loved the smell of the leather, the way the shiny surface caught the light and the slithering rasp that the laces made as she pulled them through the holes.

Chris reached over and stroked her thigh, but Jude brushed him away with the back of her hand as she might brush off a fly.

'You can look, but not touch. Those are the rules, take it or leave it.'

He looked contrite. His hand moved on his cock, while his other hand cupped his balls, stroking and pulling them. His manhood stood up proudly between his muscular thighs. Jude slid along the sofa to get out of range of Chris's inquisitive fingers. When she had laced the left boot up to the ankle, she turned her attention to the right. Above the ankle the eyelet holes were replaced by curved horizontal hooks. The long laces had to be guided round each hook, in crisscross fashion, and pulled tight. She worked methodically, crossing the laces and winding them round the hooks. At the top of each boot she tied the laces in a bow and tucked them inside. She stood up and walked around a little, treating Chris to a view of herself and the boots from all angles.

'You look gorgeous.' Chris's voice was husky and low.

Jude put her hands on her hips and lifted her left leg. She rested her foot on the edge of the sofa. 'You can touch it, if you like.'

Chris looked at her for reassurance. 'Go on. You know you want to.'

He stroked the shiny leather with his fingers, carefully and reverently, as if it were a fragile vase that might break into a thousand pieces. Jude could see that his hand was shaking. His other hand moved rhythmically on his erect member.

'Does it feel good?'

Chris nodded.

'How about this?' She lifted her foot and stroked the boot's spiky heel along his thigh.

Chris gasped.

'Good. And how about this?' With her toe she nudged his hand away from his cock. She ran the heel up and down the length of his shaft before pressing its tip gently against his scrotum.

'Oh, yes.' His voice was barely a whisper.

'Now get on with it. I don't pay you for wanking, remember.' She moved her chair away from the table and sat down in front of Chris, her legs spread wide. From this position she knew he could see both her pussy and the boots. She picked up her plate and began to eat.

Chris watched her, his hand moving on his cock. She concentrated on her sandwich, pretending not to look at him. She brought her knees together, hiding her crotch from his view, and Chris's face assumed the expression of a little boy whose mummy has just taken away his sweeties. His hand stopped moving.

'Please let me look at it.'

Jude ignored him.

'Come on, Judy, you know what I want.' His voice was full of arousal and frustration.

'How do I know what you want unless you say so? If you can't express yourself properly, how can I be expected to give you what you want?' She crossed her legs and went on eating.

'Please, just open your legs so that I can see your cunt. Is it too much to ask?'

'Well, since you asked so sweetly . . .'

Jude put her plate on the table and opened her legs wide. She shifted her weight on the chair, sliding her pussy right to the edge of the seat. Reaching down, she used both hands to spread the outer lips, exposing herself to Chris's hungry gaze.

'Take a good look, now. Because looking is all you'll be doing.'

'Fine by me,' he whispered.

He moved his hand steadily on his cock. Jude loved the way his nostrils flared as he breathed out. Hair fell over his eyes. His square jaw looked even more manly when his teeth were clenched in response to his growing arousal.

Chris's hand moved rapidly on his cock. He lay back against the sofa, his legs wide. Sweat trickled down his face. Breath burst out noisily between his parted lips.

'You're always wanking, aren't you? Didn't your

mother tell you not to play with it in public? You can't leave it alone, can you?'

Chris smiled briefly and winked at her. He pulled hard on his scrotum as he worked his cock. Jude could see his ball-sac tightening and thickening as he became more aroused. His purple helmet peeped over the top of his fist as he pumped. The muscles and tendons in his spread thighs were taut and straining.

'Why don't you pinch your nipples, Chris? I love watching you hurt yourself.' She couldn't take her eyes off him.

He reached up with his free hand and pinched his right nipple between thumb and forefinger. His face contorted in pain and he moaned softly. Jude could see the tips of his fingers go white as he squeezed. He exhaled deeply, hissing in pain.

'Isn't that better? My pussy's getting wet. I get all worked up when you hurt yourself. Hurt yourself some more for me.'

Chris wanked his cock frantically as he abused his nipples. He started to moan and his breathing became more erratic. Jude leaned forward to get a better view. Her skin felt tingly all over and she was getting distinctly moist. Watching Chris pleasure himself turned her on enormously, in spite of her pretended indifference. Her apparent lack of interest and her refusal to join in were designed to arouse him and demonstrate her control. When she finally let him touch her at the end of their working day, he'd be aroused and compliant, just the way she liked him.

'That's good. I'm going to have to play with your nipples myself later; you're getting me all hot and wet. If you're a good boy I might even suck you. Would you like that, Chris? Do you want me to take your cock into my hot, wet mouth and suck you until you come?' She reached down with both hands and spread her labia again. 'Can you see how wet you've made me?'

'Oh, yes.' Chris's voice was throaty and deep. His eyes were closed now. She wasn't sure if he was answering her, or merely giving voice to his own excitement.

'Can you feel my mouth on you, Chris? Can you feel the slick, velvety warmth of it engulfing your cock? I want you to come in my mouth. I'm sucking the come out of you. I want to feel it sliding down my throat. I want to taste it. Are you going to come for me?'

Chris was panting and moaning. His torso was covered in sweat. Suddenly, he pulled the foreskin down hard and she knew he was about to come. Hot sperm pumped out in a wide arc and landed on her boots. He groaned and swore under his breath. His come decorated her boots like a broken strand of pearls.

His eyes snapped open and he looked directly at Jude. He got to his knees and began licking her boots clean. He licked up the spunk, covering the leather with his wet tongue. When the boots were spotless, he wiped his face with his fingers then licked them clean, all the time gazing at Jude. He sucked each finger carefully as if he didn't want to waste a single drop. When he had finished he looked down briefly at his softening manhood, then smiled at Jude.

'Is that better?'

He nodded.

'Now come and eat your main course before the coffee gets cold.' Jude kicked a chair away from the table, making room for him.

Chris sat down. Jude poured him a cup of coffee and added milk and sugar. He picked up his sandwich and examined it.

'Yummy, cream cheese and walnut, my favourite.'

Jude smiled. 'I got Alma to make it specially. I have to keep my favourite model happy. She adds a touch of cinnamon to the cheese.' She leaned forward and whispered, 'It's supposed to flavour your sperm.'

'I'll let you know.'

'Thanks. And you never know . . . I may find out for myself. After work.'

At the end of her working day Jude kissed Chris goodbye on the doorstep then walked into the kitchen to see what Alma had cooked for her evening meal.

Alma Grandes had been with Jude for years. Born in Andalusia, she'd come to England in her teens yet still spoke English with a heavy accent, though she understood it perfectly. In private, she and Jude often conversed in Spanish. Jude had lived in Barcelona for a year after she'd finished art college and still owned a small house there.

Alma stood at the big kitchen table chopping vegetables.

'*Hola*, Alma. What's for dinner? You haven't forgotten Alan Fox is coming, have you?' Jude spoke in Spanish.

'Of course not. I'm making paella; I know how much he enjoys it. Dinner will be ready for eight, ten past at the latest or it will spoil.'

'Alan enjoys everything you make. And I wouldn't dare keep you waiting; I know how seriously you take your cooking. We'll be ready at eight. Have you opened the wine?'

Alma nodded. 'It's in the dining room. Everything's ready. The dessert is in the fridge, you just have to pour cream on it.' She wiped her fingers on her apron and picked up an envelope of photos. 'Do you want to look at these? They're from my nephew Joaquin's first communion.'

'Of course.' Jude took the packet of photos. She pulled out a chair and sat down at the table. 'That can't be Joaquin? Hasn't he grown? I wouldn't have recognised him.'

'Yes, it must be at least two years since you've seen him.'

21

'Is it that long? Pablo and Maria's wedding?'

Alma nodded. 'Maria's already expecting her second child. I booked my ticket for Easter today. I can't wait to see them all again.'

Alma limped across the room and washed some vegetables under the tap. In her youth, she had been an inspired flamenco dancer and used to earn her living cleaning during the day and performing at night. She'd had to give it up after a bad road accident had left her with a steel plate in her thigh and one leg shorter than the other. Jude had offered her the job of housekeeper and secretary while she was still in hospital, and it had seemed like the ideal solution for them both. She lived in the spacious basement of Jude's town house. She was fiercely loyal to Jude and had long ago become used to her employer's unconventional lifestyle.

'Did anyone call today?' Jude asked as she slid the photos back in their envelope and put them down on the table.

Alma nodded. 'Dee rang to remind you about the party at the weekend. I told her I'd make some tapas for you to take along.'

'Thanks, Alma, that's very kind of you.'

Alma shrugged. 'She is a good friend. And she's missing Sadie, I can tell. When is Sadie back from New York?'

'A couple of months yet, I think. You're right, Dee's definitely feeling lonely. Did anyone else call?'

Alma wiped her fingers and picked up several slips of paper from the table. 'Here are the messages I took.'

Jude took the notes and leafed through them. 'I'll have to call Mannheim's tomorrow about the sculpture they want for their Amsterdam office, can you remind me?'

'So you'll be going to Amsterdam?'

'Sounds like it. Thanks, Alma. See you later.'

The last message was from Michael Read and consisted only of his phone number. Jude walked upstairs to her bedroom, stripped off her clothes and tossed them into the laundry basket. She went through to the en-suite bathroom and ran a bath.

Back in the bedroom, she picked up the message from Michael Read, sat down on the bed and lifted the phone. Jude punched in the number and listened to it ring. She was just about to hang up when it was answered.

'Hello?' He sounded out of breath.

'Hello. This is Jude Ryan, I hope I'm not disturbing you.'

'Not at all. Thank you for returning my call.' He lowered his voice. 'It's good to hear from you.'

Jude felt tingly all over. Mr Read was obviously aware of the effect of his voice.

'Did you call for a reason, or were you just feeling sociable?'

'I called to ask you to dinner next Monday evening, if you can make it.'

'Yes, I think I'm free. That would be fine.'

'Excellent. Shall I pick you up? Can we say eight-thirty?'

'You'll have to pick me up from the Walker gallery in Kensington, do you know it? I'm going to a private show.'

'I know it. I'll pick you up at eight. See you then.' He hung up.

'Arrogant pig,' mumbled Jude as she walked into the bathroom.

After dinner that night Jude and Alan sat in the living room drinking coffee. A fire crackled in the grate and the lights were low. Jude reclined against one end of the sofa, looking at Alan. His hair was a light shade of blond usually only seen in small children. It sparkled in the firelight. Freckles sprinkled his face and body, emphasising his pale skin. Mellow jazz played in the background.

Jude had met Alan at Goddess, a femdom, fetish nightclub. His obvious confidence coupled with his sense of humour and open acknowledgement of his sexual needs was something Jude had found hard to resist. From the very beginning he had been submissive to Jude. It was something that they both took for granted. He was unfailingly obedient and he deferred to her. She accepted his willing submission as a natural part of his personality.

Jude had been rather surprised when she learned that, in the vanilla world, he could be authoritative and demanding. He was unfailingly polite and reasonable but there was something about the tone of his voice that left no doubt that he knew he would be obeyed.

Jude didn't know why the discovery had come as such a shock, but it had. She had never been one of those dominant women who regards any man who wants to submit to her as a wimp. It had been her experience that all sorts of men chose to be sexually submissive, and wanting to worship her didn't automatically make him a weakling. On the contrary, it was often very confident and powerful men who sought the release of obeying a mistress. Jude believed that only a man whose sense of self and personal power was strong and unshakeable could voluntarily hand control over to another person.

There were exceptions, of course; men who believed in the innate authority of women and the worthlessness of men and regarded themselves as little more than dirt beneath her feet. But they had never interested Jude. She had always been attracted to confidence and strength in a man and Alan had both. He juggled a demanding job and his unusual personal life with consummate ease. He had a laconic sense of humour and somehow seemed to remain relaxed and unconcerned no matter what pressure he was under.

As far as Jude was concerned, Alan's most attractive feature was his laid-back attitude. He gave the impression that nothing mattered to him. He regarded work, with its politics and backbiting, as a game he played for his own amusement and a little money. He greeted problems and deadlines with a shrug of the shoulders and a wry smile. Nothing got to him and nothing ever disturbed his sense of calm. He was positively relaxing to be around.

Now she thought of it, perhaps that was why his public behaviour had seemed so out of character. His quiet expectation of obedience somehow didn't seem to suit a man who saw the world as nothing more than an extended joke.

Jude loved his contradictions. He was obviously masculine yet eager to wear drag. He was proud and powerful yet he submitted to her totally and he was open to trying anything that might prove amusing, no matter how extreme. Jude found these qualities irresistibly attractive. Alan was an easy and exciting companion and Jude always enjoyed spending time with him.

'I love Chet Baker. I've often wondered how such a tortured soul could produce such wonderful music.' He stroked her forearm with one finger.

'It was precisely because he was tortured, don't you think?' Jude put down her cup.

'The creative mind theory? Madness and genius often coexist in the same mind – Van Gogh, Tony Hancock, Dostoyevsky, Isaac Newton even?'

'Perhaps. There's something about the way creative people look at the world that's completely different. They see beauty where other people just see the ordinary. Doesn't it follow that they'll also see agony when other people don't?'

'Are you speaking from experience?' Alan smiled at her. 'Should I have brought you a straightjacket instead of flowers – just in case?'

Jude laughed. 'No, I think you're safe – though, I must say, I could probably put a straightjacket to very good use. I wouldn't say I'm a depressive, not by any means, but I certainly seem to experience more highs and lows than a lot of people. I love extremes. I adore seeing how far I can go, wherever that leads.'

'Yes, you're certainly fond of extremes. Sometimes I think there's no end to the perversity and wickedness of your mind.' He put down his cup and took her hand. He turned it over and brought it to his mouth, kissing her palm.

'Are you complaining?'

He shook his head. 'No, not at all. In fact, if I were a religious man I'd get down on my knees and thank God for the sheer, twisted wickedness of your imagination.'

'Well, I may not be God, but I do love to be worshipped, so why don't you get down on your knees anyway?'

Alan released her hand and slid to the edge of the sofa. Jude caught his wrist.

'But first, I think you ought to undress. Don't you think that's a good idea?'

Alan nodded and stood up. He kicked off his shoes and bent to remove his socks. He unbuttoned his shirt and pulled the tails out of his trousers. He laid it over the back of the sofa. He unzipped his trousers and slid them down over his legs. Jude could see that he was already half hard. His growing erection strained against the front of his soft cotton boxers. A small spot of moisture darkened the material over the tip of his cock.

Alan stepped out of his trousers and pulled down his boxer shorts. He slid them over his muscular thighs, revealing his circumcised manhood. His blond pubes were neatly trimmed and his balls were completely shaved. Jude insisted that he keep it that way because she thought it made his cock seem on display for her pleasure. He slid to his knees.

'I think you should start by kissing my feet. Take off my stockings first.'

Alan unbuckled Jude's shoes, slipped them off and moved them to one side. He folded back the bottom of her dress and unclasped each stocking, then rolled the right one down carefully and placed it inside her shoe. He repeated the procedure with her other stocking then lifted one of her legs, supporting its weight.

He brought her foot to his mouth and began kissing her toes. At first he covered them with tiny kisses, then he began to nibble and lick. He nipped at the ball of her foot, squeezed the pad of each toe between his teeth. He licked her entire sole with the flat of his tongue. He slid his tongue between her toes, licking deeply and sensually.

Jude closed her eyes. Alan sucked deeply on her big toe, drawing it into his mouth and nibbling the pad. With his thumbs, he massaged her sole, using firm pressure.

Jude felt a wave of tingles begin at the nape of her neck and creep across her scalp: a delicious prickle of pleasure. The sensation spread over her face and neck and down her body, bringing alive every nerve ending.

Alan gently lowered her foot to the carpet and turned his attention to the other one. Jude slid off the straps of her dress and pushed it down to her waist. Her nipples protruded, hard and red, emphasising the smallness of her breasts. She began to tease her engorged nipples with her nails.

Alan was sucking on her toes now, squirming his tongue between them like an eel. His mouth was soft and slick and unbelievably hot. Every so often she felt his teeth nip and she gasped with pleasure.

'Enough, Alan.'

He lowered her foot.

'I think I need to feel something inside me now.' Jude spread her legs.

Alan raised himself up on his knees and took his erect cock in his hand.

'No, Alan. That's not what I meant. You know better than that. My pleasure comes first. Once I'm sated I may permit you to come. But then again, I may not.'

Alan blushed and his entire face turned red. He lowered his head and looked at the floor. 'I'm very sorry, Ma'am, I forgot myself, please forgive me.'

'If you give me a really good fisting, I might think about it. You'll find some lube in the sideboard, though I doubt if you'll need it.' Alan went over to the sideboard for the lube and Jude rearranged the sofa cushions to support her back. She reclined with her open crotch at the edge of the seat. Alan was the only man who'd ever managed to fist her and she loved it. She'd done it occasionally with Dee, but she had tiny hands and it had never felt as intense and erotic as it did with Alan.

Alan returned and settled down between her legs. He took off her panties then parted her labia and stroked her clit with his thumb. Alan had a way of touching her that she particularly responded to. He massaged her pussy with all five fingers and only touched her clitoris casually and occasionally at first, using his thumb. It was almost a flick; an accidental brushing of fingers, gradually becoming more deliberate and definite. It always aroused her quickly and powerfully.

After a while, Alan began including her pussy's opening in his massage. At first he circled his fingers round the edge, teasing her, then gradually he began to push them inside.

Jude always loved that first moment of penetration. The agonisingly slow and exciting slide past her outer muscles and the sheer, animal fulfilment as they finally slithered home. Alan slipped two fingers inside her and quickly located her G-spot. She quivered with pleasure.

He thumbed her clit and Jude murmured her appreciation.

Alan's curled fingers began to massage her G-spot and Jude felt her arousal step up a gear. It wouldn't be long before she experienced her first orgasm. It wasn't uncommon for her to undergo a wave or cluster of climaxes, each one growing stronger and finally culminating in one huge orgasm that left her feeling totally weak.

She pinched and twisted her own nipples as Alan's experienced fingers worked on her pussy. He slid in a third finger and pressed hard on her sensitive G-spot and Jude came for the first time. It was a gentle, delicious orgasm like the first waves rippling on the beach as the tide roars inexorably behind it. Jude exhaled softly.

Alan fucked her firmly with three fingers, all the time using his thumb to stimulate her swollen clit. 'I think we could do with a bit of extra lube; I don't want to hurt you, darling,' he said.

Jude opened her eyes and looked down at him. His body was bathed in sweat and his cock jutted out, its tip purple. She nodded her assent. He slipped his fingers out and picked up the lube bottle with his other hand. He squirted a big blob into his palm and rubbed both hands together, spreading the gel. He slid three fingers back inside her. The lube felt cold but quickly warmed as he moved inside her.

He rubbed his thumb on her clit and pressed his fingertips into her G-spot. She came again, another gentle orgasm that made her tingle all over.

'That's good, keep going. Nice and strong.' She stimulated her own nipples. He slipped in a fourth finger and she came again as it slid home.

Jude was panting hard. Her eyes were closed and her fingers excited her reddened nipples. Alan slid deeper and she felt her muscles relaxing to accommodate his knuckles. She loved the sensation of being full and stretched.

Jude moaned and whimpered. She was on the edge of orgasm all the time. Alan would move inside her in a particular way – a flick of the clit or just the right amount of pressure on her G-spot – and she'd come again. They were sort of mini-orgasms that promised more to come and turned her arousal up a notch.

Alan had all four fingers insider her now. He pressed his fingers down inside her, massaging her sensitive G-spot all the time. He withdrew his fingers halfway and Jude felt bereft for a moment, even though she knew what was to come. When he re-entered her, his thumb was folded into his palm and he gave her a few shallow gentle strokes while she relaxed to accommodate all five of his fingers.

Alan used his other hand to stroke her clit. He fisted her slowly, his hand sliding further inside her with every stroke. Jude felt full and stretched and every nerve ending in her body was working overtime. She came again and her pussy gripped Alan's invading fingers.

Soon, all five fingers were inside her up to the top of the thumb, with just the broadest part of his hand and the thumb knuckle protruding. Alan rotated his hand slowly, all the time pressing down. His hand slid inside her and Jude felt her pussy yield as he entered her fully.

Alan flicked her clit with his thumb and fingered her G-spot and Jude began to come for the final time. Ripples of pleasure began in her pussy and spread upwards and outwards. She arched her back. She pulled hard on her engorged nipples. She groaned and sobbed.

The ripples became a surge and Jude began to roar. Blood rushed in her ears, her heart beat like a drum. A tidal wave of orgasm crashed over her and she felt her cunt pulse round Alan's hand so powerfully she was sure it must be hurting him.

At the peak, she dug her nails into her nipples and pressed her crotch down onto Alan's hand. She gasped for breath, guttural cries hurting her throat. Gradually, her pussy softened and her heart slowed. She lay with her eyes closed, getting her breath back.

She opened her eyes and looked at Alan. He was grinning from ear to ear, his hand still buried inside her.

'Am I forgiven?' he asked.

'I suppose what you really mean is "Can I come, please?" Isn't it?'

He looked sheepish and nodded.

'Do you think you've earned the right?'

'That's for you to decide, obviously, Ma'am.'

'Why don't you start by removing your hand?'

Carefully, he slid free then waited for further orders.

'Now clean it, I don't want you making any mess.'

Alan looked directly at her and licked his hand clean. He lapped up all the moisture and sucked each finger clean.

'Good. Now, how would you like to come? And don't mumble, you know I hate it when you're half-hearted and whiny about what you want.'

'I'd like to come in your mouth, please Ma'am, if I may.'

Jude sat up and slid to the edge of the seat. She opened her mouth. Alan leaped to his feet and his erection was directly in front of Jude's face. His cock was thick and straining and a strand of shiny moisture dangled off the end. Jude could smell his arousal.

She massaged his balls, rolling them around inside the scrotum. She pulled, slowly but firmly. Alan groaned and his thigh muscles tightened. Jude reached into her shoe for her discarded stocking. She pulled on Alan's balls, stretching out his scrotum, and wound the stocking several times round the top of his ball-sac, trapping his balls. She tied the nylon in a bow.

'Pretty,' she murmured to herself.

She wrapped her hand round the base of Alan's cock and took it in her mouth. She swallowed it to the root and sucked hard. Alan shuddered. She looked up at his face, knowing he would be watching her. Their eyes met and Jude could see the hunger and love there.

She slid her lips up and down the length of his rigid cock. She could smell his musk and taste the salty pre-come. She deep-throated him, relaxing her muscles. She loved the sensation of a man's cock filling her mouth, her nostrils buried in his pubes, his balls banging against her chin.

Alan's thigh muscles strained and twitched. He was breathing hard and fast. He was clammy and hot. Jude knew he was on the edge. She stepped up the pace, establishing a rhythm. Alan reached down and laced his fingers through her hair. His hips rocked and he fucked her face.

Jude loved this moment of no return, when the man's need was the only conscious thought in his head and his body responded on autopilot. She knew that Alan couldn't stop now if his life depended on it. All that existed for him was his cock and her mouth and his imminent, inevitable orgasm.

Her mouth moved constantly, answering his thrusts. She wrapped one hand round his scrotum and pulled down firmly on his balls. Her other hand snaked between his buttocks and found his opening. She pressed one finger against his sweat-slick arsehole and pushed.

Alan howled with pleasure as she entered him and he erupted in her mouth. His hips rammed forward, filling her mouth with cock and spunk. She swallowed mouthful after mouthful of hot liquid. His dick beat in rhythm with his pounding heart and Jude felt as if she actually had his life in her mouth.

Alan's legs trembled and he put a hand on her shoulder to steady himself. Jude felt his arsehole pulsating round her invading finger. She looked up at his face. His eyes were tight shut, his mouth was open and he was panting hard. A bead of sweat dripped off his chin and landed on her face.

He began to shrink and soften in her mouth and his muscles relaxed. Jude released his cock.

'Was that good?' she asked.

Alan nodded, emphatically. His eyes opened. He used both hands to wipe the sweat from his face.

'Well, I've only just started, so why don't we take ourselves up to the bedroom and see what the rest of the night holds?'

Alan smiled. 'You'll be the death of me.'

'You say that like it's a bad thing . . .'

Three

Chris and Jude sat in the back of a taxi on the way to House of Harlot.

'I'm really looking forward to trying on the costume.' He lowered his voice; 'I love rubber. So tight and clingy, like you're being embraced.'

'So sweaty, so constricting.'

'That's part of the fun. You're conscious of what you're wearing all the time, so you feel aware and sexy.'

'Tell me an occasion when you don't feel sexy.'

He shot her a smile. 'When I've got a hangover. Or the time I got dysentery in Goa, I don't think I had an erection for a week.'

Jude sat next to him, her thigh pressed up against his. They were holding hands. She slipped her hand out of his and explored the front of his jeans.

He looked down at her, raising one eyebrow in mock surprise. 'What do you think you're doing?' he asked.

'Checking to see if you've got over your dysentery.'

The cab pulled up outside House of Harlot. Inside the shop, Jude sat and waited for Chris to come out of the changing room. His costume had been made for a special job. Her client was a gay man with very specific fetishes concentrated mainly around rubber and bondage. He'd bought quite a bit of Jude's work, finally asking her if she'd do some specific commissions. Jude knew that the paintings hung in his dungeon and she occasionally liked to imagine the kind of sights her work might witness.

Chris came out of the changing room and she stood up to admire him.

'What do you think?' he said. 'It fits like a second skin, doesn't it?'

He wore a short black catsuit, ending halfway down his thighs. Wavy red flashes spread out from the edges of the suit like fingers of flame caressing him. At the groin, it was a shaped pouch designed to accommodate Chris's testicles and penis. Jude could see that to fit himself into the pouch he had had to squeeze his genitals through a small, tight opening and this had the effect of thrusting them forward. He was half erect, his rubber-covered cock sticking out at a 45-degree angle. Jude wondered if there was room enough inside if he got properly hard. She stroked his belly through the latex.

'Yes, it's positively obscene. I think I can see that little mole you have on the base of your cock, and is that the outline of your foreskin?'

He smiled and nodded.

'What does it feel like?'

'Like someone's got my cock in their fist and is squeezing very hard. It's lovely.'

'Go over there and walk around a bit so I can see it from all angles.'

Chris walked away from her and she looked at the costume from the rear. The suit emphasised his muscular legs, making them look smooth and perfect. It clung to his buttocks as though it had been painted on and Jude thought it made his bum look like two perfect plums. It was sleeveless and low at the front, displaying his nipples.

As he turned, he shimmied his shoulders and tassels attached to his nipples wiggled. The tassels covered his natural nipples with a small black cone arrangement, inside which Jude knew there was a nipple clamp biting into his flesh in accordance with the customer's request.

'I'll have to practise until I can make them twirl.'

'Do they hurt?' Jude went over and pulled on one of the tassels.

He shook his head. 'I'm conscious of them, but they're not really painful. You wouldn't be able to wear them for long if they were.'

'Doesn't it hurt your cock? If you get a stiffy, isn't it going to cut your circulation off?'

'No, it's fine. It stretches and the tighter it gets, the better it feels.'

Jude laughed. 'Pervert.'

'And you're not? I know there's a rubber item or two in your wardrobe, as well.'

'And the only reason you know that, Chris, is because you've been in there trying on my dresses . . .'

'OK, OK. I'll peel myself out of this. Why don't you try something on? I spotted a lovely rubber nurse's outfit over there and some fabulous boots. Go on, have some fun.'

'Yes, why not? I can always do with something to put me in the mood.'

Chris disappeared into the changing cubicle and Jude browsed the racks of clothes. There was something for every taste and fetish. Impossibly high heels with the foot at such a steep angle you probably couldn't walk in them, thigh boots with sharp metal stilettos, rubber nun's habits, air hostess outfits and police uniforms.

There were skirts, dresses, catsuits, hats, underwear, gloves and stockings. Jude wasn't particularly into rubber but she couldn't help being turned on. Designed to arouse both wearer and onlooker, the outfits were unambiguously erotic. Corsets cinched in waists, pushed out breasts and emphasised hips. High heels altered the centre of gravity, forcing the wearer to walk with a sexy wiggle, and rubber clung to the curves, concealing nothing.

'How about that one? The corset with the buckles. I can see you in that.' Chris appeared suddenly to part the clothes on the rack and select a garment.

'Hi, Chris. How did you manage to get out of that suit so quickly? I thought you'd be in there for ages.'

'I got one of the assistants to help me. He said it was like peeling a banana. Try this one.' He handed her an off-the-shoulder, boned rubber dress. 'Purple looks divine on you.'

Jude selected a few items and took them into the changing cubicle. She tried on the rubber dress Chris had suggested, but she didn't like it. She looked at her reflection in the cubicle's mirror. It was a wonderful dress, but it was really built for someone with more cleavage.

She took it off and put on a floaty black dress and, over it, a waspy corset. She thought she looked like Morticia Addams. The Goth look was popular in the fetish scene, but Jude had never seen herself that way.

The final outfit was a pair of very high, patent-leather thigh boots with a long zip all the way up the front. There was a scarlet mini skater-skirt and a black corset that left her breasts bare. She loved it. Chris was right about rubber clothing making you feel as though you were being embraced by a lover. It held her in a tight embrace and grew warm in response to her body heat.

She came out of the cubicle and did a slow twirl.

'It's beautiful,' he said, 'the skirt is lovely. The way it flares out from the corset makes you look really curvy. And the boots are fantastic. They make me want to be walked on. I've got a massive great erection just thinking about it.'

'It is lovely, isn't it? I think I'll buy it. I need something new to wear to clubs and I know I'll regret it if I don't buy these boots. They make me feel so masterful.'

'I'm beginning to think I might regret it if you do buy them.'

Back at work Chris was restless. His constant erection and the occasional furtive handling of his cock left Jude in no doubt as to the cause of his unease. Though she knew it was cruel, she actually liked him to feel frustrated while they were working. His arousal gave an edginess and immediacy to the paintings that she liked.

Chris still had an adolescent's libido and, if she let him, he'd masturbate several times a day. Jude deliberately restricted his opportunity for release because it enabled her to capture his sexual hunger on canvas. Chris played along because he knew that she always let him come in the end and he'd learned that, if he let her take charge, the orgasm she finally permitted him to have would be worth waiting for.

He didn't really consider himself submissive, but he had no hang-ups about going along with his partner's fantasies. He'd long ago learned that a woman's sexuality was often more powerful and complex than a man's and if he let his partner have full rein he was usually in for a very good time.

They were friends and lovers as well as colleagues and Jude always said that if they defined their relationship with a title they'd be putting limits on it, which neither of them wanted to do. Sometimes she even called him her muse.

'You're restless, darling. Can you try and keep still? And leave your cock alone, please. I'm trying to paint it and you keep covering it up with your hand.'

'Can you blame me? We've spent half the morning trying on sexy outfits, I haven't come since I had my shower this morning and the only relief you've given me is a quick fondle in the back of a cab.'

'You've got a one-track mind, Chris.'

'So have you. It's not like you're Mother Teresa. I know half the time your knickers are dripping when you paint me. I just don't understand how you can concentrate when you feel like that. I know I can't.'

'Well, that's the difference between us, isn't it? I've got self-discipline, but you –'

'Rely upon you to discipline me,' Chris interrupted. 'I know. And I'm a lucky man. But sometimes it's so frustrating I want to kick over your easel and ravish you on the floor.'

'Do you think you could make it the sofa? Otherwise I might get splinters in my arse.'

'Please, Jude, it'll only take a couple of minutes, can't I fuck you?' he whined. Chris was practically begging.

'Sorry, darling. You know the rules; they're there for a reason. I tell you what, though – I could see you this evening, but there's a catch.'

'A catch?' Chris sounded suspicious. 'That's not fair, you know I'm so horny I'd agree to anything. You could ask me to shave my head, or marry Alma, and I would.'

Jude laughed. 'I'll tell her, you never know, she may take you up on it. But it's nothing like that. I have to go out to dinner this evening and I know I'm going to be pretty horny when I get back. It would be really nice if you were here when I got home.'

'No, it's fine. What time shall I come over?'

'I don't suppose I'll be back until around eleven. Tell you what, why don't you just stay? Alma will make you dinner, you can watch TV, or listen to music, get a video – whatever you want. Then you'll be all ready and waiting when I get back. What do you think?'

'Sure, I never turn down Alma's food. There's just one problem . . .'

'How do you survive until eleven?'

He nodded.

'By thinking about what I'll do to you if you don't. That should be motivation enough. And no playing with yourself. I want you to wait for me, understand?'

Chris nodded and stuck out his bottom lip in an exaggerated sulky pout. 'I promise I won't play with your toys while you're out,' he said.

Jude looked at her watch. 7.58. She wondered if Michael Read would be on time. Submissive men were invariably punctual. Alan always arrived on the dot of the appointed hour and Jude often wondered if he sat in his car outside waiting for the minutes to tick round.

But Michael clearly didn't see himself as submissive. He'd made it obvious he was confident he could persuade her to submit to him. It would be much more likely that he'd be late for their appointment just to make a point. Well, it had been a long time since Jude had called anyone Master and she certainly didn't plan on changing her ways just for Michael Read.

Jude wandered around the gallery watching the other guests. Private shows always bored her. They were full of critics who looked at every item with disdain no matter how original, and friends and family of the artist who thought it was all fantastic in spite of the evidence of their own eyes. And both factions seemed intent on consuming as much complimentary alcohol as their stomachs would hold.

The artist responsible for tonight's show was a good friend of Jude's. Jude was delighted that her friend's work was getting the recognition it deserved at last. Mia had real talent and the confidence and courage to explore it to the full. Yet she was modest and self-effacing. They'd met when Jude had done some master-classes at the art college where Mia had been a student and they'd quickly developed a rapport.

A waiter walked past carrying a tray full of champagne.

'Excuse me.'

The waiter stopped and turned.

'Do you think I could have a glass?' Jude smiled at

the young man. He held out the tray and she took one. 'Thank you.'

'You're welcome, Ma'am.' The waiter performed a small formal bow, a sharp nod of the head that signified his respect, then turned and walked away.

'I must say, you certainly seem to have the knack of getting men to obey you. That waiter couldn't have been more obsequious if he had tried.'

Jude turned and looked at Michael. 'I don't know. He could have got down on his knees. That's the minimum I usually require. That's the second time you've sneaked up on me. If I didn't know better I'd think you were stalking me.'

Michael laughed. 'No, no, that's not my style at all.'

'I'm glad to hear it. Have you had a chance to look around? Mia's work is fabulous, isn't it?'

'Yes, I had a quick look. I like it a lot. I'd read that you were her mentor; I think I can see your influence in her work.'

'Really?'

'Indeed. Not the subject matter, of course, but the breadth of her vision and the sensuality of the way she paints flesh. There's quite an echo, I think.'

'Perhaps. Shall I introduce you to Mia before we leave? I'm sure she'd like to meet you.'

Michael nodded. 'I'd love to.'

Jude took Michael's hand and led him across the room to where Mia was talking to a tall young man with glasses.

'Excuse me, Miles,' said Jude, 'would you mind if I stole Mia away for a second? There's someone I'd like to introduce her to.'

'Not at all.' Miles spoke politely enough, yet his expression didn't quite match the civility of his words. 'I suppose I have been rather monopolising her. I'll get myself something to eat and perhaps we can have another talk later, Mia?'

41

'Of course, Miles. I'll look forward to it.'

Miles walked off in the direction of the buffet.

'Over my dead body. Thanks for rescuing me, Jude. I've been trying to get away for twenty minutes.' Mia smiled at her friend.

'You're welcome. I got the impression it's more than your artwork he's interested in.'

'And who can blame him?' put in Michael. 'If I hadn't come here to meet the lovely Jude I assure you I'd be fighting Miles for the privilege of talking to you.'

Mia laughed. 'Sorry, I should have introduced you two. This is Michael Read and this is my friend, Mia Ransome.'

Mia and Michael shook hands.

'Of course. I saw your exhibition at Dee Kane's gallery. I find your work intriguing. Powerful. And from what I saw, it certainly seems to provoke strong reactions.'

'And what sort of reaction did it provoke in you, Miss Ransome?'

'A purely artistic one, I assure you.' Mia blushed.

'Ah, well, I can't tell you how disappointed I am.'

Mia laughed. 'I'm sure you'll get over it. But I should go. I've just spotted a producer from the *South Bank Show*; they're interested in doing a profile of me. I'd better steer him in the direction of the champagne. Thanks for coming, Jude. Nice to meet you, Michael.' Mia gave Jude a kiss on the cheek and walked away.

'What a delightful young lady.' Michael's eyes were fixed on Mia's retreating rear.

'Do you ever have a day off? Have you taken a sacred vow to seduce every woman you ever meet, or perhaps you're just so insecure you don't feel like a man unless you can get a girl's interest.'

Michael smiled. 'Can I help it if women find me attractive? Shall we go, if you're ready? I made our reservations for eight-fifteen in the end, so we don't want to keep them waiting.'

'Of course, I'll get my coat. But I hope you've reserved a table for three, because your ego is obviously so enormous it's going to need a chair all to itself.'

Michael laughed with genuine amusement and, for the first time, Jude saw warmth in his eyes. 'I feel suitably chastened. You certainly know how to put a man in his place.'

'So I'm told. But let me assure you, Michael, you ain't seen nothing yet.'

The restaurant Michael had chosen was a small, family-run Italian a few streets away. They started with mixed antipasto and garlic bread. Then Jude ate veal in pepper sauce while Michael had a *bucatini carbonara*. They shared a good bottle of Barolo.

'I love Italian food,' said Jude. 'This veal just melts in your mouth. The continentals have the right attitude to food. They realise it's a sensual experience – something to linger over and share. We English are far too puritanical about it.' She cut a piece of veal.

'I can't picture you being puritanical about anything. You're obviously something of a hedonist. Let me top up your glass.' Michael poured more wine.

'I don't think so, Michael. My definition of hedonist is someone who pursues pleasure to the exclusion of all else. He doesn't care if he hurts other people in the process. That's not my style. I suppose, if I had to give myself a title – and I tend not to, titles are so limiting, don't you think – I'd prefer to call myself a sensualist.'

'If it feel's good – do it? A fine philosophy.'

'I think so. Though I admit that sometimes it can be just as much fun to indulge in things that feel bad.' Jude leaned forward and spoke softly. When she'd finished speaking she popped a morsel of food into her mouth and began to chew. She licked her lip slowly, looking directly into Michael's eyes.

Michael met her gaze. He took a sip from his wine glass. 'When she was good, she was very, very good. But when she was bad . . .'

'Exactly.' Jude finished eating and put down her cutlery. 'Tell me, Michael. What was your first kinky experience? Is it a recent thing or have you always been a pervert?'

Michael laughed. 'Oh, I've been on the left-hand path for as long as I can remember. I'm afraid my soul must have been damned long ago.'

'Does that path lead inevitably to damnation? I'm not sure I think so. Didn't William Blake say, "The road of excess leads to the palace of wisdom"? It's much more apt, I think.'

'Possibly. I'd certainly like to think so. At any rate I very much look forward to our journey along the road of excess.' He tipped his glass at her.

'You know what they say,' replied Jude. 'A journey of a thousand miles begins with a single step. Are you brave enough to take that step?'

'I don't lack courage, I assure you. But you asked me about my first experience. I must have been about ten. I was playing cowboys and Indians with my next-door neighbour, Cheryl. She wasn't really my friend. I usually played with her brother, Mike, and other local boys but they all had the measles and Cheryl and I were the only ones who weren't in quarantine. I was the cowboy. She captured me – I can't remember how it happened now – but she tied me to a tree at the bottom of her garden. I think she used a couple of skipping ropes. Then she picked up an old garden cane and started whipping my legs with it.'

'How old was Cheryl?'

'I don't know, a little older than me. Twelve, perhaps?'

Jude raised her eyebrows. 'I see, an older woman. You were clearly very advanced for your age. Did she whip you hard?'

'Oh yes, she was merciless. It stung like hell. I had bruises for weeks afterwards. I struggled against the ropes, but she'd tied them really tight. It was useless. They dug into my skin and the cane stung my legs. I was crying and screaming for her to stop, but she wouldn't listen. It turned out she was getting her own back because Mike and the boys would never let her join in our games.'

'And how did you feel? What was going through your mind?'

'I don't know: shame, humiliation, excitement. All sorts of things I couldn't possibly name mixed up in one overwhelming, arousing package. Then all of a sudden she dropped the cane and untied me. I begged her to do it again several times after that, but she wouldn't.'

'So you lied when you said you'd never turned the tables? How very naughty of you.'

'I wouldn't really count that as indicating a submissive nature. After all, I didn't consent to it, or even know what she was going to do.'

'Ah, classic avoidance of responsibility. Some people prefer to believe the dominant partner is responsible for their submission, that it's not their free will.' She leaned forward and lowered her voice. 'But we both know differently, don't we?'

'Well, it was the one and only time that I was ever on the receiving end and, as I said, I've never felt tempted to repeat the experience.'

'Until now?'

'Your charms are considerable, Jude. But even so, I still don't feel inclined to change the habit of a lifetime.'

'So why are you here?'

The waiter came and took away their plates. Michael said nothing. He sat looking at Jude, a half smile on his lips.

'You're hoping that you might persuade me to change sides?'

Michael nodded and Jude began to laugh.

'If that's the case, Michael, I am afraid you are in for a very long wait. The day I let a man dominate me they'll be ordering snowploughs in hell.'

'Fortunately, I am a very patient man.'

'Hello, darling.' Jude called out to Chris as she let herself in. She walked into the living room, where Chris was lying on the sofa watching TV. He sat up as she entered then clicked off the picture with the remote control. He was dressed in tatty jogging pants and a sweatshirt but still managed to look sexy and stylish.

'Am I pleased to see you! My cock's been so hard all evening I'm sure I could crack nuts with it.'

Jude walked over to the sofa and kissed him. She sat down beside him. 'Well, I'm here now. And, you'll be pleased to know, I'm just as horny as you. What have you been watching?'

'Oh, just a video, nothing special.'

Chris sounded evasive and Jude thought she saw him blush. She took the remote control out of his hand and pressed the button. The TV screen flashed into life. A huge close-up of a woman's mouth sucking on a cock filled the screen. Jude looked at Chris and shook her head in disappointment.

'You've been watching porn? I bet you've been playing with yourself too, haven't you? Didn't I make it clear I didn't want you to?'

'I know, I know. I was so worked up, I didn't think it would matter. But I didn't come, I promise you.'

'Then what are those screwed-up tissues doing on the floor? And don't tell me you've got a cold.' She picked up one of the discarded tissues and sniffed it. She instantly recognised the distinctive scent of sperm. 'Chris!'

46

'Damn! I meant to flush those.' He hung his head. 'I'm sorry, Jude. I just couldn't help it. Forgive me?' He smiled.

'Maybe I will, maybe I won't. But you're lucky I'm so horny myself, because if I wasn't I'd probably just send you straight home and go to bed with my vibrator.'

'I know I've been a very naughty boy but I'm pretty sure I can do a much better job than your vibrator.'

'I'm counting on it, Chris. Why don't we go into the playroom?' Jude stood up and held out her hand to Chris. She led him up the stairs, past the floor where the bedrooms were, past the studio and up a narrower flight of stairs to the attic.

The loft in Jude's house had been converted into a sort of playroom. It was basically one large space, a vertical wall at either end and the sloping sides of the roof on each side. Dormer windows cut into the roof provided light during the day and were covered by blinds at night. At one end of the room a door led into a bathroom.

A series of bars, hooks and rings were fixed to one wall, providing convenient attachment points. A St Andrew's cross occupied the opposite wall. There was a black leather whipping bench, a spanking horse and a piece of furniture that looked like a massage couch which could be adjusted into a variety of shapes to suit Jude's mood or the nature of the scene. Built-in cupboards housed her toy collection.

'I suppose I should start by undressing,' said Chris as they entered the room. He began to strip.

'It's certainly a good start. Let me see if I can find something for you to put on.' Jude went over to the toy cupboard and opened it. She selected a leather body harness, some shackles and a short riding whip.

'Put this on.'

He strapped himself into it quickly and efficiently, even though it looked like a meaningless tangle of leather straps.

'I can tell you've done that before.' Jude leaned against the edge of the whipping bench, watching Chris.

'Once or twice; you know I have.' He spread his legs and manipulated his genitals carefully through the steel ring that formed the bottom of the harness. 'Ouch. This bit always makes my eyes water.' He fastened the last buckle and stood up straight, waiting for Jude's next order.

Straps went over each shoulder and joined another that circled his chest. They met at a large metal ring, from which another strip of leather went down the front of his body to a waist strap and, from there, connected to the cock ring. At the back, two straps from the cock ring travelled diagonally over each buttock and linked to the waist strap at the side.

'Lovely. But I think it needs something else.' She went over to the toy cupboard and found some crocodile nipple clamps. She attached the clamps to Chris's nipples. He let out a long hissing breath as the teeth bit into his flesh. Jude turned the screw, adjusting the grip, and watched Chris's face, assessing his reactions. When his eyes widened in alarm and he bit his bottom lip she gave the screws one more turn each. She pulled on the chain connecting the clamps, stretching Chris's nipples.

'Bitch,' he said, his voice full of pain.

'You know you're not allowed to speak to me like that, Chris. You disobeyed me earlier and played with your worthless cock when I'd specifically told you not to, now you've started insulting me. You obviously need to be punished.'

'Yes, Ma'am. I'm sorry.' Chris hung his head.

'It's a bit late for an apology. I told you I was going to punish you and you know I always keep my word. Bend over the spanking horse.'

Chris stepped forward and bent over the horse. He winced as his clamped nipples made contact with the leather, but Jude pushed him down until he lay flat and

48

let the bench take his weight. She knelt and attached steel cuffs to his wrists and ankles, then locked them to the rings on the horse.

Jude moved to the top end of the bench and began to undress slowly. She'd deliberately placed herself in Chris's eye line, but her striptease was methodical rather than titillating. She knew he'd be more aroused by her disdain than a deliberate attempt to arouse him. Jude could see Chris's neck muscles straining to keep his head high as he watched her.

Jude stripped down to her stockings and suspender belt, leaving on her high heels. She got a ball gag from the cupboard and fitted it to Chris, then fetched her strap-on harness and buckled herself into it. She made a show of selecting a suitable dildo, conscious of Chris's eyes on her. Finally, she chose an eight-inch black silicone cock as thick as her wrist and fitted it into place. She put a bottle of lube down by the foot of the whipping horse and picked up the whip.

Without warning, she brought the whip down hard across Chris's buttocks. It swished through the air and cracked loudly as it made contact. Chris's whole body jolted in pain.

'Did that hurt, darling?' She hit him again. 'Then perhaps it will remind you to obey me in future.' Jude whipped him twice across the fattest part of his arse then stepped back to admire the darkening stripes.

Chris was struggling. He twisted his body and strained against the cuffs. Jude loved it when he resisted. She always saw acquiescence and resignation in a sub as a sign that she needed to step up the pace.

She whipped him again; three hard strokes one after the other, leaving a row of angry slashes across his flesh. The leather bench creaked as Chris struggled and thrashed. He was hyperventilating, the sound of his breathing amplified by the constriction of the gag.

Jude walked around the bench and knelt by his head. She stroked his hair, pushing his fringe out of his eyes. She wiped the sweat off his face and stroked his cheek, calming him.

'Good boy,' she said, her voice soothing and comforting. 'I know it hurts. It'll be over soon. I know you can take it – that you want to take it for me. Are you ready for some more?' She looked into Chris's eyes. He nodded. She kissed his forehead.

Back in position she aimed six rapid strokes at Chris's left thigh, followed by the same on the right. Chris was panting hard and fighting against his shackles.

'Just a few more, then we'll turn you over.' She brought the crop down on Chris's arse and he shuddered in pain. Raised red stripes glowed against his pale skin. She hit him again and he grunted through his gag. Another stroke, and another. Chris struggled and fought.

Jude gave him three more strokes in quick succession and Chris's muffled howls filled the room. The bench wobbled under him as he fought.

She stepped back and admired the inflamed slashes on Chris's otherwise perfect flesh. At the bottom of one cheek a line of small bruises darkened the skin.

Chris had stopped struggling and lay defeated, with his head lowered and his eyes closed. His chest heaved and he was covered in sweat. A string of dribble dangled from the side of his ball gag. Jude unshackled Chris. She sat him up on the edge of the bench and carefully detached the nipple clamps. He wailed through his gag and brought his hands up to cover his sore nipples. Jude gently but firmly moved them away then gripped each nipple between thumb and forefinger. She squeezed hard and Chris's body began to quiver. He gripped the edge of the bench, his knuckles turning white. His frantic breathing throbbed inside Jude's skull.

50

She released his nipples and embraced him. He wrapped his arms round her and held her close. Jude held him, stroking his back until he became calm.

'Now I want you to lie on your back. That's right.'

Chris lay back against the bench. Jude lifted his legs and bent his knees, placing his feet at the edge of the bench.

'Now, I want you to open your legs, keep your feet together. That's it.'

Chris spread his knees, pressing the soles of his feet together.

'And put your hands behind your head. Good boy.'

He complied.

Jude picked up the whip and brought it down on his right nipple. Chris jumped but held his position. Jude could see that it took every ounce of his effort. She whipped his nipple five more times then did the same to his left. Jude could see the pain and fear in Chris's eyes, but he didn't move. His cock pointed at the sky, signalling his arousal in spite of all the signs to the contrary.

She moved round the bench and whipped the sensitive inside of Chris's upper arm. He flinched, screwing up his eyes in pain. Squeals of protestation escaped through the gag and he thrashed his head from side to side.

'Is it too much? You've only got to say, Chris, and I'll stop.'

She whipped him slowly on the vulnerable and exposed flesh of his inner arms until each had received half a dozen strokes. Jude positioned herself by Chris's other end and laid a slash against his inner thigh. His legs came together and his knees curled up towards his chest. He was panting hard, his chest heaving with pain. His cock was hard and swollen.

'Open your legs.' She spoke quietly, but her voice left no doubt that she expected to be obeyed.

Chris complied, his legs trembling. He closed his eyes tightly and held his breath. She laid a stroke across his bared inner thigh. Chris snorted loudly, the noise escaping down his nose. He held his breath again and Jude could tell that he was only keeping himself still by force of will.

After two more strokes, Chris was trembling. A trail of shiny pre-come quivered at the tip of his rigid cock. Jude held his left knee and whipped the thigh six times in quick succession. When she'd finished, he was howling through the gag and his chin was slimy with his own dribble.

Jude sat him up and removed the gag. 'I bet your jaw must ache.'

Chris nodded.

'Did you enjoy that?' She wiped the sweat and drool off his face.

Chris nodded, then shook his head, then nodded again.

'Both,' he said. 'You know how it is.'

'Indeed I do. Pain and pleasure, the divine dichotomy.' She leaned forward and kissed him on the mouth. He embraced her, pressing their bodies together. She wrapped her arms around him. She could feel his heart beating against hers. Chris covered her face with tiny kisses. She brought her mouth up to his ear.

'I think it's time for me to fuck you.'

'Yes,' he said, 'fuck me so hard I can't sit down for a week.'

'You may regret saying that. Get down on your knees. Suck my cock.'

Chris slid to his knees and opened his mouth. He looked up at Jude, his eyes eloquent with need. She forced her silicone cock past his lips and pressed both hands on to the back of his neck, forcing him to take it all.

'Do it like you mean it, Chris.'

He sucked her fake cock with wild enthusiasm. His eyes were closed. He wrapped one arm round her hip, pulling her close. His other hand reached up and found a nipple. He pinched it hard, making her gasp. She fucked him between the lips, thrusting her rubber dick hard into his mouth.

'I've got to put it in you. Why don't you bend over?'

Chris spat out her cock and scrabbled to his feet. He bent over the edge of the whipping horse, thrusting his arse at her. Jude picked up the bottle of Astroglide and squirted a big dollop into her hand. She slathered half the lube onto her cock and massaged the rest of the gel into his eager hole. She used her fingers to part his cheeks, exposing the brown, wrinkled opening. It seemed to wink at her as she slipped a slick finger inside. Chris gasped as she found his prostate and parted his legs, allowing her entry. He planted his feet flat on the floor and braced himself against the edge of the bench.

Jude fucked him with two fingers, stretching his hole. It rippled round her fingers as she explored him and she felt as though it was inviting her in. A third finger followed and Chris began to moan.

She removed her fingers and placed the tip of her slippery cock at the entrance. She pressed forward and Chris groaned softly as she slid inside. She allowed her weight to move her forward, pushing her cock home. Soon, it was buried up to the root inside Chris's hungry arse.

She began to move, sliding in and out as she held onto his hips. Chris groaned as she hit bottom and mewled in frustration as she withdrew.

'That's good. Fuck me harder, please.'

'You asked for it.' Jude wrapped her fingers round the chest strap of Chris's harness and began to fuck him hard. She braced her feet against the floor and thrust into him. She pulled on the harness as she fucked him, pressing her cock home with power and passion.

'Oh my God!' Chris held onto the bench for support.

She rode him like a horse, gripping the harness. She filled him with her cock, ramming it into him with all her strength. Sweat poured down her body. Sobs and wild cries escaped her throat, a frenzied echo of her lust. Her hair flew round her head and fell in her eyes. Jude's entire body tingled with pleasure.

She plunged her cock into him with all her strength. The leather straps cut into her hands as she pulled on them. Chris's body was dragged backwards as she tugged the straps. He was panting and moaning, rocking his own hips in rhythm with hers.

Jude rammed herself into him. She tugged on the straps and they gave way, coming free in her hands.

'I want you to fuck me, Chris. Help me get out of this thing.' She took a step back and her cock slid out of him with a plopping sound. Chris dropped to his knees and began unbuckling Jude's harness with trembling fingers.

Both of them were covered with sweat. The room smelled of sex. The sound of panting filled the air. Chris had freed her from the harness and he pulled it down, dropping it on the floor. He got to his feet and sat on the edge of the bench. He lifted Jude and sat her on his lap. She reached down and positioned his cock. She pressed down and it slid home.

She wrapped her arms round Chris's neck and held him close. Her sweat-slick chest slid against his. Chris held on to her and rocked his hips. She bounced on his cock, loving the way it stretched and filled her.

Jude bucked and writhed. Her hardened nipples brushed against Chris's chest. His tongue was in her mouth. He tasted of garlic and wine and toothpaste. He smelled of sweat and arousal.

Her cunt felt hot and liquid and a shiver of delight shot up her spine like electricity. She arched her back. Chris's mouth was on her throat. He licked and sucked. She gasped as his teeth bit into her skin. He licked and nibbled his way down her chest and found her nipple.

He teased the sensitive nub with his teeth and she gave a little yelp.

She was coming, her cunt contracting around Chris's cock. Heat spread through her body and she started to sob.

'Fuck!' Chris drew out the word into one long syllable as he began to pump out spunk.

Jude was moaning and crying, her whole body responding to her orgasm. She rode on Chris's cock like a madwoman, grinding her crotch against his. Her nails dug into his shoulders and she leaned backwards, arching her spine. He held her tight, his strong hands gripping her hips. She screamed, a long, loud note that seemed to go on for ever, then collapsed against Chris.

He stroked her hair and rocked her while she recovered. Finally, she sat up and smiled at him.

'How was it for you, darling?' she asked.

Four

In the taxi home from the restaurant Michael couldn't get Jude out of his mind. She was an exciting woman. Her intelligence and self-confidence brought a slight edge of superiority to her obvious sexiness. Somehow, in spite of himself, Michael found that hard to resist.

He knew she was attracted to him; she'd spent the whole evening flirting. Yet, the sexual banter had been more intellectual than anything else. In fact she had seemed rather amused by the whole thing.

Michael wasn't used to being a source of amusement. Under normal circumstances, he'd have found Jude's gentle mocking something of an affront. He was used to women hanging on his every word. That was the way he liked it, and he tended to gravitate towards women who looked up to him and were keen to obey.

Yet when Jude made fun of him he hadn't felt at all insulted, though he wasn't sure he could give a name to how he did feel. Part of him enjoyed the repartee and the slight sexual *frisson* their verbal duels had created. Another part of him, somewhere deep inside, found the whole thing slightly humiliating, as though she were mocking him and questioning his manhood.

She behaved as if she was convinced he was pretending to be dominant. As if she could somehow see into his soul and knew, beyond doubt, that he longed only to submit to her. Michael knew this wasn't true.

He'd been a top for years and it had never once crossed his mind to switch roles. The very idea turned him off completely. Yet, the funny thing was, he couldn't seem to muster up the sense of outrage that Jude's assertions ought to arouse. Instead, there was unease, shame and somewhere underneath it all, a slight shiver of excitement.

Jude was an intriguing woman, all right. Well, she had another think coming if she believed she could get him to submit. He'd hadn't met a woman yet who couldn't be persuaded to obey him in the end.

There was something unspeakably thrilling about breaking a woman who insisted she was dominant. The look of total surrender in her eyes as she finally accepted the inevitable was intoxicating and almost spiritual. Michael could make any woman kneel and beg to serve him and Jude was no different.

As the taxi turned off Cheyne Walk into Edith Grove, he realised he was far too hyped up and horny for sleep.

'I've changed my mind. Can you take me to Putney, please? Fulham Palace Road?'

'OK, guv, your wish is my command.' The driver did a U-turn.

Michael knew Carrie would be awake. Ever since she had given him a copy of her key he knew she had been desperate for him to make a surprise visit. Until recently, Carrie had been his secretary, but that all seemed like another life now.

Six months ago Michael had decided to take redundancy and concentrate full time on his art career. While working as a banker in the city he had always dabbled in art and had managed to build up a respectable reputation, but he'd never had enough time to devote to his work.

He and Carrie were fond of each other and, though they got together less frequently now they weren't working together, she was still a regular sex partner. He knew that Carrie would like nothing more than for the two of them to become a proper couple. Michael had considered it more than once, but in his heart, he knew that it wasn't really what he wanted.

She was a lovely woman, a loyal friend and a sexy and compliant lover, but there was something missing. Call it chemistry, if you like, but whatever it was, Michael knew he couldn't settle for less. He longed for that indefinable spark that made his heart lurch and his cock stiffen at the mere thought. Try as he might, he just couldn't feel that way about Carrie and he was far too fond of her to let her settle for anything less than she deserved.

Michael paid the driver and climbed up two flights of stairs. He tapped on the door and after a few minutes it opened a few inches to reveal Carrie's familiar face in the gap. She smiled.

'I wondered who it could possibly be. Why didn't you ring the bell downstairs to let me know you were coming up?'

He stepped inside. 'Hello, Carrie. I let myself in with the key you gave me. I thought about letting myself into the flat and surprising you in bed, only I was worried you'd think I was a burglar.'

'You'd have given me a heart attack, I'm sure.' She embraced Michael.

He gave her a quick hug and walked through to the living room without waiting for Carrie to follow.

'What were you doing? Have I interrupted?'

'Not a lot. Watching TV and eating chocolate. To be honest, you're a very welcome interruption. And, as it happens, I'm ovulating, so I'm rampantly horny.'

'Aren't you always?' He picked up the open box of chocolates and ate one.

Carrie plumped the sofa cushions and rearranged some magazines on the coffee table.

'Don't fuss,' he said. 'And what are you wearing? You look like a housewife who's let herself go to seed.'

'It's my nightie. I know it isn't very glam, but I wasn't expecting you.'

'Well take it off. And isn't it time you got down on your knees where you belong?' Michael took off his jacket and sat down.

Carrie was five feet tall and petite. Her diminutive size always made Michael, who was a rather slender man, feel huge. Her long dark hair was curly and springy. When they made love it grew wild and messy and Michael always thought it made her look as though she had been electrocuted. Her figure was extremely curvy, the perfect hourglass. Her crowning glory was her full, round breasts, topped by enormous, dark nipples.

Carrie took off her nightie and threw it onto the sofa.

'And the knickers. You know I like you best when you're naked.'

She slid out of her knickers and knelt in front of Michael. He grabbed a handful of her hair and gently pulled on it to tilt her head back. He kissed her, exploring her hot mouth with his tongue. With his free hand he reached for one of Carrie's fat nipples and rolled it between his finger and thumb until it hardened and thickened. She made a soft grunting sound in her throat and arched her back.

Michael kissed her throat. He dabbled his eager tongue into the hot hollows of her collarbones and down the upper slope of her left breast. Carrie gasped as his mouth found her nipple. He caught it between his teeth and pulled it into his mouth. His fingers found her other nipple, pinching and pulling. Her breathing was rapid and loud. Michael could feel her warm, chocolate-scented breath on his face.

'Shall I bite it?' He brushed his thumbs over the tips of her excited nipples. 'Do you want to feel my teeth digging into your nipple? Do you want to feel the delicious, hot shiver of pleasure between your legs as I hurt you?'

Carrie nodded. He squeezed her nipples, slowly increasing the pressure. Her dark eyes burned. Gazing into the eyes of his woman as he gave her the pain she so badly needed had always been a huge turn-on for Michael. It was a moment of profound, naked intimacy.

She exhaled heavily, responding to the pain. He squeezed her nipples harder, the tips of his fingers turning white. Her eyelids fluttered and then closed.

Michael knew that she was turning her awareness inward, concentrating on her body's responses. She was going into 'subspace', a state of mind brought upon by profound submission to a master and said, by those who'd experienced it, to be somewhat akin to meditation. Michael had seen it often enough, and could easily recognise the signs. Carrie usually reached subspace via tit play and Michael was more than happy to provide the necessary stimulation.

He released Carrie's nipples and she moaned in disappointment. He stroked her breasts, holding her close and rubbing his lips against her face.

'Shall we go into the other room where we can play properly?' He spoke softly. 'Then I can give your big, beautiful tits the attention they deserve.' He kissed her, pressing himself against her naked body. Her skin was hot and slightly clammy.

In the bedroom, Carrie opened the bottom drawer of her dressing table. She knelt by the bed, waiting for instruction. Michael sorted through the toys in the drawer.

'It's a shame that you don't have room for a proper dungeon here. Having the right tool for the job makes things simpler. It gives one so much more scope for wickedness.'

'Oh, I don't know. You always manage to improvise somehow. You're quite capable of the most depraved wickedness with nothing more kinky than a silk scarf and the belt from your trousers.'

'Or failing that, my teeth.' He knelt beside Carrie and brushed her hair away from her neck. He kissed her throat, bathing the soft skin with his tongue. Her heaving chest betrayed her excitement. He began to suck and nip, drawing the delicate skin into his mouth.

Carrie extended her neck, tilting her head back until her long hair brushed the carpet. Michael used his teeth, biting her. Her breathing was loud with lust and urgency.

'I want to come. Please!'

'Of course you do. That's the idea.' He bit her nipple. 'To get you so hot and worked up you feel as though you might explode.' He bit Carrie's other nipple. 'But exactly when, how and if you get to come is entirely up to me. Isn't that right?'

'Yes.' Though Carrie had readily agreed with him, it was obvious too that every cell in her body wished that she was the one in control of her relief. And yet they both knew that submitting to him, and whatever that entailed, was precisely the relief she desired. It was a contradiction that Michael found intensely arousing.

He fished a pair of metal handcuffs out of Carrie's toy drawer.

'Get up.' Michael walked over to the door and closed it. Carrie followed meekly behind. 'Now, stand here. Hands above your head.'

He fitted the handcuffs and attempted to loop the chain over the coat-hook on the back of the door.

'You're just a bit too short. I can't quite reach. Go and find a pair of high heels and put them on.'

Carrie went over to the wardrobe and found some shoes. She held them up for Michael's approval.

'No, no. What about that pair of sandals with platform soles and the strap round the ankle?'

Carrie found them and sat on the bed to put them on. She fiddled with the straps and buckles. Excitement and her cuffed hands made her clumsy. Finally she had them fastened and she walked back over to Michael. She pressed her back flat against the door and raised her hands over her head.

'That's better. You're still a bit short but if you stand on your tiptoes for a second . . .'

She complied and Michael looped the chain over the hook. He selected a coil of cotton rope from the drawer. He found the centre of the rope and looped it around her neck, then wound one of the loose ends round and round her left breast, pulling it tight.

Carrie's chest heaved as he worked. His cock began to stiffen.

'You've obviously done that before, Michael. It feels good.'

'Wait a little while, you may change your mind. When the rope starts cutting off your circulation, your tits will be hypersensitive. That's when I'll use my whip on them.' He finished winding the rope around her right breast and fastened both of the ends behind her back. He stood back to admire his handiwork. 'It's called a rope bra. I think it looks beautiful. How does it feel?'

'Tight. My tits are beginning to tingle.'

'Good.' Michael picked up a small, multi-tailed leather whip. 'This should make them tingle even more.' He drew the soft tails of the whip up Carrie's body. She gasped. Michael drew back his arm and she flinched, expecting pain. He flicked his wrist and the whip made contact with her left breast.

'That didn't hurt, did it?'

Carrie shook her head. 'It sort of tickles. It's quite nice, actually.'

Michael flicked her other breast. He watched her face as he brought the whip down, alternating sides. He whipped each breast in turn, barely making contact with the leather tails. Carrie's chest was thrust forward, eager for the whip. Her eyes shone, her lips were parted and moist.

Michael knew he wasn't hurting her yet. He was tantalising her, warming her up and getting her ready for the kiss of the whip. Pleasure and pain were only divided by a narrow margin and, by keeping Carrie constantly aroused, he knew that margin would blur and eventually dissolve. He knew that if he teased her, preparing her to expect pain but providing pleasure, then gradually cranking up the pace, by the time he did start hurting her she'd be so excited and aroused that she'd be incapable of distinguishing between the two.

He ran two fingers along the length of her slit. 'You're dripping, you slut.' He brought his wet fingers to her face and smeared the shiny moisture on her lips. 'You want the whip, don't you? You want me to whip your tits and pussy and make you come?'

'Yes!' The word hissed out of Carrie's mouth.

Michael pinched a nipple, making her wince. 'Yes, what? That's no way to address me, is it?'

'I'm sorry. I mean, yes, Master. I want you to whip me please, Master.'

'All in good time.' Michael wandered over to the toy drawer. He held up a leather ball gag. 'Since you can't seem to address me properly, I think we'd better stop you talking altogether.'

'Please, Master, no. You know how much I hate it. It makes my jaw ache and dribble just pours out of my mouth. It's so . . .'

'Humiliating? Exactly, my love. Now, hold your head still while I put it on. Open your mouth.'

Carrie opened her mouth for the orange rubber ball. Michael pressed it gently past her teeth. Her mouth closed around the ball. He fastened the buckle at the back. The gag seemed to amplify her excited breathing. Michael's cock was hard.

'Now, I think it's time I made myself comfortable.' He slid his sweater over his head and threw it onto the bed. He toed off his shoes and kicked them out of the way. He was out of his trousers and pants in one movement and his rigid cock swung free.

'See how excited you've made me?' He stroked his cock. 'You look irresistible when you're all helpless and naked. When I've finished whipping you I'm going to have to put my cock in you and fill you with my spunk. Would you like that? Speak up?'

Carrie's eyes burned with excitement and assent. He leaned in close and caressed her cheek with his thumb. She rubbed her face against it, eyes half closed.

Michael stepped back and looked at Carrie. The height of the hook forced her to stand upright, forcing her bound breasts forward. Her wild hair was damp with sweat around her face. Her chest rose and fell visibly as she breathed through the gag. She was tense with anticipation and arousal, her thigh muscles trembling.

'You want it, don't you?'

Carrie nodded, frantically.

'You want me to whip your tits and pussy?'

Again, she nodded her agreement.

Michael lowered the whip and swung it upwards. The leather tails landed with a thwack on Carrie's swollen pussy. Her body stiffened. He whipped her again and the slight trembling in her legs became a definite wobble. Michael whisked the whip against each inner thigh in turn and Carrie moaned. The gag strangled the sound.

He whipped her between the legs, bringing the tails down on her pussy and thighs. Red stripes glowed against her pale skin as it kissed her. He used the whip on her mound and belly, making her gasp and buck. Soon her legs, crotch and abdomen were crisscrossed with scarlet. Carrie cried into the gag. Her head hung, spittle dribbled from the corner of her mouth and down her chin. Tears shone in the corners of her eyes.

Michael lifted her head and wiped her face. He kissed her eyelids and cheeks. She nuzzled her face against his.

'Look at me.'

Carrie's eyes snapped open and she gazed into his eyes. Michael gazed back. He leaned his body against hers, pressing his hard, wet cock against her belly.

'Do you feel that? That's what whipping you does to me. I'm going to put it in you in a minute, but first I've got to finish the whipping. So far, I've completely neglected your beautiful tits, and that will never do.' Carrie's eyes were shining with excitement and entreaty. 'Are you ready?'

She nodded.

'If you want me to stop at any time, you only have to ask.'

Michael swung the whip. It swished through the air and landed with a thud against the meat of Carrie's right breast. She gasped and struggled. He whipped the other breast and her body hit the door, making it bang. He brought the crop down on each breast in turn, establishing a rhythm. The impact made her tits jiggle and dance. Welts formed, darkening her pale skin. Her nipples grew hard and thick.

Tears ran down her face. Spit dangled off the gag and trailed down onto her chest. She was panting. Michael concentrated his strokes on her swollen nipples and Carrie began to roar. Her body bucked and twisted. Her hips gyrated. Michael could smell her excitement.

He dropped the whip and held her close, soothing her. Gently, he undid the gag and let it fall. He wiped away the spit. Carrie covered his face in kisses.

'Please, please, fuck me. Let me come.'

Michael laughed. He kissed her on the mouth, tasting her salty tears. 'Patience is a virtue, darling. But then again, what would you know about virtue?'

He went over to the toy drawer and rummaged through its contents. He selected a pair of crocodile clamps and fitted them to Carrie's swollen nipples. She gasped as the serrated metal bit into her delicate flesh.

Michael lifted her up, releasing the handcuffs. He carried her over to the bed and threw her on it. He forced apart her thighs and rubbed his face against her wet pussy. Carrie moaned and rocked her hips. He slipped three fingers inside her and she squealed.

'I'm so close . . . Put your cock in me and I'm sure I'll come straight away.'

'Your wish is my command.' Michael stood up and held his cock in his hand. He rubbed it slowly. 'If you want my big, hard cock to make you come, who am I to deny you? Now, turn over.' He flipped her over onto her knees and climbed onto the bed behind her. He slid it deeply into her cunt then withdrew instantly and pressed its tip against her tight arsehole.

'Oh, you bastard!'

'I'll make you pay for calling me that later.' Michael rubbed his helmet back and forth along her slick cleft. He pushed down against her rear entrance, waiting for it to yield. Carrie thrust her round arse high into the air, pushing back against him. Her hole began to soften and his cock slipped inside. She was wet and tight and as hot as a furnace. His helmet slid past her sphincter millimetre by millimetre.

Carrie groaned, a long, guttural sound that deepened as he entered her. He held onto her hips, pulling her onto his dick.

He tilted his hips back, pulling slowly away from her. His cock withdrew until just his helmet was inside. He stayed perfectly still for a moment, tantalising her. He knew she wanted him to push inside her again, to fill her with his meat. She fidgeted under him, trying to coax his cock back inside. He held her still. She understood. He wanted her to be still, to wait.

Slowly he slid his cock back inside her. His fat helmet pushed into her gut. He fucked her in slow motion, his rock-hard manhood sliding tantalisingly in and out of her arse.

His thrusts picked up speed. He ploughed her arse rhythmically. Sweat dripped into his eyes. He blinked it away. He was panting hard, tensing the muscles in his belly and buttocks as his arousal grew. He held on to her hips. A ball of tension formed in his belly. Gradually, it tightened, deepened. He was on the edge now. About to explode.

He was fucking her hard, his balls banging against her wet slit with each thrust. He shut his eyes. The knot at the base of his belly focused and broke. A jolt of pleasure shot up his spine, making him gasp.

Michael pumped out jizz inside her tight hole. His whitened fingers dug into her flesh as he pounded her. He roared; a deep, animal sound that hurt his throat. He gave one more thrust, burying his cock deep inside her.

He was out of breath and suddenly tired. He wiped the sweat out of his eyes and collapsed over her back. He rolled them both onto their sides, his softening cock sliding out of her with a plop. He reached round and removed her nipple clamps, making her gasp. He fiddled with the knots of her rope bra and loosened it, releasing her breasts. He curled himself around her and kissed her shoulder.

'That was lovely, darling. Do you mind if I stay the night? I'm sleepy all of a sudden.'

'Of course you can stay the night, you know that.' Carrie wriggled against him. 'But haven't you forgotten something?'

He shook his head. 'No, I don't think so. Shall we get under the covers? I'm almost dropping off.' He hopped off the bed and slid underneath the duvet. Carrie sat up and looked at him.

'Don't tell me you're not going to let me come? You can't be serious. You get me all hot and worked up then leave me high and dry? I'll never get to sleep if you don't let me come.'

'You know your orgasm is under my control. I'm not ready for you to come yet.' He held the covers back for her and she got inside beside him. He wrapped her arms round her and kissed her. 'I never said obedience would be easy, did I? If it wasn't difficult, it would be meaningless.'

'I know that's true, but how would you like it if you'd got right to the edge then weren't allowed to come?'

'Oh, I'd hate it, but we aren't talking about me, are we? Tell you what, as I'm in a benevolent mood, if you come to my place after work tomorrow I promise that I'll let you come . . .'

She kissed him.

'Eventually.'

Five

Next morning, Michael caught a taxi outside Carrie's and was home before nine. He had agreed to be interviewed by one of the Sunday supplements. He was delighted when the journalist turned out to be a woman. He knew that with a little judicious flirting, he could easily get Leah Oakley on his side. She'd write a favourable article and, if things went well, he might even fuck her.

They sat on the sofa in his living room drinking coffee. Leah was tall and slim. She wore a black wool sheath dress that emphasised her slenderness. Her hair was the colour of a raven's wing and was cut into a sleek, asymmetric bob. Her lipstick was scarlet and her eye make-up dark and smoky. She leaned back against the sofa cushions, her body elongated and languid.

'Great coffee.' She put her cup on the coffee table.

'Thank you, Leah. I get it from a deli I know in Little Italy. It's expensive, but if you want the best you should be prepared to pay for it, don't you think?'

'I can see you're a man who's used to the best of everything. This flat, for example; it can't come cheap.'

'You're right. It was scandalously expensive. But then I was a banker in a previous life, as you know. I assure you I couldn't have afforded it on a meagre artist's income.' He picked up the cafetiere and refilled her cup.

'Hardly meagre, I wouldn't have thought. Some of your pieces sell for thousands.'

'Some of my pieces are worth thousands.'

She laughed. 'You're very' – she paused – 'confident. Aren't you?'

'I think arrogant is the word you've been groping for.'

'Actually, I was politely avoiding it. It's bad manners to antagonise your host. Especially when he serves such excellent coffee.'

'I'll have some sent round to you. That way you can enjoy it in the comfort of your own home and be as rude as you like.'

She took a sip from her cup. 'I get the impression you might prefer me to be rude.' She looked into his eyes.

'Shall we get down to business? I've set up some examples of my work in the dining room if you'd like to come through.' He stood up.

'Oh . . .' Her disappointment was obvious. 'I was hoping that you'd let me look into your studio. After all, it's the artist's natural habitat.' She got to her feet.

'Unfortunately, I don't have a studio in the flat. There isn't room and the light is wrong anyway. I rent one. It's in the city. A bit of a trek nowadays, but it was handy when I was working nearby. I've thought about finding one nearer, but I'm used to it now. And I've done some of my best work there, so I'm a bit superstitious about it. I know that sounds silly.'

'Not at all. In fact it makes you seem, I don't know, a little more human I suppose. I was beginning to think you were a control freak.' She smiled at him. Michael liked the challenge and confidence he saw in her eyes. There was no hint of apology or uncertainty in the way she looked at him. He realised he was beginning to feel aroused.

'I must admit I do find control rather compulsive but, you're right, there's much more to me than that. Isn't that what makes people so interesting? Complexity? And let's face it, who wants to be simple?'

She laughed out loud, throwing back her head. Her dark hair shook. Her tongue was just visible between her teeth. Her cheeks formed into little round apples and her eyes crinkled.

'You look completely different when you're laughing.'

'Better, I hope?'

'Different – more wholesome. As if the journalist's mask of indifference and ennui has slipped, revealing the woman underneath.'

'I don't think anyone's ever accused me of being wholesome before . . .'

'And now you're blushing, how sweet.'

She covered her cheeks with her hands. 'If you were a gentleman, you'd pretend you hadn't noticed.'

'Leah, my dear, I may be many things, but I assure you a gentleman isn't one of them. Let's go through to the dining room.'

'Shall I make a fresh pot of coffee? Or perhaps you'd like a drink.'

'Actually, I'd love a gin and tonic, if you have it. I feel I need a drink after seeing your work.'

'You found it arousing?' Michael went over to the drinks cupboard.

'Well, it's intended to arouse, isn't it?'

'Of course. But you didn't answer my question.'

She sat down on the sofa. 'Oh yes, it worked on me, all right. In fact, it's a toss-up between the gin and tonic and a cigarette. Only I gave up smoking years ago.'

He laughed. 'I'll just pop into the kitchen for some ice. Make yourself comfortable.'

Michael put ice in their drinks and cut some slices of fresh lime, poured salted cashews and olives into bowls and put it all on a tray. He carried everything through to the living room and put it down on the coffee table.

He sat down beside Leah on the sofa and handed her a drink. He clinked their glasses. She took a swallow.

'Lovely. G and T tastes so much better with lime.'

'Of course. And we've already established I'm a man who likes to have the best.'

'Tell me, I'm curious. The things you include in your art – are they real or staged?'

'What do you think?' He smiled.

'I can't decide, to be honest. I mean, it's pretty obvious you do kinky stuff in private – why else would it find its way into your art? But I can't make up my mind if your art records it, or merely mimics it. I thought I'd be able to tell, but I can't.'

'Does it have to be either? Nobody asks Patricia Cornwell or Ed McBain if they murder people for research, do they?'

'That's very true. But art imitates life, doesn't it?' She kicked off her shoes and put her feet up on the sofa.

'Imitates, yes, but does it have to recreate it? The old masters painted classical subjects – Rubens' *Rape of Lucretia*, Rembrandt's *Blinding of Samson*. Do you suppose they really made their models do those things? I doubt it.' He put his glass down.

'Of course I don't, but you're not actually denying it, are you?'

'Perhaps.' He smiled.

Leah reached across and touched his hand. 'You're not going to tell me, are you?'

He shook his head.

'Isn't there any way I can find out?'

'Perhaps.' He held her hand. 'But it's strictly between us, not for publication.'

'I can keep my mouth shut when I have to.'

'When will the article appear?'

'This Sunday.'

'Then I can meet you one day next week, if you like.'

'And you'll tell me your secret?'

'Let's just say I'll put you out of your misery. Assuming you'd like that.'

'I can put up with it in the name of art, I'm sure. Let me give you my card.' She picked up her handbag. 'I work from home most of the time, so unless I have a deadline I'm pretty flexible.'

'I'm banking on it.'

Michael climbed out of the taxi in Whitecross Street and paid the driver. A young woman sat on the doorstep of the studio reading a newspaper.

'Sorry, Jenny. I got held up.'

She looked up. 'About time. I was going to give it another five minutes and go home.' She stuffed the paper into her bag. 'It's bloody freezing on this cold step with no undies on.'

'And that's my fault, I suppose?' He fumbled in his pocket for his key.

'Well, if it was up to me I'd have my thermals on.'

'Tight clothing leaves marks on the skin.' He opened the door.

'I know, I know. But I bet you wouldn't be such a purist if it was you freezing your arse off.'

'Maybe I'm not wearing any either.'

Jenny laughed and shook her head. 'Nah. Otherwise you wouldn't waste five minutes messing about with your key. You'd get inside quick before Jack Frost turns your todger into an icicle.'

She went through the door and ran up the stairs. Michael could hear Jenny's feet thumping against the steps. He picked up the post, switched on the light and went up.

'I've put the kettle on.'

'Thanks, Jenny.'

Michael hung up his coat. He went over to the office area, sat down and leafed through his mail. Several faxes had arrived overnight. He tore off the shiny, curled paper and scanned the messages. Jenny put a cup of coffee on the corner of his desk. He looked up and smiled, then picked up his mug and swivelled his chair to look at Jenny.

She walked to the end of the room and put her coffee on the floor. She took off her clothes and put on a loose silk robe. Jenny had white blonde hair. Long and wavy, it hung down to her hips. Michael thought it gave her a fairy-tale princess look. Her figure was slender but curvy, and her small, pointed breasts terminated in pale pink nipples. Her fair skin was flawless and her eyes were violet-blue.

Her delicate colouring gave her a sort of purity and fragility Michael never quite felt he managed to capture. But, when naked, there was something liquid and lascivious about her body and the way she used it that was so out of keeping with her apparent innocence that the onlooker couldn't help feeling as if his gaze had somehow defiled her. Jenny switched on an electric fan heater and sat down to drink her coffee.

The studio was a disused warehouse close to Petticoat Lane market. Michael used the lower floor for storage and the upper storey was divided into a kitchen area, an office and the studio. One wall had been replaced with floor-to-ceiling windows. It had cost a fortune, as he'd had to have the roof reinforced, but a studio needed light and the result was spectacular. It flooded the building with daylight, no matter what the weather. The one drawback was that it was always cold, in spite of central heating. Jenny refused to take her clothes off unless he let her use the fan heater.

At the far end of the room things were set up for his latest painting. A double bed was covered by a red velvet throw. To one side there was a sofa and a screen behind which the model could undress, though Jenny never bothered. She stripped off the moment she came in and in the summer didn't even bother with the robe. She sat on the sofa, her legs stretched out, drinking her coffee and reading the paper.

Michael put that day's post in his in-tray and threw the envelopes and junk mail into the bin. He drained his cup.

'Are you ready to roll?'

Jenny got up and took off her gown. 'Sure, I'll just get some lube.'

'And I'll get the bottle.' He opened a small cupboard and brought out a resin replica of a champagne bottle. He walked over to her, smiling.

Jenny lay down on the bed and spread her legs. She opened a tube of lube and applied a fingerful to her pussy.

'Why not let me do that?' Michael knelt on the edge of the bed. Jenny spread her pussy lips with both hands and he slid one finger inside.

He frigged her cunt, then leaned forward and kissed her clit.

He slid a second finger inside her.

'There can't be many models who'd be prepared to do the things I do in the name of art. Though I'm not sure if you can call a painting of me fucking myself with a champagne bottle art. That feels lovely.' She relaxed back against the bed.

'Art, like beauty, is in the eye of the beholder.' He slid in a third finger.

'Especially if the client's prepared to pay for it.'

'Don't be so cynical, Jen. You feel as though you're ready now. What do you think?'

She nodded. He squirted a blob of KY onto his fingers and coated the neck of the bottle with it. He positioned it at her entrance and looked at her for confirmation that she was ready, then slowly pushed it home. Jenny gasped as it entered her.

'At least it's Bolly, darling.'

'That's true. If you've got to fuck yourself with a champers bottle, it might as well be the best.'

A wine importer had seen a previous painting of Jenny and had asked Michael to paint her frigging herself with an empty bottle of Bollinger. And it had to be Bolly – he'd even specified the year. He wanted the label to be clearly in view and readable. He'd also specified that he wanted her completely naked, except for a pair of black leather gloves and lying on a velvet cover. Every detail had to be just right. He'd even demanded to approve Polaroids of the set-up before Michael could begin. Michael was happy to oblige his clients' fetishes, especially when their pockets were as deep as the wine importer's. He'd decided it was too risky to use a real bottle, though – there was a possibility of it causing an embolism – so he'd had a perfect replica made by a firm that specialised in resin sculptures. Even so, they had to be careful around Jenny's more sensitive areas.

Jenny couldn't hold the pose for more than ten minutes, so she took frequent breaks. She stretched her legs and had a cigarette while Michael worked on the background. She wandered across to him and looked over his shoulder.

'How do you make that velvet look so . . . velvety?'

'Talent.'

She leaned close to the painting.

'Are my cunt lips really that red?'

'When you're turned on they are.'

'I'll have to take your word for it.'

'You can always get a mirror and check it out for yourself.'

'I've usually got better things on my mind.'

'Are you ready to lie down again? I need you for the next bit.'

'Sure.'

'We don't need the bottle this time; I'm working on

your face and hands. But don't forget to put your gloves back on.'

Jenny padded back over to the bed. She sat on the edge and pulled off the thick woollen socks she wore when not posing. She put on the gloves and lay down.

'A bit to the right. Tilt your head back a bit more. Now, spread your hair out over the bed. That's right.'

She arranged her hair. 'Is that OK?'

'Perfect, my slutty Rapunzel.'

The light was beginning to fade and Michael's shoulders ached. He put down his paintbrush and looked at his watch.

'Shall we call it a day, Jen?'

She sat up and stretched. 'Fine with me. I'll get dressed unless you have anything else in mind.'

He went over to the bed. 'Not tonight, darling. I'm expecting someone at home. I have to get moving.' He put out his hands to help her up.

'You are a meanie. You make me lay there all afternoon with my cunt on display and now you want to send me home without relief?'

He took Jenny in his arms. She rested her head against his chest.

'It gets to me too. You know it does. Can't you feel my stiffy?' He rubbed his crotch against her. 'But I need to get home tonight. If I had the time you know I would. However, if you're desperate . . .' He glanced meaningfully at the freezer where he'd just returned the bottle.

Submissives were invariably punctual. Michael knew that Carrie would arrive on the dot of seven. He shaved and took a quick shower. He slipped into a silk dressing gown and poured himself a glass of wine.

His flirtatious encounter with Leah and the erotic

77

nature of his painting had left him edgy and excited. Extended periods of arousal always made Michael feel restless and anxious. Sometimes he deliberately provoked the condition because he believed it made him more creative. He channelled his heat and excitement into his art and it somehow took on a life if its own. The artwork became the tangible representation of his arousal. If he got it right it was contagious. His sexual excitement was passed on like a virus to anyone who looked at the finished piece. But after several days his cranked-up sexuality became unbearable and counter-productive and he had to find an outlet.

Michael finished his drink and put it aside. If only Carrie weren't so punctual. He was impatient for relief. If he hadn't gone to her flat after his date with Jude last night he'd have been far too excited to get any work done today. Damn Jude Ryan.

All day thoughts of Jude had intruded on his work. It was so unlike him. No matter what was going on in his private life, he'd never had any difficulty remaining focused during working hours. Yet Jude had somehow managed to insinuate herself inside his mind.

The acquiescence and longing he'd seen in Leah Oakley's eyes when she had handed him her card had barely moved him. And while it was true that painting Jenny had turned him on, Michael had found himself speculating about Jude as he worked. He wondered if her cunt lips grew red and fat like Jenny's when she was aroused. Did her eyelids half close and flicker as she was about to come? Were her small breasts pointed like Jen's or round?

Michael loved that moment of excitement and discovery when he first undressed a new lover. Sometimes it was surprising. A demure ice-queen may turn out to have the body of a stripper, or a slutty vamp might wear a tight red dress that hides virginal white undies. The moment, when it finally came, always crackled with anticipation and arousal. For Michael it was the first delicious submission of many.

When he met a woman he desired he knew his curiosity would eventually be satisfied. Once he turned on the charm and began to flirt it was inevitable. Yet with Jude, his desire was still tinged with a hint of unease that he couldn't quite name. What's more, he knew that little shiver of discomfort was, in part, responsible for his heightened state of arousal.

She'd be a challenge, he knew that. But he'd conquered women who insisted they were dominant before. In fact, he rather enjoyed it when a woman put up a bit of resistance. The hunt was always as exciting as the kill. But there was a niggle of discomfort attached to his intended seduction of Jude that he could neither ignore nor understand. It burned in his belly like dread or excitement; he couldn't decide which.

The doorbell rang, and he glanced at the clock. Carrie was dead on time. He got up and went to the door.

'Hello, darling.' She stepped inside and lifted her face for a kiss. Michael pulled her close, pressing his body against her.

'Shall I take your coat?'

Carrie took off her raincoat and handed it to him. Underneath she wore only a black satin corset and stockings.

'Delicious.' Michael tweaked a nipple, making her gasp. 'Follow me.' He turned and walked down the hall. Carrie's stiletto heels clip-clopped against the parquet floor behind him.

Michael opened a door at the end of the corridor and held it open for Carrie. One end of the room was a home gym with weights and a running machine. The apparatus at the other end were designed with a much more sinister purpose in mind. It was dominated by a black leather whipping bench and a suspension rig.

Along one wall, whips, chains, and clamps hung on hooks, the tools of Michael's trade.

'I'm pleased you remembered to wear your collar.' Michael went over to the wall and selected a leather dog lead.

'Yes, Master.' Carrie got down on her knees.

Michael fastened the lead to the ring on her studded collar and pulled it taut. He moved towards the whipping bench, expecting her to follow. Carrie progressed slowly on hands and knees, like a dog. Her bottom wobbled lasciviously as she moved and her breasts swung free of the corset.

Michael patted the leather bench. 'Climb aboard.'

The whipping bench had a long rounded section, the shape of an elongated barrel, for the victim to lie across. She could either bend across the long side standing up, or lie her body along its length, resting her legs against the specially shaped leg supports. Carrie climbed onto the bench, placing her legs against the supports. Her bottom was forced high into the air, displaying her crack. Michael preferred this position because she could maintain it comfortably for some time and because it gave him easy access to her cunt. Or her arse if he was in the mood.

Carrie stretched out her hands and Michael locked her into the leather straps attached to the bench. He moved round to her feet and did the same to her ankles. Then he fastened a long strap round her waist. He slapped her raised arse with the flat of his hand. She gasped.

'Are you ready, darling?'

'Yes, Master. I'm ready.' Her voice was breathy and deep.

Michael ran his finger along the length of her slit. He rubbed his wet finger on Carrie's upper lip.

'It looks to me as if you're not just ready, you're eager.'

'More than eager. Desperate.'

Michael squatted down and looked into her face. He smiled.

'Desperation is a bad thing, my darling. You're playing into my hands. If you're desperate to come I have all the power.'

'You always have all the power.' She lifted her head and looked into his eyes.

He shook his head. 'I only have the power you give me.' He kissed her cheek. 'But let's get down to business.' He stood up and opened his dressing gown. Carrie was straining her neck, lifting her head to look at him. He rubbed his hard cock against her face. She twisted her head, trying to get it into her mouth. Michael walked away. He put down his dressing gown and selected a long, thin riding whip and a black leather blindfold. He swished the whip through the air several times as he walked back over to the bench.

He tucked the whip under his arm and knelt to fasten the velvet-lined blindfold over Carrie's eyes. He buckled it behind her head. When he was satisfied that she could see nothing he walked round to the foot of the bench.

Michael could see the moisture pooled between Carrie's plump lips. Her breathing was ragged and loud. He pressed his thumb against her tight arsehole and she wriggled against her restraints. He leaned forward and kissed her once on each upturned buttock, then took a step back.

Michael raised the whip into the air and flicked his wrist, making it swish. Carrie flinched then exhaled in relief. Michael cut the air with the whip several times without hitting her. Her body was taut and tense. She was holding her breath.

'You want it, don't you?' He swished the crop again.

'Yes ... No ... you know what I mean.'

'Yes I do, darling.' The whip cut across both cheeks. Her body jolted, making the leather cuffs creak. 'You dread the pain ...' He brought the whip down on her thigh. 'Yet you hunger for it.' He whipped her other thigh and she gasped. 'And wanting it brings you shame.' The whip slashed across her arse three times, leaving red streaks. 'And that shame excites you. The more excited you become, the more pain you need. You don't understand it, but the hunger is so powerful you can't ignore it. Am I right?'

'Yes, yes. I need it.' Carrie was out of breath.

He knelt down and stroked her inflamed flesh, feeling for the raised marks like a blind man reading Braille. He bent his head and kissed them. Carrie wriggled against her bonds.

Michael stood up and looked at his handiwork. His cock twitched. He whipped Carrie slowly. The whip cut through the air and landed with a crack. He lashed her arse and thighs. She struggled and bucked, pulling against the cuffs. A crisscross pattern of scarlet stripes stood out against the pale flesh. The swish of the whip, the creak of leather and his own excited breathing played counterpoint to Carrie's frenzied cries.

His cock was rigid, its tip wet with pre-come. He was tempted to plunge it into one of her eager holes and satisfy himself, but he knew that anticipation would make the inevitable moment of release all the more delicious for both of them. He dropped the whip and bent to unbuckle Carrie's ankle cuffs. He unfastened the waist strap and wrist cuffs and helped her to get up.

'Let's go and lie over here, where it's more comfortable.' He took her hand and led her over to a chaise longue at the side of the room.

She sat down and he knelt in front of her. Michael held Carrie's hips and pulled her to the edge of the couch. Michael's whole body felt alive. His skin prickled with pinpoints of excitement. His cock dribbled pre-come. He kissed her neck and pulled her close. Michael reached down and slid his rigid cock home. She sighed as it filled her.

She gripped his shoulders. Her fingers dug into his flesh. Michael fucked her slow and deep. He rocked his hips, making sure that her clitty rubbed up against his pubes on the in stroke. Carrie fell into his rhythm and tilted her own pelvis to create the stimulation she needed. Her cunt was like hot, wet velvet, gripping him. Carrie's body began to tremble. Michael pulled her closer.

Carrie started to moan and sob. Warm tendrils of delight spread out from his groin. He held on, waiting for Carrie to come before he let himself go. He pressed his cock into Carrie's pussy, riding the waves of pleasure. Her fingernails cut into his shoulders. His chest heaved in rhythm with his shallow breathing. He loved to come inside Carrie's tight cunt. The sensation of her muscles gripping his rigid member as he pounded her, somehow intensified his climax.

The carpet grazed his knees as he fucked her but he didn't care. Carrie was out of breath. She held on to his shoulders, rocking her hips in rhythm with Michael's frantic fucking. She moaned loudly with every thrust. She was practically screaming now, animal sounds of lust that made Michael's cock tingle. She was coming at last. Michael held her tight. Her sweat-slick body slid against his. Her cunt tightened and pulsed round his cock. He counted them: one, two, three, four. His own orgasm began with a flutter in the base of his belly.

Michael grunted loudly. He held on to her arse, pushing his cock into her. He watched Carrie's face. She was panting, gasping as she came. Sweat filmed her upper lip. A single teardrop trickled down her cheek. Michael's cock moved inside her like a piston. He pounded her hard. Damp hair clung to his face; he was panting. He arched his back.

Watching Carrie as he came always made him feel slightly ashamed, as if he were spying on some deeply private moment. The sight of her beautiful face at the moment of fulfilment always filled him with tenderness and lust.

He gripped her hard and gave one long, deep thrust. He circled his hips, grinding his crotch against hers. His cock pumped out hot sperm inside her. His whole body was taut and trembling. Carrie's full lips seemed to be smiling in secret amusement.

Gradually his breathing returned to normal and his cock began to soften inside her. Carrie reached out and wiped sweat off his face with her thumb. He caught her hand and kissed her palm.

'Does that feel better?'

'Yes, though waiting for it was agony.'

'Good things always come to those who wait.'

'Don't you mean those who wait always come?'

Carrie and Michael shared a meal of risotto and salad and half a bottle of cold Frascati. He invited her to stay the night, but she had an important presentation in the morning and needed to be up early. He called a taxi for her and kissed her goodbye.

As he got ready for bed, he noticed that the catalogue on which Jude had written her phone number was lying on his bedside table. He checked his watch. Ten-thirty. A night owl like Jude was bound to be awake. He picked up the phone and dialled.

Six

Jude had invited him to dinner, the next evening, at her house in Spitalfields. As Michael's office was only a short walk away it didn't make much sense to go home first. That morning he put clothes into an overnight bag so that he could shower and change before walking over to Jude's.

He stood in front of the mirror in the studio's small bathroom, naked except for a towel round his waist. He smeared foam onto his face in preparation for a shave. He put a fresh blade into his razor and stroked it down his cheek. The blade rasped against his stubble as he shaved. He rinsed off the foam, splashing water onto his face from the running tap. He pulled off the towel and stepped into the shower cubicle.

Michael was a little disappointed that Jude hadn't sounded more enthusiastic on the phone. He hadn't been able to get her out of his mind and he'd rather hoped that she felt the same. Of course, it was possible that she was just playing it cool.

Yet, if he were honest with himself, Jude's coolness and unreadability somehow added to her allure. She seemed mysterious and self-contained and somehow complete. She gave the impression that she didn't need him or anyone else, but that she might be persuaded to take him to bed if it seemed like an entertaining enough diversion. The way she looked at him left him in no doubt that, as far as she was concerned, if he did end up in her bed she'd be lowering her standards and doing him an enormous favour.

Though it was totally out of character, Michael was beginning to wonder if he might agree with her. His hackles didn't rise and, no matter how hard he tried, he couldn't muster up the expected sense of outrage. Instead he felt a niggling bead of discomfort in his belly that he couldn't find a name for. Part of the sensation, Michael knew, was the usual excitement that accompanies any new relationship. But there was something hard, unfamiliar and a little scary underneath it that he didn't recognise.

In the couple of days since he'd last seen Jude, that little knot had grown into a lust for Jude that was so intense it was almost tangible. It kept him awake at night and had him reaching for his cock when he should have been concentrating on work.

He turned on the shower. Water splashed onto his face. He reached for the shampoo and washed his hair.

Michael climbed the three steps up to Jude's door and rang the bell. After a few moments it was opened by a middle-aged woman, wearing a dark dress and a white apron. She smiled at him.

'Mr Read?' She spoke with a European accent Michael couldn't quite place. Spanish or Italian, if he had to guess. He nodded. 'Come in. I am Alma, Jude's assistant.' She closed the door behind them. 'Let me take your coat.' Michael removed his coat and handed it to her. Alma folded it over her arm. 'Jude has asked me to show you into the dining room and make sure you have a drink. She will be down shortly.'

As Michael followed her down the hall he noticed that she walked with a pronounced limp. The dining room was impressively large with an Adam fireplace and original plaster mouldings.

'What would you like to drink?'

'Red wine, if you have it.'

'Of course.' She moved over to the table and poured wine into a glass from an open bottle. She handed it to him. 'I must see to the food. Jude will not be long. She says to make yourself at home.' She leaned in confidentially. 'She likes to make an entrance.' She smiled enigmatically and disappeared through the door.

Michael wandered around the room. The walls were a pale, matt green that reminded him of cream stirred into pea soup. A tall glass-fronted cabinet stood at one end of the room displaying an impressive collection of blue and white china and eighteenth-century glass. In the centre of the room a long table covered with a white linen cloth was set for dinner. A silver candlestick holding red candles gave a flickering light. Beside it was glass bowl of crimson roses. The silverware looked real and the china, Michael recognised, was Wedgwood. Between the two long windows there was a console table with a hi-fi system and a rack of CDs. He wandered over and looked through the titles, selected a recording of Bach's piano études and put it on to play.

'That's one of my favourites.'

Michael turned around. Jude stood in the doorway. The light from the hall had turned her into a silhouette. He couldn't make out what she was wearing but he thought he could see shiny leather boots. She stepped into the room. His cock stirred.

Jude was dressed in long black boots that laced up to the knee. They shone in the light and terminated in cruel, silver stiletto heels. Her black velvet dress had a tightly boned bodice reminiscent of a corset and soft horizontal pleats in the front that made her belly look rounded and womanly. Michael could imagine the feel of her curved belly in the hollow of his hand as he embraced her from behind.

'You look . . . breathtaking.'

'Thank you.' Jude received the compliment as if she believed it was her right. 'And you look rather handsome yourself this evening. But tell me – do you always wear black?'

He looked down at his clothes. 'I suppose I do. I've never consciously thought about it.'

'Oh, come on, Michael. I can't imagine there's anything about you that isn't conscious or deliberate. I'll bet you think it makes you look mysterious and brooding and . . .' – she walked over to him and leaned close – '. . . just a little bit dangerous. Don't you?'

'Actually, I had rather hoped it suited me.'

'Oh, it does. But you know that, of course. In a dissolute, vampiric sort of way.'

He smiled. 'I was aiming for the Bryan Ferry look, rather than Dracula.'

'Well, both are interesting, in their own way.' She poured herself a glass of wine. 'It all depends if you want your man to sing to you or suck you.' She sipped her wine.

'And which do you prefer?'

'I'm not sure, Michael. Can you sing?'

He laughed out loud.

Alma popped her head round the door. 'Are you ready for dinner?'

'Yes, Alma, thank you.'

After dinner, Jude and Michael drank coffee in the living room. Jude leaned back against the sofa. Her shiny boots gleamed. Her dark eyes glowed.

'Have you thought any more about exploring your submissive side?' She picked up a chocolate truffle from a plate on the coffee table and popped it into her mouth.

He smiled. 'Is it possible to think about something that doesn't exist?'

She sucked on the truffle in her mouth. 'Perhaps. Philosophers write about God even though there's not a shred of proof that he actually exists. Or the unicorn: beautiful, desirable yet mythical.'

'I'm sorry, Jude, but I think you'll find my submissiveness as elusive as the unicorn.'

'Nonsense, Michael. I know it exists; I've seen it. And so have you.'

Michael felt the hairs on the back of his neck rising. His face burned. 'I think you must be mistaken.'

'On the contrary. I have an infallible radar for submissive men.'

'Nevertheless . . .'

She leaned forward and the dark cleft between her breasts came into view. She looked him in the eyes.

'I've seen the way your hand shakes when you pour my wine. I've seen the little sheen of sweat on your upper lip. I know that when you look at these boots you imagine the heel digging into your flesh.' She put her mouth right by his ear. Her hot breath warmed his skin. 'And I know you lie awake at night handling your cock as you fantasise about being naked at my feet.'

She ate another chocolate.

Michael realised he was holding his breath. Inside his underwear things were decidedly cramped. 'You're wrong, Jude.'

She shook her head slowly. 'I haven't been wrong yet.'

'So you are infallible? I'm impressed. Are you omnipotent too?'

'Well, I might not be in God's league but I think you will find I know how to use my power.'

'I don't doubt it. What a pity I will never find out.'

'Never is a long time, Michael.'

The following Wednesday Michael and Jude had arranged to meet in the turbine hall of Tate Modern at 11.30. They'd see the Joseph Beuys exhibition together then have lunch in the restaurant. Michael arranged to call on Leah Oakley at 9 a.m. If he satisfied himself with Leah, he reasoned, his date with Jude wouldn't be clouded by arousal. He wasn't sure why, but the thought of being aroused in Jude's company again somehow made him feel at a disadvantage.

Leah lived in an attic flat in Belsize Park. Michael plodded up five flights of stairs. As he rounded the last corner he saw Leah standing inside the open door. She was dressed in dark-green cargo trousers and a tight black T-shirt. Her feet were bare and she wore no make-up.

'I feel like Sherpa Tenzing reaching the summit of Everest. I should have brought a Union Jack.'

Leah laughed. 'I should have warned you about the stairs.'

'I shall consider it my aerobic workout for the day. And anyway, I'm hoping it will turn out to be worth the climb.'

They went inside.

'Why don't you go through to the living room – it's that way. I'll just pop into the kitchen and make us some coffee.'

In the living room, Michael sat down on the sofa. Opposite him, French windows opened onto a small balcony with plants in pots and a chair and table. Floor-to-ceiling bookcases had been built into the alcoves either side of the fireplace. On the opposite side of the room a cello leaned against a chair. The walls were white and would have made the room seem stark but for the many paintings that hung on them.

Some Michael recognised as prints – Matisse, Turner, Sickert; she clearly had eclectic tastes. But many of the paintings were obviously originals. He recognised Ben Clarke, Helen Chadwick and an early Sarah Lucas self-portrait.

Leah came into the room carrying a tray.

'I hadn't realised you were such an art-lover. You've got quite a gallery here.'

'Well, I'm hardly Charles Saatchi, but I do love to look at beautiful things. One of the perks of being an arts correspondent is that galleries often let me have a discount. Do you see anything you like?'

He looked into her eyes. 'Yes, the moment I walked in the door.'

She laughed. 'Among my paintings, I mean.'

'Is that a Jenny Saville over there?' He pointed.

'Yes. I bought it at her first show, so it was very reasonable. I like her work. It has echoes of Lucien Freud, don't you think?'

'I do, yes, though her nudes aren't quite as grotesque.'

Leah handed him a cup of coffee. 'Do you think they're grotesque? I wouldn't say so. Did you see the exhibition at Tate Britain a few years ago? I thought his paintings of Leigh Bowery were among the most beautiful I'd ever seen.'

'Let's just say he doesn't flatter his subjects . . .'

'True, but he shows you who they really are. It's as if he somehow manages to paint their souls. It's only oil paint and canvas, I know, but you almost feel that if you put out your hand and touch the surface you'll feel flesh, do you know what I mean?'

Michael nodded. 'I had no idea you were such a passionate woman, Leah. And you play the cello?' He nodded towards the instrument in the corner.

'Yes, I do. I went to the Guildhall. I'd planned to play professionally, but it didn't work out. I drifted for a while after I finished college, then a journalist friend asked me to review a couple of concerts and things sort of snowballed.'

'But you obviously still play.'

She nodded. 'Oh yes, I couldn't live without it. There's something about making music that sort of – I don't know – completes me somehow. It lets me express myself in a way that nothing else does. In a way I feel I'm most myself when I'm playing.'

'I hope you'll let me hear you play.'

'Perhaps. I get terribly nervous when there's anyone listening. That's the main reason I don't play professionally.'

'Nevertheless, I look forward to a private performance one day.' He drank some coffee. 'You look different today.'

'This is the casual version of me, the at-home me. You did say you preferred me when I looked more wholesome?'

'Yes, I prefer you when you're not hiding behind your professional mask.'

'Well, I'm not hiding today.' She looked into his eyes.

He returned her gaze. 'Has anyone ever told you that you have lovely eyebrows? Very expressive.'

'They haven't, thank you. Did you see the article on Sunday?'

'I did, thanks. It was very flattering.'

'Honestly? You thought that? I'd have said it was professional and objective. I just happen to like your work.'

'Really? Then I'm surprised you don't own one.'

'I can't afford one! As you pointed out last week, some of your stuff sells for thousands.'

'But you have a Jude Ryan, I notice.'

'Yes. I've had it a while. I certainly wouldn't be able to afford her stuff now.'

'What do you think of her work? Nice coffee, by the way.'

'You're teasing me. You know very well it's the coffee you had sent over. I like Jude's work. It's bold, even controversial sometimes. Yet she always seems to imbue her subjects with a sense of humanity. She's not just shocking us for effect, they're real, whole people.'

'Do you see any of Jude's influence in my work? It's one of the things people often say.'

'The subject matter, yes, but yours are much darker,

much starker. The kinkier images anyway, not the vanilla stuff.'

'Is that a good thing or a bad one, do you think?'

'I'm not sure yet, to be honest. But you still haven't told me your secret. Are the things in your paintings staged or real? I'm dying to know.'

She was leaning against the back of the sofa, her legs curled under her. Michael thought he could see the outline of her nipples under her tight T-shirt.

'Then I hope the answer doesn't disappoint you. Sometimes they're real, sometimes not. The darkroom, for example, at my new exhibition, is real. I filmed a session – with the model's agreement, of course – and then edited it and had the finished film made into a loop. And if I paint people fucking then, yes, they really fucked when they sat for me. At least, they fucked some of the time. Most of the time they're just posed in the appropriate position. You can't expect anyone to keep it up for hours on end, after all.'

'And do you get aroused, standing there watching people fuck all day?' She exaggerated her pronunciation of the word 'fuck', rolling it around in her mouth like a treat.

'Again, sometimes I do, sometimes not. It's often rather clinical, actually.'

'But sometimes you do? The darkroom or some of the kinkier images? If you're really doing those things to a woman, it must have an effect on you?'

He shrugged.

'Of course. I'm not made of wood, after all.'

'Actually, I was rather hoping that you were.' She leaned forward and put her hand on his crotch.

'Do you think my cock is like Pinocchio's nose? It grows if I'm telling a lie?'

'Why don't we go into the bedroom and find out?'

'How can I say no?' He leaned close and whispered. 'But will it be vanilla or are your tastes . . . a little more dark?'

She gave him a long stare. 'I think it's time I came over to the dark side.'

Leah led him down the short hall and into her bedroom. She stood in the middle of the room and pushed her hands down hard into her trouser pockets. The gesture seemed casual, but Michael knew she'd hidden her restless hands in case they betrayed her nerves.

'If you imagine that I'm going to promise to be gentle with you, I'm afraid you're going to be disappointed.'

'But I don't want you to be gentle. That's the point.' She maintained eye contact. Michael laid his open palm against Leah's cheek. She closed her eyes and pressed her face onto his hand.

'I think you should start by getting undressed.' Michael sat down on the bed.

'Do you want me to do a striptease?'

'No, I just want you to take your clothes off. Slowly, while I watch.'

She crossed her arms and gripped the hem of her T-shirt. She pulled it off over her head and threw it onto a wicker chair nearby. Underneath she wore a black lace bra. Dark nipples peeped through the sheer fabric. Leah reached behind her and unhooked it. She tossed the bra aside.

Her breasts were small but full. Her nipples were the colour of strong coffee and they were erect. They seemed even more obvious, impudent almost, against the pale cream of her skin.

'I'm surprised you wear a bra. You don't need one.'

'I think a bra makes me look a bit bigger; I need all the help I can get.' Leah slipped out of her trousers.

'Nonsense, they're quite big enough. Don't wear a bra when I see you in future. Now, take your knickers off. Slowly.'

Leah's knickers were made from the same sheer lace as her bra. They were cut like French knickers or shorts, but they clung to her body, hugging her curves. At the top there was no waistband, and the front dipped down in a V that revealed her navel. She slid them slowly over her hips and stepped out of them.

She stood with her hands at her side, looking at him, waiting for instruction. Her chest moved visibly as she breathed. He could just hear the soft rush of breath as she exhaled. Her lips were parted and moist. Her eyes glowed.

'Now, I want you to turn round, so I can see if your arse is as pretty as the rest of you.'

Leah turned. From the back, her curves were more evident. Her bottom was heart-shaped and plump, her legs long and shapely.

'Open your legs a little. A bit more, that's right. Bend over.'

Leah bent at the waist. The dark cleft of her crack stretched a little wider.

'Good. Now I want you to reach round with both hands and hold your cheeks apart.'

Leah hesitated, then complied. She pulled her buttocks open. Though he couldn't see her face, Michael knew it was burning with shame.

'I'm glad you decided to obey me, Leah. As you will find out, there are consequences for disobedience. A little wider, please, I want to see your arsehole.'

Leah pulled her cheeks open, revealing the dark bud of her hole.

Michael squatted behind Leah. He used both thumbs to spread her buttocks a little wider. He looked at her puckered opening. He blew on it and she gasped.

'Have you ever let a man fuck you in the arse, Leah?'

'Yes . . . yes, I have.'

'And did you enjoy it? And don't forget, you must be honest.'

'Yes, I enjoyed it.'

He sat back down on the bed.

'And do you ever play with it, stick your finger in it when you masturbate?'

'Yes, I do.'

'You're a dirty little girl, aren't you? Stand up now, and come over here. Get on the bed.' Michael slid along the bed, making room. 'That's right, lie down. Open your legs. Wider.'

Leah lay back against the bed and opened her legs. Her dark pubic hair was neatly trimmed. Her lips were a slightly darker shade of the same coffee colour as her nipples and plump with blood.

'It's a little peculiarity of mine, but I prefer my cunts to be naked. Next time I see you you'll have had yourself waxed. Is that understood?'

'Of course, whatever you want.'

'That's right. Whatever *I* want, you're obviously learning. But just in case you're in any doubt. I *never* lick a pussy that has hair on it. And I'm assuming you do want me to lick your pussy, Leah.'

'Oh, yes.'

'Then you'll do as I say. Now, I want to look at your cunt. Hold your lips open for me.'

She reached down and spread her cunt. The inner folds of her pussy were a rich, dark red that was almost purple. Her hard clit peeked out of its hood as if begging for release. Around her opening she was shiny with moisture. A single bead of juice ran down and was lost between her cheeks.

'Are you aroused, Leah?'

'Yes! Can't you see how wet my cunt is?'

'Indeed I can. I just wanted to hear you say it. There's nothing quite as erotic as hearing a woman admit she's helpless with lust.'

'Well, do something about it then!'

'All in good time.' He stroked the inside of her thigh. Leah moaned. 'But you'll have to learn to control your impatience because, as I'm sure you've realised by now, we're operating on my timetable, not yours.' He bent his head and kissed her belly button. Her whole body quivered.

'Do you have any toys? I think it's time we had some fun.'

'I've got a couple of vibrators in my bedside drawer and some anal beads.'

'Is that all? No handcuffs or whips?'

'Of course not. I'm new to this, you know.'

'Then I shall have to improvise. Fortunately for you, I have a vivid imagination. Get up, and sit on the edge of the bed.' He opened the bedside drawer and took out the vibrators and beads. 'Don't you have anything I could tie you up with? Ropes, belts?'

'There are some silk scarves, hanging over the bed-knob there.'

Michael took one of the scarves and covered Leah's eyes with it. He wound the length round her head several times and tied the ends.

'Can you see? What am I doing now?' He stuck out his tongue.

'No idea.'

'Good. Move over a bit and get on your knees.'

Leah slid over to the middle of the bed and did as he said.

'Put your hands behind your back.' Michael used another of the scarves to tie her wrists. He pulled the silk tight, making sure she couldn't work it loose.

'Now bend over.'

She leaned forward slowly, then hesitated.

'I'm going to fall, I can't support myself.'

Michael flipped back the corner of the duvet and picked up a pillow. He placed it in front of Leah. He held her by the shoulders.

'Lean forward. I've put a pillow down for your head. You can't fall. You can rest your forehead on the pillow, or your cheek if you want to.' He helped her into position. 'Is that OK?'

'Yes, that's fine. I think I can hold this position for a while.'

Michael climbed off the bed and quickly undressed. He was already half hard. He put his clothes on the wicker chair then looked around the room for anything he might be able to use on Leah. At her dressing table he picked up bottles and jars, smelling them. In the mirror he could see Leah's reflection, arse high in the air, body rigid with anticipation and excitement. Her loud breathing filled the room. He picked up a hair-brush and tossed it onto the bed.

'Do you have any lube?'

'Sorry, no. There's a jar of Vaseline on the dressing table, I think.'

'Buy some for next time.' Michael picked up the jar. He pulled his belt out of its loops and carried it over to the bed.

He opened the Vaseline and smeared it on the first few inches of the anal beads. The beads were threaded on a thin rod rather than a string and were semi-rigid, with each bead larger than the previous one. He pressed the first small bead against her hole and pushed it inside. She gasped. He pushed slowly, sliding the beads inside her one at a time. Her arse seemed to swallow them, each little intrusion eliciting a moan of protest or delight; Michael couldn't decide which. He managed to get about half the bead wand inside her before he met resistance. He left the end hanging out of her. It dangled down like an obscene tail.

Michael's cock was fully erect, his balls tight and hard. He looked down at Leah. Her entire body was quivering. She was so wet that her cunt glistened in the light. He touched her buttock with his fingertips and she arched her back. He stroked her cheeks with the flat of his hand. He slid his thumb along the damp crack of her arse and she tilted her hips up to meet him, hungry for his touch.

Michael stroked her bottom with both hands, one palm for each peachy cheek. At first his touch was gentle and soft, but gradually, he increased the pressure. The sight of her upturned arse was almost impossible to resist. For a moment, he considered pulling out the beads and sliding his cock in their place. He massaged and rubbed her skin, digging in his thumbs. Leah was panting loudly. Her bound hands were formed into fists behind her back. She moved her hips, making her tail of beads jiggle and dance.

He massaged her arse with strong hands. He squeezed her flesh between thumb and fingers. He pummelled and pinched. Her skin grew pink and hot. He tapped her buttocks with the flat of his hand, barely making contact at first. His taps became slaps and Leah's panting became moans. Stinging slaps made her gasp and reddened her tender flesh.

Michael's cock was rigid. Its tip glistened with pre-come. He took it in his hand and slid his foreskin backwards and forwards over his helmet a couple of times. He picked up the hairbrush and began to spank her. Leah's face was buried in the pillow. She struggled, but the scarf round her wrists was tight and wouldn't budge. Her usually sleek hair was messy and damp. She made a sharp little cry of pain every time the brush landed.

He dropped the brush. 'You're making far too much noise.' He went over to the chair and sorted through their discarded clothes for her knickers. He got another silk scarf and climbed back onto the bed. He stuffed Leah's knickers into her mouth then wrapped the scarf around her face as a makeshift gag.

Michael picked up his belt. With the buckle against his palm, he wrapped the belt round and round his hand until he had a workable length. He brought the end of the belt down on Leah's upturned arse. She roared into the gag. He whipped her again, bringing the belt down on each buttock in turn. Michael's cock twitched. The belt thudded down and Leah's body shuddered. Her bead tail wagged frantically.

He uncoiled the belt and put it down. He flipped Leah over and sat her up. He held her close, stroking her back and hair. Her heart pounded against his. He kissed her neck, licking her salty skin. Leah moaned. He reached behind her and untied her hands. She wrapped her arms around him, pulling him close. He pushed her damp hair away from her face and laid her down again.

'Spread your legs. I want you to play with yourself.'

Leah didn't need telling twice. Her right hand was between her legs, fingers frantically rubbing her swollen clit.

'Use both hands, I want to see what you're doing. I want to see you fingering your wet cunt. And you are wet, aren't you? I can see it, dribbling down the crack of your arse. There's even a wet patch on the bed where you've been lying. You're nothing but a slut.'

Leah nodded her head in mute agreement. Michael watched as she spread her lips and fingered her clit. The inside of her pussy had darkened to a deep aubergine. Arousal had also darkened her cunt lips and made them plump and puffy.

'Stick two fingers into your hole. I want to see you fuck yourself.'

Leah slid two fingers in, groaning softly as they slid home. Michael leaned forward and brushed her nipples with the flat of both hands. Robbed of her vision, Leah's other senses were operating on overdrive. The unexpected sensation turned her body rigid and made her moan.

Michael flicked her nipples with a fingernail. Her back arched and a long, noisy breath hissed down her nose. He began to roll her nipples between thumb and fingers and she snorted into the gag. Leah's fingers moved frantically between her legs.

100

'It goes without saying, that you're not allowed to come until I give you permission. So perhaps you ought to slow down a bit, after all there's so many more things we can do first.'

Leah stopped wanking and put her hands on her belly.

'But you mustn't stop, Leah. I merely told you not to come. I didn't tell you to stop.' He pinched her nipples hard and she put her hands up to cover them. Gently, he took both of her hands and put them back on her pussy. Obediently, she spread her lips and began to finger herself. 'That's better. Since this is your first time I shall overlook your disobedience.' He bent his head and sucked on her nipple. She gasped and arched her back. 'However, I assure you I won't be so generous next time. But now, I think it's time to fuck you.'

Michael knelt between her legs and slid his hands underneath her buttocks. He pressed the tip of his cock against her cunt and thrust his hips forward, entering her. She gasped her appreciation through the gag. He put her ankles over his shoulders and wrapped his arms round her thighs.

'Play with yourself while I fuck you.'

He pumped hard. Leah had both hands between her legs, rubbing her clit. Her hot cunt gripped him. Michael's hair fell over his face, sweat prickled in his armpits.

The erotic charge of his verbal seduction and Leah's inevitable submission had kept Michael at the pitch of arousal. It wouldn't be long before he would burst inside her. He reached out a hand and pinched one of her nipples. Leah's body bucked and her cunt rippled around his cock. He pinched harder, pulling and twisting it. Her nipple stretched and elongated, pulling her breast out of shape. Leah mewled into the gag.

Michael held on to her thighs and rammed his cock into her. His balls smacked against her bottom on every stroke. Now and then, the wand of beads in her arse would dig into him, but he didn't care.

He was sweating and panting hard. His hips pounded. He released her right nipple and gave the same loving attention to its twin. He pinched and pulled, stretching out her small breast into a point. He filled her hot cunt with his cock, ramming it home. Her knuckles pressed into him as her fingers worked her clit between them. Her mouth moved fruitlessly under the silk gag.

Her legs banged against his head as he hammered into her. The back of her thighs stuck to his chest. His groin ached for release. His balls were tight and hard inside their thickened sac. Leah was practically screaming now, her howls muted by the knickers in her mouth. She rubbed her clit. Her back arched and she screamed. The sound pierced the air in spite of the gag, and Michael knew she was coming. He reached underneath her and pulled out the beads in one quick motion. Leah's body bucked and twisted and she howled into the scarf.

He wrapped both arms round her thighs and fucked her hard. He was close, just a few more strokes and he'd be there. One, two, three. He gave one final deep thrust and his cock exploded inside her. He grunted and gasped. He filled her with his hot spunk. He circled his hips, grinding his crotch against her. Sweat dripped off his face. His legs felt weak.

Leah lay exhausted, both hands still clamped over her cunt. She was breathless and red in the face. Dribble ran down her chin. Michael leaned forward and uncovered her mouth. He pulled out the knickers and wiped her wet face with them.

'Did you enjoy that?'

'Yes, I did, couldn't you tell?'

'I had an inkling, yes.' He lay down beside her and removed her blindfold. He took her in his arms. 'But I must say, I don't remember giving you permission to come. Let's just say that you owe me one.' Michael looked at his watch. 'I'm sorry, darling, I'll have to get moving soon. But there's one last thing I'd like you to do for me.'

'Anything.'

'Anything? You don't even know what it is yet.'

Michael kissed her. He took her by the hand and led her down the hall to the living room. He sat down on the sofa.

'I want you to play for me.'

Leah opened her mouth to speak, but the look on Michael's face told her that refusal was out of the question. She moved the cello aside and sat down. She positioned the instrument.

Leah sat silently for several long moments with her bow poised on the strings. Above the instrument's opulent body her naked breasts seemed out of place. Michael felt an illicit shiver of delight. Her hair was matted and frizzy. Her cheeks were still flushed pink, an afterglow of her orgasm. She began to play. Long, deep, resonant notes echoed round the small room.

Within a few bars he had recognised Max Bruch's *Kol Nidrei*. Leah had unknowingly chosen to play a piece that Michael knew well. His favourite version was by Jacqueline du Pré and he listened to it often while he worked.

She played with her eyes closed. Michael watched her hand on the neck of the cello. Her fingers moved with strength and delicacy. When she played a vibrato note her hand rocked in a sort of controlled flutter that made the cello sing.

Michael couldn't take his eyes off her. The music Leah was creating seemed alive and tangible. It hung in the air like smoke. It resonated in Michael's ears. It vibrated inside his chest.

Leah's parted legs held the sumptuous curves of the cello in a lover's embrace. She rocked and swayed. Her chest heaved. Her parted lips were red and puffy. An expression that Michael could only describe as rapture transformed her face. Her bow moved over the strings and her fingers flew along the cello's slender neck.

Michael was on the edge of his seat. The music resonated through his bones, consumed him. He could see that Leah was totally absorbed by her playing, lost in it. Her music was more than just notes on a page, learned mechanically and reproduced. She was playing from the heart, allowing her soul to sing through the strings of the cello. He could hardly breathe.

As Leah reached the last few notes of the coda it dawned on Michael that he'd seen the same expression on her face when he had made her come. When she played the final triumphant note and lowered her bow his cock was rigid.

She opened her eyes.

Seven

After the exhibition Jude and Michael had lunch. Sun streaked through the glass walls of the restaurant. Waiters hurried by with laden trays of food. The room smelled of fresh coffee and garlic. Their table was by the window, overlooking the river.

'I'll have the goats' cheese and tomato tart and a rocket salad, please. And a glass of red wine.' Jude handed her menu to the waiter. His fingers touched hers and lingered for a moment. His dark eyes gazed into hers. She smiled.

'Tagliatelle for me . . . and I'll have a glass of red wine as well.'

'Pasta for the gentleman and goats' cheese tart for the lady. Can I get you anything else?' Though he was addressing them both his eyes were fixed firmly on Jude.

'Perhaps some sparkling mineral water?' She smiled at him.

'Certainly, madam.' He walked away.

Michael laughed.

'Do you think I'm funny, Michael?'

'No, no, not at all. It's just that you were rather . . . blatant.'

'The waiter, you mean?'

'Yes, you had him practically eating out of your panties.'

'You find that inappropriate?'

105

'No, but bad manners, perhaps.'

'Oh, I see, your masculine pride is wounded. I should only have eyes for you.' She smiled.

'When you say it like that it makes me sound rather . . .'

'Shallow? And just a little arrogant, perhaps?'

'Perhaps, but at least I can rely on you to put me in my place.'

'This is new territory for you, isn't it? I get the impression that you're rather out of your depth.'

The waiter arrived with their drinks. Jude looked up at him and smiled, deliberately provoking Michael.

'You make me sound like an inexperienced teenager on his first date.'

'I'm not making you do anything, Michael. Not yet. But perhaps that's how you feel.'

He laughed. 'I like to consider myself a man of the world. I think my social skills are adequate. I've plenty of experience of seducing women, you know.' He lowered his head and smiled at her, looking up at her through his dark lashes. Jude was sure that most women found the gesture irresistible.

'Perhaps you are, but that's not what's happening here, is it?'

'I don't understand. I'm a man, you're a woman, as they say. We're obviously attracted to one another. I wine and dine you, we get to know each other and eventually things become more intimate. Isn't that the way it works?'

'So you see seduction, as you call it, as a process that inevitably concludes in my capitulation? I'm the prey and you are the hunter?'

He laughed. Jude thought she could detect a little nervousness in his voice.

'You make it sound rather clinical but, yes, that's traditionally the way it goes, isn't it?'

The waiter brought their food.

'Tradition is a nasty word. What does it mean when you think about it? Predictable, habitual, boring. Who wants that? I like to think of myself as something of an iconoclast.' She took a sip of wine. 'But perhaps that's where we differ, Michael. You cling on to the tradition of seduction, as you call it, because it's habitual and somehow comforting. You put it on like an old jacket that's worn thin on the elbows and doesn't fasten properly, but you keep it because it's cosy and reassuring and familiar.'

'Are you accusing me of being unadventurous? I may be many things, but surely I'm not that? You only have to look at my work to know that my sexual tastes are very broad indeed.'

'True. But perhaps you're just a little bit ... What's the right word? Complacent?' She cut into her tart. Though her eyes were on her plate she knew Michael was staring at her.

'How can you accuse me of that, of all people?'

Jude put down her fork. 'Because you hide behind your work. You think it proclaims to the world that you're a libertine, a sexual adventurer. You think there's no woman alive you can't conquer and maybe that's true. When all the time the ultimate adventure is staring you in the face and you're too blind to see it.'

He threw up his hands in exasperation. 'I'm afraid you've totally lost me now.'

She looked into his eyes. 'Where's the thrill in seducing yet another woman? Maybe you could get me to submit too. But pretty soon the thrill of victory would fade and you'd be jaded and restless again. My friend Dee has a saying: "If you always do what you've always done, you'll always get what you've always got." You need to break that cycle, Michael, if you really want to expand your boundaries. What are you afraid of?'

'What makes you think I'm afraid of anything?'

107

She leaned in close. 'Because I can smell it. The tired old patter you trot out, the practised little gestures you think women find irresistible. They're masks you hide behind. Take them away and you're lost. But that's where the real journey begins, don't you see? If you let your barriers down the possibilities are limitless. You'll feel things you only ever dreamed of. You'll be free. And all you have to do is toss aside the mask and let the man underneath really trust another human being for the first time in your life.'

'You make it sound like paradise. I'm almost tempted.'

'You're more than tempted, Michael, you're desperate.'

He laughed. 'I'm really not sure.'

'I think you are.'

Michael looked away. His fingers fiddled with the tablecloth.

'Suppose I agree to what you want. What would you . . . what would you do to me?'

'You want a menu? You know that isn't the way it works. If you decide it's what you want – and we both know it is – then you just have to trust me.'

'You make it sound so simple. I don't think you realise how hard this is for me.'

She reached across the table and held his hand. 'Of course I do.'

His thumb stroked the back of her hand. He looked down at the table, unable to meet her gaze. 'Then help me.' His voice was soft and uncertain.

'I will, I promise. I'll be your guide, your counsellor, your friend and your lover. When you take your first step into that dark void I'll be there holding your hand and I'll be there beside you every step of the way.' She reached out her hand and touched his cheek. He turned his head and kissed her palm. 'But first, you need to take responsibility for your own desires. After today, if you want to see me you've got to let me take charge. I don't want you to contact me again unless that's what you want. Do we understand each other?'

He nodded.

'I'll look forward to your call.'

Next day, when Jude came downstairs from her studio after work she noticed that the light on the answerphone was flashing. She pressed the button.

'Hi Jude. This is Michael Read. You told me I shouldn't contact you again unless I wanted to submit to you.' He took a big breath and exhaled loudly. 'Well, I'm calling. So . . . I agree to your terms, I suppose, and I look forward to hearing from you. I think you know my number but just in case you can't lay your hands on it . . .'

Jude picked up a pencil and copied down the number. She clicked off the tape, picked up the phone and dialled.

'Michael Read.'

'Good evening, this is Jude. I'm not disturbing you, I hope?'

'No, not at all. I suppose you got my message?' Michael sounded nervous but was doing his best to hide it.

'Yes, I did. That's why I'm calling. Are you free tomorrow evening?'

'I can be. What time?'

'Shall we say seven o'clock?'

'That sounds OK.'

'Now, there's something I want you to do for me before you come over tomorrow.'

'Yes . . .'

'There's no need to sound so nervous, it's just a simple instruction, nothing sinister.'

'It just feels very unnatural and a bit scary agreeing to your terms blindly without knowing in advance what you're going to ask me to do.'

109

'I know. But you'll do it nonetheless.'

'Yes, I'll do it, of course.'

'It's a very small thing really, Michael, it shouldn't present you with any difficulty. Starting today, you are not permitted to come without my permission.'

'You mean I'm not allowed to masturbate?'

'To masturbate, or to have an orgasm with another person.'

'You're banning me from having sex?' Michael didn't bother to keep the outrage out of his voice.

'No, I'm merely insisting that you seek my permission to have sex, even if you are the only party involved.'

'You will let me do it occasionally, won't you?'

Jude laughed. 'Of course, don't worry. But you are not permitted to masturbate, or to have any sexual contact with another person until you come here tomorrow.'

'So you'll let me come then?'

'Not necessarily, Michael. You know how it works, I'm sure.'

'Yes, I do. It's just that I never expected to be on the receiving end of it.'

'Then it will be a new experience for you.'

'OK, Jude. I will arrive at your house tomorrow night completely chaste. And, no doubt, rampantly horny.'

'Well, I sincerely hope so. I'd hate to be the only one.'

Michael laughed.

'You do understand what you're agreeing to, Michael? This is what you want – you're sure?'

There was a long pause. Michael's breath snorted loudly into the mouthpiece. 'You know the answer to that, Jude. I know I wouldn't admit it at the time, but everything you said to me yesterday was true. I want this. In fact, I need this. Do you understand?'

'I do.' Jude cradled the phone. 'I'll take good care of you.'

'Thanks. So . . . I arrive tomorrow at seven and?'

'It begins.'

'You're not going to give me any clues, are you?'

Jude laughed softly. 'No. But it will be OK, I promise. You just have to trust me.'

'I do, Jude, otherwise I couldn't even contemplate doing this.'

'Thank you. And that's an excellent beginning, don't you agree?

Next day Michael was restless and distracted. His stomach was queasy from a combination of eager anticipation and what he could only describe as trepidation. He was irritable and edgy and found it hard to concentrate. Eventually he'd admitted defeat and sent Jenny home early in a taxi. He sat at his desk and pondered his options.

Under normal circumstances Michael would have dealt with any feelings of unease by masturbating. It might not be a sophisticated solution but it was cheap, always available and a hundred per cent effective. He'd unzip his flies, take his cock in his fist and within five minutes orgasm's soothing hormones would have worked their magic. Yet Jude had specifically forbidden it and obviously expected to be obeyed.

Jude wanted him to be aroused and frustrated; that was the point. She wanted him to be so worked up and overwrought that he'd arrive at her house trembling with excitement and eagerness. He'd often used this ploy himself over the years, but had never dreamed it was so powerful.

Michael walked over to the kitchen area. He picked up the coffeepot then changed his mind. Caffeine wouldn't help. He opened the fridge and poured himself a glass of juice. He was sure he could handle a few hours of frustration if he had to, especially if it meant depriving Jude of the satisfaction that his disobedience would provide. But there was something else gnawing at him; something dark and unfamiliar that was harder to ignore. It sat in his belly like a rock, making him feel nauseous and putting him off his food. It whirled inside his brain, filling him with doubts and worries. If only Jude had given him some clue about what his submission might entail.

Michael leaned against the kitchen counter. He had no frame of reference, no previous experience to guide him. The only comfort he could find came from Jude's assurance that she'd look after him. She'd be there by his side, she had said, holding his hand every step of the way.

Michael laughed out loud as realisation dawned. He was afraid – Jude was right. It was such an unaccustomed emotion that he hadn't been able to name it at first. It pumped inside his brain, ran through his veins like infected blood. He was terrified of what Jude might do to him – no, that wasn't it. He was terrified because he felt completely out of control. He was helpless, lost and impotent. Jude had all the power now, and he had given it to her.

Jude wasn't like the other supposedly dominant women he had known. From the very beginning he'd been aroused by her genuine strength and authority. She'd cut through his banter and practised charm and seen the real man underneath. And it was that man inside who he usually took such care to hide from the world that wanted Jude. Needed her.

Michael trusted her. He wouldn't be doing it otherwise. He had put himself in her hands and he had total faith that she'd look after him. She was only asking him to do what he'd done to others hundreds of times. There was nothing scary about pain and humiliation, was there? And Michael knew that he didn't lack courage. He'd taken risks all his professional life and had actively sought new experiences that would broaden his outlook. He was man enough to cope with anything Jude asked. He was certain.

He looked at his watch. It was just after four. He'd take the Tube home then get ready for his appointment with Jude. He got his things together and left.

Michael's taxi pulled up outside Jude's house at 6.45. He'd deliberately arrived early because he didn't want to risk being punished for lateness. But it wouldn't do to be early either, so he planned to walk through to Middlesex Street and stop off in one of the many pubs.

It was a chilly evening. He turned up his collar and stuffed his hands down into the pockets of his overcoat. He turned into Middlesex Street a few hundred yards from The Puzzle. Inside the pub it was warm and smoky and practically empty. Michael made his way to the bar. He took a note out of his wallet and waited to be served.

'What are you having?'

'That's a good question. Tonic water, I think. Ice and lemon.' He'd have liked a drink, but he was sure Jude would be able to smell it on his breath and he wanted to create a good impression. He paid for his drink and found himself a seat.

He sipped his tonic water. He'd hoped it might help to settle his stomach. He'd barely eaten all day. When he reached out to pick up his glass his hand was shaking. He couldn't remember the last time he had felt so nervous. Yet the funny thing was, under his trousers he was already half hard. He didn't understand the power Jude had over him, but it was impossible to ignore. He looked at his watch. It was five to seven. He swallowed his drink and left the pub.

On the short walk to Jude's house his erection grew harder. It rubbed uncomfortably against the material of his boxers. He was willing to bet that when he undressed for Jude they would be stained dark with pre-come. He adjusted his underwear and walked up the steps to the front door. He rang the bell.

113

After a few moments a light came on and, through the glass, he could see a figure approaching down the hall. The door opened.

'Hello, Michael. Come in.'

Jude was wearing a black gypsy skirt and a velvet top that clung to her curves. Her dark hair hung down her back. She was smiling. Michael stepped inside.

'Take your clothes off, please.' She closed the door behind him.

'I'm sorry?'

'You heard me, Michael. Take your clothes off. Now. You can fold them and put them on this chair. And make sure you do fold them. I can't abide untidiness.'

He took off his overcoat, folded it carefully and laid it on the chair. He did the same with the rest of his clothes. Soon he was naked except for his boxers and his socks. His stiff cock tented the front of his underwear. Michael felt his face colouring with shame. His cock grew harder. He slid his hands under the waistband of his underpants and pulled them down. His erection stood out in front of him, advertising his arousal and his shame. He moved his hands to cover it, but Jude slapped them away.

'No need to hide it, Michael. I've already seen it. I assume you followed my orders and you haven't been giving it a sneaky rub?'

'No, Jude. I did as you asked. I haven't laid a finger on it.'

'And did you find that difficult?' She placed her outstretched finger under the tip of Michael's cock. She lifted her finger, feeling its weight.

'I found it almost impossible, Jude.'

'Good. While you're here I'd prefer it if you addressed me as Mistress, or Ma'am, whichever you choose. Is that understood.'

'Yes, Jude . . . Yes, Ma'am, sorry.'

'Now, I'd like you to get down on your knees, please.'

She picked up a thin leather dog collar from the hall table.

Michael got to his knees. She fitted the collar round his neck, sliding a finger underneath it to make sure it wasn't too tight. She fetched a small gold padlock from the table and locked him into it. The collar was tight but not uncomfortable. The inside was rough and slightly cold, but he knew his body heat would soon warm up the leather. He loved the weight of it and the way it embraced his neck like a lover's fingers. He looked up at Jude.

She lifted her skirt up to her waist. Underneath she wore black stockings and suspenders that looked as though they were connected to a corset of some kind. Shiny black boots with viscously spiky heels reached to her knees. She wore no panties and Michael could just see a glimpse of her dark-fringed pussy under the bottom of the corset.

Jude turned around. She swished the back of her skirts up to her waist and bent over slowly, knowing that Michael would be drinking in every detail of her body. Her bottom was round, her skin ivory-pale and smooth. His eyes followed the length of her dark cleft to her plump pussy. Michael's heart pounded. She reached behind her with both hands and spread her cheeks, revealing her tight, chocolate-coloured arsehole.

'Lick it.'

Michael leaned forward. He stuck out his tongue and lapped at her arsehole. He flicked around the puckered edges, he pushed its point against her opening. She smelled of coconut body lotion and her own, indefinable, womanly scent. His cock twitched. His heart thumped inside his chest. Her warm, damp pussy pressed against his chin.

'Use your whole mouth, please. Show me some enthusiasm. I want you to taste it, not poke it with the tip of your tongue as if you're trying not to touch it.'

He opened his mouth wide and pressed it against her warm cleft. He smeared his wet tongue against her skin, he sucked and nibbled. He licked her hole, pressing his tongue into it, rimming her. Michael could hear her breathing hard. She pressed her arse into his face, rocking her hips slightly. Her pussy had softened and grown wet. Her juices smeared against his chin. His cock tingled.

Jude stepped away and dropped her skirts. Michael's disappointment was almost painful. She picked something up from the table and attached one end of it to the D-ring on his collar. She tugged on it and Michael realised that it was a lead. A sudden rush of heat flashed through his body, making him feel light-headed.

'We're going upstairs to my playroom now. Normally, I'd make you do it on your knees like a dog, but since you wouldn't be able to negotiate the stairs you may walk upright. She pulled on the lead, expecting him to follow.

She led him up three flights of stairs to the attic. Jude had obviously spent a lot of time and money equipping her dungeon. Michael found himself experiencing an odd combination; curiosity about her set-up and growing alarm. His armpits prickled with sweat and his heart was beating double time.

Large equipment dominated the centre of the room and an impressive array of smaller equipment and whips hung along one wall above a series of drawers, the contents of which he could only guess at. There was a bed at one end of the room and a door, which stood ajar, leading to a bathroom.

Jude led him over to the centre of the room and made him kneel in front of the whipping bench. She attached the end of his lead to a shackle set into the bench, near the floor. The lead was pulled taut, preventing him from lifting his head. He heard Jude moving about. He guessed she was undressing. He could hear her picking things up and putting them down as she moved quietly around the room.

He turned his head, trying to steal a peek at her, but the lead was at its limit. He looked down at the ground. She hadn't told him that he couldn't look at her, but she hadn't said he could either and he certainly didn't want to risk her displeasure. He knew he was sure to incur it at some point, but he didn't want to provide her with ammunition.

Jude's shiny boots came into the range of his vision. Though his whole body ached to see the rest of her, he kept his eyes pointing at her toes. Something touched the back of his neck, making him shiver.

'Down.'

The authority in Jude's voice was impossible to ignore. He knelt forward, raising his arse into the air. He felt her foot on the back of his neck, pressing his face against the floor. The floorboards smelled dusty and stale. It repulsed him. He turned his head on its side. The heel of Jude's boot gently nudged him in the cheek. It was little more than a tap, but left Michael in no doubt that her next reminder would be far less gentle if he failed to comply. His face was millimetres from the dirty floor. The tip of his nose brushed against the rough surface of the wood. Her foot on the back of his neck pressed downwards.

'I forgot to ask Alma to clean the floor this morning, so I'd like you to mop it with your tongue.'

Michael opened his mouth to protest but was answered with the weight of her boot against his neck. There was obviously no room for negotiation. The tethered lead pulled at his neck. The floor stank. The sole of her boot dug into his flesh. His cock was rigid, trapped between his thighs and his belly. His heart beat a frantic tattoo in his chest.

'I'm waiting, Michael, and I'm a very impatient woman. I wouldn't make me wait much longer if I were you.'

He licked the floor. The wood was rough and dry. The dust got into his throat and made him want to cough. It tasted bitter and dirty and gritty. It was like licking sandpaper. He tongued the floor as if his life depended on it. His urge to obey her was irresistible and tinged with a feeling of humiliation that he found inexplicably, intensely arousing.

His trapped cock grew harder, drooling pre-come onto his belly and thighs. Sweat dampened his hair and ran into his eyes. He licked the dirty floor, lavishing it with his tongue as if it were her open pussy.

'Now my boots. I want you to polish them with your tongue so that I can see my face in them.' She put one shiny foot in front of his face.

He crawled a little closer, risking strangulation as the lead pulled taut. He licked her boots, wetting the surface with his tongue. He sucked on the pointed toes. He ran his tongue up the length of his shin and down her calf. He was panting and breathless. The smell of leather filled his nostrils like nectar. She lifted her foot and ran the tip of her heel along his bottom lip.

'Suck.'

He opened his mouth and took the slender heel into his mouth. Jude moved the heel, sliding it in and out of his mouth, fucking him. He sucked on it with eyes closed. His mouth warmed the cold heel. Its tip grazed his tongue as it fucked him.

'That's enough for the moment. Kneel up on your haunches while I undo your lead.'

He released her heel reluctantly and sat up. His head swam a little when he was upright. Jude bent to unbuckle the shackle and he caught a glimpse of her long black corset. He tingled all over.

'Now, lie over the bench.'

Michael got to his feet. Jude's bench was from Fetters, like his own, so he knew what to expect. His stomach lurched. He leaned along the bench, lifting his legs onto the supports. He lay still while she fastened the straps. The bench had straps that fastened around the ankle, calf and thigh. There were similar straps for his arms and wrists and a waist strap, with a shaped back guard to protect against accidental kidney damage.

Jude took her time fastening the straps, checking them for tension. Michael had performed this ritual himself many times and was well aware that his victims had always found it an intensely powerful moment.

The leather was cold against his skin. As she fastened each shackle his sense of helplessness and the accompanying arousal increased. When she had tightened the waist strap he felt like a sacrificial lamb. The thought stiffened his cock and sent his pulse racing.

'What do you think is going to happen now, Michael?' She ran her finger along the length of his spine, making him gasp. 'You don't imagine I've gone to all the bother of shackling you to this very expensive whipping bench just because I like the look of your arse in the air, do you?' She tapped his backside with the flat of her hand.

'No, Mistress.'

She stroked his bottom and he felt like purring.

'That's a good boy, you're catching on. But I forgot – you've played this game before, haven't you? Hundreds of times, I'm willing to bet. Except it wasn't you strapped down helplessly and waiting to be punished. It feels different, doesn't it? You've already started to sweat. Your breathing's changed. Blood's pounding in your ears. You can feel cold air against your naked skin. Your genitals are on display and your arse is held high, ready for whatever punishment I decide to mete out. And there's not a damn thing you can do about it. What's it like to be on the receiving end, Michael? Do you think you could get used to it?' She squatted by his head and spoke into his ear.

'Yes, Mistress. It's incredible. I never want it to stop.'

'Really? Well let's see if we can change your mind. Tell me, Michael, do you prefer the stinging kiss of the crop or the thud of the cane? Perhaps you like the cat, with its biting leather tails, or the bullwhip. You can take someone's skin off with a bullwhip, did you know that?' She ran a fingernail up the crack of his arse. Michael's body went rigid and he let out a soft moan.

'But I forgot, you're a virgin. We need to break you in gently. We've got to toughen up that tender skin. We'll start with the crop and save the big guns for later.'

Michael heard her heels clip-clopping over to the wall to select a whip.

'Actually, I'm rather partial to the crop. A simple little tool.' She swished it through the air. Michael clenched his buttocks in expectation of pain but none came. 'It's light, portable, cheap and effective. It can provide any kind of stimulation from a gentle caress . . . ' – she trailed its leather tip along his spine – '. . . to the burning sting.' His body juddered as the crop swished down on his arse. 'Yet it's discreet and unpretentious. It's not ostentatious like the bullwhip, or blatant like the cane yet it's one hundred per cent effective. And, if necessity or mood dictates, the handle can double as a thoroughly serviceable dildo.' He felt the blunt end of the crop pressing against his arsehole. He struggled against his bonds.

'No!'

The crop bit him across the buttocks. He moaned.

'No? I thought we had an understanding, Michael.'

The whip slashed across his arse half a dozen times in quick succession. Michael gasped and pulled against the shackles.

Jude bent down and lifted his head up by the hair. She looked into his face.

'Either you submit, willingly, to whatever I choose to do to you, or I untie you and you go home. Those are the terms you agreed to. And, just in case you're in any doubt,' she added. 'If you choose to go home, I shall consider our agreement at an end.'

'You mean you won't see me again?'

'I see we understand each other. Now, what's it to be?'

'I'd like to stay, please.'

'Thank you.' She kissed his cheek and released her grip on his hair.

'Now I'm going to whip you. You can scream and struggle as much as you like because I've had the foresight to ensure that my playroom is thoroughly soundproofed. So feel free to express yourself. To tell you the truth, I find the sound of a man in pain rather arousing. Sooner or later, I'll want to come. The more I hurt you the hornier I'll get. Eventually, my cunt will be so wet that it drips down my thighs.' She stroked his bollocks with a fingernail, making him wriggle and buck.

'Once or twice I've almost reached orgasm while whipping someone; all it took was a little touch from a willing tongue to tip me over the edge. I bet you'd like to do that, wouldn't you, Michael? You'd like to press your tongue against my crack, suck on my clit and make me come in your mouth?' Her fingernail traced up the length of his crack and circled his hole.

'Yes!'

Michael lay motionless along the bench, waiting for it to begin. His chest heaved. His thigh muscles had developed a little quiver that was totally beyond his control. His sweat had made the leather slick and slippery. His cock was so rigid it was almost painful. He held his breath.

He could hear Jude's breathing. The floorboards groaned and creaked as she shifted her weight. The crop swished through the air. She whipped his arse, each stroke cutting across both cheeks, making them burn. He groaned, exhaling loudly with each stinging cut. He was on fire. Adrenaline rushed through his brain, making him light-headed and flooding him with pleasure. The whip only stung for a second, a brief moment of intense pain that instantly became the most exquisite pleasure.

The crop slashed across his arse time after time. Michael knew she was deliberately changing direction to cover his buttocks with a crisscross of angry stripes. The whip landed on his thigh and he yelped. She whipped each thigh in turn, putting her whole weight behind the crop. His skin was on fire. He burned with pain and pleasure, he couldn't tell them apart any more. He struggled against the shackles, making the leather creak. Sweat poured off his face. His cock rubbed against the sweat-covered leather.

Hoarse animal cries escaped his throat. His body shuddered and shook. His skin was aflame. He was practically screaming; urgent cries of protest so loud they hurt his ears. His senses were overloaded. Pain and pleasure and helpless need mingled into a nameless intensity so powerful that it frightened him. He wanted her to stop because he honestly felt he might die of pleasure, yet another part of him wondered if death might not be a price worth paying.

Tears welled in his eyes and ran down his forehead into his hair. He was sobbing and gasping, completely out of breath. The crop lashed him. Every pore was alive with pleasure. His cock was as hard as granite.

'I love you!' Michael didn't know where the words had come from but, having said them, he knew they were true. Jude was the only woman who truly understood him. She gave him what he needed.

Michael heard the crop fall to the floor. Suddenly she was behind him, her body pressing up against his arse. She ran her hands over his welts, careful not to hurt him.

'Have you ever been fucked up the arse, Michael?' Jude's voice was deep and throaty with lust.

'No, I haven't. A finger, sometimes, but nothing bigger.'

'No? Well there's a first time for everything. Open wide.'

Something cold, hard and wet pushed against his hole. It pressed forward, nudging at his opening. At first he was confused. It was a dildo, he supposed, but it was moving forward with some considerable force. He had no idea she was so strong. Then it slid into him, millimetre by delicious millimetre, and realisation dawned. At some point she'd buckled herself into a strap-on and she intended to fuck him in the arse with it.

'Can you feel that? It's my cock. It's not as big as yours, so there's no need to get worried. I'm starting you off gently to begin with. There's another, smaller cock on the inside of my harness that fits inside me. And over my clit there are some delicious little nubbly things. As I fuck you, my dildo fucks me. It's an ingenious arrangement, don't you think? If we're lucky we might even manage to get off at the same time.' She shifted her weight, pressing her cock a little deeper.

'I don't know about you, Michael, but I'm pretty close. It isn't going to take much to tip me over the edge.' She gave a short thrust, making him gasp. 'You can come whenever you want to. I think you've earned it.'

'Thank you, Mistress.'

Jude held on to his hips and pressed her cock home. It slid inside him all the way. He could feel Jude's belly pressing up against his arse. It chafed against his injured flesh, but he didn't care. She withdrew, sliding her fake cock out of him, until only the tip was inside. She rotated her hips, teasing him, then pressed it home again.

Michael's balls were riding his shaft. His cock drooled pre-come, wetting his thighs and belly and making everything slippery. His arms hurt. The cuffs bit into his wrists. His helplessness somehow intensified his excitement. He rocked his hips, meeting her thrusts.

She leaned over him, panting and breathless. Her long hair tickled his back. Her fingers dug into him as she held on. She was pumping him hard. He was seconds away. He was gasping and groaning, rubbing his trapped cock against the leather as she fucked him. Jude began to moan and grunt. She was pumping hard, short fast thrusts that made his body jerk.

Michael was coming. His cock pumped out spunk. Jude let out a long, keening wail. She held on to his hips, ramming her cock into his willing arse. She bent over his back, sobbing and trembling as her orgasm took hold. His sperm wet the leather. His arse contracted around Jude's cock.

Jude held on tight. Her fingernails cut into his flesh. Her body pressed against his. She quivered and shook. She sobbed and cried.

Slowly, she relaxed. Her muscles softened. She pressed her body against his back and laid her head against him. She stroked him, running her hands up and down his back. She kissed him on the shoulder.

Afterwards Jude had filled her bath for him and sat on the edge as he soaked. She wiped his face with a damp flannel.

'You're an incredible woman, Jude.'

She smiled. 'And you're an incredible man.'

He shook his head. 'I'm nothing compared to you.'

She laughed. 'And you said you weren't submissive . . .'

'How did you do that to me?'

'I didn't do it to you, we did it together, that's the point. It's symbiotic, if you like. I need you as much as you need me. Which of us really has the power, do you think?'

'Both of us, I suppose.'

'Exactly. It's a perfect balance. What's more, it's pure, naked intimacy. I know it sounds the wrong way round, but I view domination as an act of giving, not receiving – no, it's both. I give you what you need and you do the same. No limits, no reservations, nothing concealed or withheld. Absolute trust, absolute openness. You can't get more intimate than that, can you.'

'You're right. And it's so powerful, so intense. There was a point when the pleasure was so overwhelming I was scared of it, do you know what I mean?'

Jude nodded. She looked into his eyes. 'I loved it when you cried. I knew you were giving me everything you had. In that moment I felt as if you were completely mine. It was beautiful.'

'It was . . . mind-blowing.'

'And this is only the beginning.'

Eight

Jude and Michael spent the weekend in sexual exploration. On their last night together they lay on the bed.

'Are you sure about this?' Michael reached across the bed and took Jude's hand. He trusted her completely. She'd been his guide and counsellor on their journey into the unknown and she'd never once let him down. Yet his stomach was knotted with anxiety and all she was asking him to do was put on a dress.

'*I'm* sure, yes. I promise you'll love it.' She squeezed his hand.

'You're probably right. It's just ... I don't know. Part of me finds the whole idea –'

'An assault on your masculine pride?'

'Yes, I suppose so. I've never thought of myself as a cissy. It's hard to get my head round it.'

Jude brought his hand to her lips and kissed it.

'I understand. But a week ago you wouldn't have thought of letting a woman fuck you up the arse. Yet you're still just as much a man as you were then. More so, as far as I'm concerned. I always say it takes a real man to let himself be dominated, and the same goes for putting on a dress. You'll be the same Michael Read as you've always been. You'll just be ...'

'Michael Read in a dress. OK. Just promise me one thing?'

'If I can.'

'Please don't let me end up looking like Lily Savage.'

'I think you'll be all right. I see you more as a sultry brunette myself. Elegant with a touch of Goth.'

'I can't tell you how relieved I am. I thought you might make me look like a fiver-a-night streetwalker.'

'A fiver? I hope you take plastic? I'll get my purse.'

Michael laughed. Jude rolled off the bed. Her nearly naked arse swayed invitingly as she moved across the room. He was so absorbed in looking at her bottom that he almost didn't notice when she pulled back the sliding door of the wardrobe to reveal racks of colourful, kinky female clothes. He was intrigued. He slid off the bed and walked over for a closer look.

'Everything at this end of my wardrobe is designed for men. The cut's slightly different and, of course, they come in larger sizes. What's your shoe size? I've got up to fifteen.'

'I'm size ten, though I'm afraid I have no idea what dress size I am.'

'No problem. I've been doing this so long I can guess a bloke's size from ten paces.'

Michael stared at the racks of clothes. They must have cost a fortune. He put out a hand and stroked a Chinese silk dress. He let out a long, low whistle.

'This is just like the dressing-up box my sister and I had as kids, only better.'

'And you told me you'd never dragged up before.'

'I hardly think that letting my little sister dress me as a princess when I was six qualifies me as a lifelong cross-dresser.'

'That's your masculine pride speaking again. Anyway, slip out of your boxers. The first thing we've got to do is give you a feminine shape.'

Michael slid out of his underpants.

'You're already half hard, naughty boy.'

'I don't know why. I thought I'd hate it. But I seem to be quite excited by the idea.'

'It's the thrill of the forbidden. Delicious, isn't it? Now, let's get you into this.' She handed Michael a black satin garment he didn't recognise.

'What is it? I've never seen a woman in anything like this.'

'That's because you've got an extra little secret lurking between your legs.' She tapped his cock, making it swing. 'To get you looking the way a woman should look, we have to use a little camouflage.'

She took the garment from him and turned it the right way up.

'You see? It's basically just a big pair of knickers, except it's got padding on the hip and bottom to give you the proper womanly shape. And here ... ' – she indicated a hole in the crotch – '... is where you put your tackle. Then the Lycra in the gusset flattens it and keeps it out of sight. It's called a cache sex.'

'Sounds painful.' Michael looked dubiously at the alien garment.

'I don't think so. I'm told it feels strange and a little uncomfortable but it isn't painful.'

'What happens if I get an erection?'

'Shall we find out?' She knelt down and held out the knickers for Michael to step into.

'That's right, now just pull it up like you do your boxers.'

Michael struggled to put it on, but it clung to his legs tightly and became tangled and twisted as he tried to pull it up.

'My boxers aren't as tight as this. Are you sure it's the right size?'

'Of course, it's just the Lycra. It's meant to cling. But you've got it all rucked up. Let me smooth it out.'

She straightened out the knickers and pulled them up over Michael's hips. The Lycra was very clingy but not unpleasant. He felt as though he was held in a tight embrace and the silky fabric was cool and soft against his skin.

'That's right. Now we have to slip your tackle into the pouch.' She manipulated his cock and balls into the right place, eliciting a sharp intake of breath. 'Then we clip the end of the pouch to the back of the waistband like this and pull the pants right up.' Jude made the adjustments and Michael felt as though a firm hand was gripping his genitals and pressing them tightly between his legs. There was constant pressure and a sense of everything being contained and compressed but, as Jude had promised, it wasn't at all unpleasant.

'And now you look like you're wearing an ordinary pair of big knickers except you're nice and flat where it counts and you've got a lovely round bum.' She gave his bottom a playful slap.

Michael ran his hands over the satiny fabric. His shape felt completely alien – and exciting.

'It feels good. I love the curves and it's really nice against my skin.'

'Good. Now we have to find something to give you a bit more shape in the middle.' Jude opened a drawer and selected an item. 'This one, I think. Red should suit your colouring. What do you think?' Jude held up a crimson waspie corset with black lace trim. 'Do you like it?'

'Oh yes. Things have suddenly become very cramped inside my knickers.'

Jude laughed. She pressed her hand against Michael's trapped genitalia. 'You're right. You'll burst them if you're not careful. Now, turn round and I'll put the corset on for you.'

Michael shivered with anticipation. Over the years, he had dressed most of his female companions in similar corsets. He was well aware of the power of fetish clothing. Corsets were both sexy, emphasising and enhancing a woman's natural body shape, and restrictive. The boning, the hooks and laces, together with the close, constricting embrace of a tightly laced corset, were firmly rooted in the world of bondage. Yet, now the tables were turned, he understood for the first time just how potent and significant it really was. Sweat prickled in his armpits. He felt light-headed

Jude laced Michael into the corset, pulling it tight. He stood with his feet apart, bracing himself against the tugging as she pulled hard on the laces. It tightened round his waist, gripping him in a relentless bear hug. It made him breathe more shallowly and forced him to stand straighter. She went on pulling the laces, increasing his bondage, tightening the unforgiving garment's grip on his body. Jude was panting and breathless from the effort.

'There, that should do. How does it feel?'

'Tight, unbelievably tight.'

Jude reached round and stroked his nipples. He shivered under her touch. 'Tight but good, I hope?' She teased his excited nipples with her fingernails. Inside the elastic confinement of his underwear, his cock grew harder.

'Oh yes. I feel like I'm trussed up and on display for your pleasure. I can't wait to see how I look.'

'Well, you'll have to cultivate patience. You don't unveil a masterpiece until it's ready, do you?' She turned him round and looked at him appraisingly. 'OK, you've got a nice round bum and the corset has emphasised your waist. Can you feel the way it holds you all in and improves your posture? If you want to be able to breathe you've got no choice but to stand up nice and straight.'

Michael nodded. 'Yes, I feel as though I'm six inches taller. What comes next? I can't help thinking I'm still a bit flat-chested for a girl.'

'That's exactly what I was thinking. Let me see what I can find.' Jude went to the wardrobe and selected a black lace bra to match the knickers. 'Put this on.'

Michael took the bra and put his arms through the straps. He pulled the cups down over his chest and reached round the back to hook it up. He pulled the two edges together, hoping that the hooks would connect. He tried over and over again, but the bra remained unfastened.

'I'm sorry, I just can't do it. Can you help?'

'Why is it that men know perfectly well how to undo a bra with one hand but they can't do one up using two?' She turned Michael round impatiently. 'No, don't take your hands away; I want you to feel the hooks, so you can work out how they go together. This bra has three separate hooks. Can you feel them?'

Michael's fingers felt clumsy and thick. It was like trying to read Braille. Finally, he managed to feel the individual hooks.

'Yes, I think so.'

'OK then, you have to find each separate hook in turn and do them up one at a time. Find both top hooks with your fingers and do them up. That's right. Now you've got the first one done up the others should be much easier. Feel for the second hook and do it up, now the third. Well done.' She fiddled with the bra, pulling it down at the back and adjusting the straps. 'And now for the filling . . .'

Jude went to the cupboard and came back with what looked like two rubber breasts complete with nipples. She held them up in front of her own modest frontage and thrust her chest out proudly.

Michael couldn't help laughing.

'I think at least one of us should have a decent pair of boobs, don't you? And since I've got no intention of wearing falsies, it might as well be you.'

'What are they made of? And how do they stay on? Won't they flop out of my bra if I lift my arms up?'

'They're silicone, like the implants, and they have glue on the back, so no, they won't fall out. And it's a good job your chest isn't very hairy, because they don't cling quite so well to fur.'

131

'I think this is the first time I've ever been glad I'm not a big, muscular, hairy bloke. Especially if it means I'm not going to rip half of it out when I peel off my fake boobies.'

'They're called "bosom friends", as a matter of fact. And you've got the perfect figure for this. You're slender and smooth and not very hairy, though we'll have to have a go at your legs soon.'

He raised his eyebrows in a parody of surprise.

'You think I'm joking, don't you? Now, let's put these on.' Jude peeled away the backing from the 'bosom friends' and fitted them inside his bra. 'Lovely. I can even see your nipples through the fabric, you slut. Stockings next, then shoes.'

Jude selected a pair of sheer, black seamed stockings with lace tops. Michael put them on, careful to make sure that the seams were perfectly straight. Jude had to show him how to fit them to the suspenders attached to his corset. They felt unbelievably silky and sexy against his skin. He rubbed his legs together and they made a delicious swishing noise and gave him a strange feeling like a slight electric shock. Inside his underwear, his stiffening cock felt delightfully constricted.

'You're right about shaving my legs, Jude. It rather spoils the effect, doesn't it?'

She smiled. 'You're really getting into it, aren't you? You'll be plucking your eyebrows next. Now shoes. How about these?' Jude picked up a pair of black patent stiletto sandals with a single strap across the instep and another that buckled round the ankle.

'They're lovely. But I don't think I'll ever be able to walk in them.'

'You might be right. OK, we'll start with something with a bit more support.' She selected a pair of suede court shoes with some diamanté trim on the front and four-inch heels.

She knelt down to help him put them on. Michael looked down at her and smiled.

'It makes a change, doesn't it?' she said. 'Me on my knees at your feet? Well, don't get used to it. I'm only down here to help you into your high heels.'

'You do look beautiful down there. But, I must admit, it is beginning to feel unnatural. I'd be on my knees in a minute if only I could work out how to get down there in these shoes.'

'Then we'd better teach you how, hadn't we? Now, walk around a bit, see how it feels.'

Michael took a few experimental steps. He wobbled unsteadily and felt clumsy and awkward. Millions of women walked on the things every day; he must be doing something wrong. He tried taking smaller steps, but even if he shuffled along without taking his feet off the ground he still felt wobbly. If he took bigger steps his ankles felt weak and he teetered dangerously.

'There's obviously a technique to this.'

'There is. Let me show you.' Jude went to the other end of her wardrobe and found a pair of shoes similar to Michael's. 'Now, watch me. Men tend to walk by putting their heels down first and then sort of rocking onto the ball of their foot and finally their toes. If you try that in heels you have no stability and you're in danger of falling off.' She demonstrated.

'I'd already worked that out for myself.'

'Right. So what you have to do is put your heel and toe down on the ground more or less at the same time. Like this.' She strutted around the room.

Michael burst out laughing. 'I'm sorry, you look so funny doing that in just your thong and a pair of "fuck-me" shoes.'

'I'll have you know there are men who'd pay good money to see that.'

'And I'm at the head of the queue, I assure you. But you've got to admit it's a bit bizarre, prancing around in a thong and high heels so that your lover can learn how to walk like a girl.'

'And you don't look bizarre, I suppose? Now, walk across the room. Let's see if you can do it without falling over this time.'

He took a couple of steps, carefully placing his foot flat on the floor as Jude had instructed. It seemed to work, though it still felt unnatural.

'That's good. Now take longer strides. And stop watching your feet. Stand up straight and look straight ahead.'

Michael walked across the room, gaining in confidence with each stride. With practice, he was sure he could learn to walk comfortably in heels.

'Try to put one foot directly in front of the other. Haven't you ever noticed how catwalk models walk? That's right. It makes you look elegant and draws attention to the sway of your bottom as you move. Good, I think you've got it now.'

Michael walked as Jude had instructed. She was right; he could feel his hips swing as he moved. It was a very feminine gait and, in normal circumstances, it would have made him feel like a cissy. But now, it was somehow natural and authentic. When he stopped in front of Jude he was breathless with excitement.

'Good. You've obviously got the hang of it. Now, kneel down. You're far too tall in those high heels. It's time we cut you down to size.'

Michael tried to kneel, but he couldn't work out how to do it. He bent each knee in turn, flexing his foot as he would when executing the manoeuvre in his normal clothes. But somehow, it didn't work. The height of his heels and the way they altered the distribution of his weight somehow made it impossible for him to get his knee to the floor.

'I'm sorry, I can't work out how to do it.'

134

'Like this.' Jude bent her left leg at the knee and slid her toes back along the carpet. 'You've been flexing your foot the wrong way, bringing your toes forward. You have to lift your foot a little and straighten your toes – point them almost. Then bend your knees and sort of slide the top of your foot along the floor like this.' She demonstrated. 'Slowly bend your knees and, before you know it, you're on one knee. Can you see?' She slid elegantly to one knee. 'Then bring your other knee down and you're kneeling. Now you try.'

Michael executed the manoeuvre with considerably less elegance than his tutor. They were both on their knees, eye to eye. Michael cupped Jude's face and kissed her tenderly. She responded, closing her eyes and pressing her nearly naked body against his. His cock lengthened inside the relentless embrace of his restrictive underwear. It felt good.

'Mmmmm, lovely.' Jude put her hands between Michael's legs and stroked his imprisoned cock, making him gasp. 'But there's plenty of time for that later. Let's get you into some clothes now.' She rose elegantly, leaving Michael on his knees. It took him a few moments to work out how to get up. Eventually he managed it by reversing the series of movements he'd used to kneel down. When he was finally on his feet again he felt unreasonably proud.

Jude was standing by the wardrobe holding up a red leather minidress. It had a fitted bodice with a zip and a skirt that flared out from the waist. It was the kind of thing he would have loved to see Jude wearing. He could hardly believe that he was about to put it on himself. A few days ago, he'd have thought such a thing impossible, yet today he could hardly get into it fast enough.

'What makes the skirt flare like that?' Michael stroked the supple leather.

'It's what we call cut on the bias. The skirt section is cut out of a circle of leather and stitched to the bodice.' Jude held up the skirt to demonstrate. 'It should draw attention to your hips and make you look curvy. Do you like it?'

'Oh, yes.'

Jude helped him into it and zipped it up.

'It's beautiful.' Michael ran his hands over the leather. 'I hope it looks as sexy as it feels.'

'It is lovely isn't it? I've got one just like it, and I always love wearing it.'

The hairs on the back of Michael's neck stood up. 'Have you? I don't suppose you'd consider putting it on for me, would you? When I'm dressed, I mean? I can't think of anything more exciting.'

'Perhaps I will. In fact, you've given me an idea . . . But first things first. Let's find you a wig and then I'll put some make-up on you. Go and sit in front of the dressing table and I'll bring everything over.'

Michael went over to the dressing table. His hips swished sexily as he walked and his stockings made a soft hissing noise with each step. He sat down and, for the first time, got a glimpse of himself in the mirror.

Though he could only see his head and shoulders, he could see the curve of his fake breasts under the clingy red leather dress. His upper arms and the exposed part of his chest looked smooth and feminine – something he had never noticed before. He could only put it down to the clothes, bringing out his inherent femininity. Didn't they say that all men had a feminine side, no matter how hard they tried to hide it?

The only jarring note was his head. His jaw was unmistakably masculine and, even though he'd shaved, he had a hint of a five-o'clock shadow. And his haircut, though not especially short, was most definitely male.

'I see you're taking a sneaky peek.' Jude's image appeared in the mirror behind his. 'What do you think?

Personally, I think you need the wig to get the full effect.'

'I was just thinking the same. Below the neck I look surprisingly girly, but above, I'm still definitely a man.'

'Well, let's see what we can do about that, shall we?' Jude held up a long, dark-brown wig. 'Shall we see how you look in this?'

Michael nodded. Having come this far, he was eager for the transformation to be complete.

'Let's turn you round, so that you can't see yourself until you're finished. Now, if you hold the wig down at the front of your head I'll pull the rest of it on.' Jude fitted the wig. It felt strange, tight and hot but Michael found that he quite liked its unfamiliarity. Every new step of his metamorphosis excited him more. It was as though he was giving himself totally to Jude – giving her his identity and becoming, under her loving hands, whatever she wanted him to be.

Jude fiddled with the wig, using a comb to primp and shape it. When she was satisfied she picked up a palette of make-up and started applying it to Michael's face with a sponge.

'This is foundation. We use a very concealing base for men, because we have to cover up your beard. It takes a little while to blend it, but it's worth it in the end.'

Michael nodded. Somehow, he felt that speaking would break the spell. He'd given himself up to the transformation and felt more submissive and acquiescent with every stage.

After the foundation, Jude carefully applied powder then blusher. The make-up brushes and sponges felt silky and sensual against his skin. He relished the unfamiliar sensations, which seemed to him like a secret ritual initiation. Goose bumps prickled his skin and his nipples were sensitive and erect.

Next, Jude brushed eye shadow onto his lids, followed by eyeliner. She trimmed a few unruly eyebrows with a pair of nail scissors.

'You're lucky, you've got such long, lush eyelashes that you don't need mascara. Why is it always men who have lovely eyelashes? Women would kill for eyelashes like these.'

Michael knew it was silly, but he couldn't help being pleased by her compliment. Finally Jude selected a crimson lipstick and applied it with a lip brush. She took a step back to admire her handiwork. She fiddled with his wig and brushed the fringe away from his eyes.

'Perfect.' Jude smiled. 'Do you want to have a look?'

Michael turned to look in the dressing table's mirror. Jude put a hand on his shoulder.

'No, over here. I've got a full-length mirror.'

Michael followed Jude over to an antique cheval mirror in the corner. It had faced the wall during Michael's transformation and Jude turned it round and beckoned him to stand in front of it.

Michael hesitated. He felt so good – so right. He didn't think he'd be able to bear the disappointment if what he saw in the mirror didn't correspond with how the clothes made him feel. He closed his eyes and stepped in front of the mirror. He took a deep breath and opened his eyes.

He could hardly believe what he saw. Though he was still recognisably himself, the person in the mirror was also undeniably female. The complicated underwear had given him an unmistakable, yet subtle, female shape. The corset nipped in his waist and forced him to adopt a more feminine posture. The shoes altered his centre of gravity, thrusting his hips out, his shoulders back and his fake breasts proudly forward. Though he wouldn't go as far as to say he was beautiful, the woman in the mirror was attractive; even striking.

'What do you think?' Jude stood behind him, smiling.

Michael could tell she was as excited by his new appearance as he was. 'I can hardly believe it's me. And yet I still recognise myself. If I met myself in a bar, I'd definitely chat myself up.'

Jude laughed. 'I know what you mean. You have a sort of Audrey Hepburn look, with a modern twist – a kinky twist. A bit like Liv Tyler, do you know what I mean?'

Michael nodded.

'You look so gorgeous I just want to ravish you.' She pressed herself against Michael's back. He watched in the mirror as one of her hands gripped a fake breast and the other moved between his legs. He could feel her body heat seeping into him. He placed a hand over each of hers.

'You're beautiful, and you know it, don't you? You can't stop looking at yourself in the mirror.' Her hand moved against his gusset, teasing his cock. 'Do you like your beautiful big tits and your lovely round bum? Your legs look gorgeous in those stockings. I can't keep my hands off you.' She massaged his breast, squeezing hard as her other hand stroked his captive member.

Reflected in the mirror Michael could see the expression of desire in his own eyes and a familiar glint of pleasure in Jude's. He could tell that she was getting off on controlling him. His helpless arousal and his trapped genitals gave her the sense of power that she craved. Seeing her obvious excitement reflected in the mirror seemed to supercharge his own arousal.

His skin felt sensitive and hot. Jude's warm body squirmed against his back. Inside his underwear, his erection was compressed and contained. Unable to stand free, it stretched the Lycra, increasing his bondage. He rubbed himself against Jude's fingers.

'Harder,' he whispered.

Jude increased the pressure, rubbing the crotch of his knickers hard.

'My nipples are stiff. Can you feel them?' She brushed them against Michael's back. 'You're so sexy in that dress. I'm all worked up.' She pressed herself against him, holding him tight.

In the mirror a half-naked girl embraced a woman in a slinky red dress from behind. One hand massaged a breast, the other cupped her pussy. The woman in the dress spread her legs wantonly, welcoming the invasion.

Michael pressed Jude's hand against his erection. His cock stiffened inside the unnatural embrace of his underwear. It felt like an iron hand, gripping him and holding him in place. To Michael, it seemed the ultimate form of bondage. His cock was Jude's captive and only she could decide if and when he would be permitted release.

He was panting. His knees were trembling and, for a moment, he worried that he might fall off his high heels. He moved his feet a little wider apart. Jude was teasing him with her long fingernails now. Running them up and down the length of his shaft. He shivered.

The women in the mirror held each other tighter now. Their intertwined bodies rocked slightly in rhythm with their growing arousal.

Jude's nails moved against his imprisoned cock, teasing him. Michael rubbed his crotch against Jude's moving hand.

'Does that feel good?' Jude whispered, her breath hot against his neck.

'Yes. Don't stop.'

Jude's nails raked against his Lycra-encased cock. His hips rocked, establishing the rhythm that would bring him to orgasm. Jude held him tight, her mouth against his ear. Her excited breathing was the only sound in the room. Her fingers worked on his crotch.

'I bet you're going to spunk into those lovely new knickers, aren't you? Dirty boy.'

Her taunting words seemed to push him over the edge. He pressed Jude's hand against his aching cock. As he came, his restrictive underwear's unforgiving grip seemed to squeeze the orgasm out of him. His legs quivered and he rocked unsteadily on his high heels. He moaned softly.

In the mirror, he saw the rise and fall of his chest, their two hands pressed against his crotch and Jude's steadying arm around his waist. She smiled as she watched him; Michael recognised the lust and tenderness in her eyes that was reflected in his own.

'Is that better?'

He nodded.

'I'm glad. Though it does mean that you're going to spend the rest of the evening in wet knickers.' She looked at her watch. 'But we'll be late for dinner if we're not careful. Why don't you go down to the dining room and have a drink while I get ready? I won't be long. I've had much more practice with this stuff than you.'

'And you've got your own boobies, that's a head start.'

Jude kissed him softly, so as not to ruin his lipstick.

'See you in a minute, Audrey.'

Michael had a bit of trouble negotiating the stairs but he eventually got the knack of it. In the dining room he poured himself a gin and tonic and leafed through Jude's CDs. He selected Annie Lennox's 'Love song for a Vampire' and put it on to play. He found the song sexy and evocative. The way the rhythm and intensity built as it progressed reminded him of a woman's orgasm. It always aroused him and he often used it as background music when making love.

He wandered round the room, looking at the various paintings, most of which he recognised as Jude's work. The sinuous shapes and skin tones of one abstract in particular caught his attention. He studied the painting's textured surface. It almost looked like magnified human skin. He thought he could even see the pores. The colours and tones Jude had used were sensual and shadowy. Annie Lennox's haunting voice seemed to perfectly complement the mood of the painting. He was sure that it was a close up of someone's skin. Something about it just seemed alive to him. He put out a finger and touched it.

'That's a particular favourite of mine. Do you like it?'

Michael answered without turning round. 'Very much. It's skin, isn't it? Human skin.'

'You're right. In fact it's six inches from the base of Dee Kane's spine. If you look closely you can see two little dimples at the top of her buttocks – I've always loved those dimples. And that shadow there,' she pointed to it, 'is where the crack begins.'

'So I was right when I suggested that you two were on intimate terms. It's beautiful, Jude. And all the more beautiful now I know what it is.' Michael turned round and looked at Jude for the first time. He gasped in surprise. 'But not as beautiful as you. You look incredible.'

'We both do.'

Jude was wearing the same red leather dress as Michael and a smaller pair of the same suede and diamanté shoes. She unzipped the bodice to show him the red waspie corset and black satin bra and pants.

'These are my own, of course,' she said, squeezing her breasts, 'though I can't help feeling that yours are rather more impressive.'

'Looks can be deceiving.' Michael massaged his fake breasts, then moved his hands to Jude's real ones. 'At least yours work.'

'Sorry to interrupt, but dinner will spoil if you don't eat now.'

Michael turned in time to see Alma bustling into the room, carrying two plates. For some reason he had assumed that they were alone in the house, even though Alma had served them dinner at around this time on the previous two evenings. She'd have to be blind not to have noticed how he was dressed.

Alma put the plates down on the dining table. She picked up an open wine bottle and poured two glasses.

'Sit, sit.' Alma waved an impatient hand. 'Good food should not spoil.'

'We're ready, Alma. I'm ravenous. How about you, Michael?' Jude looked at him expectantly.

Michael had rather hoped that she wouldn't draw attention to him. It probably wasn't very realistic, but he'd imagined that if he kept quiet Alma might not recognise him. Oh, well, he certainly had no intention of slinking about as if he was ashamed of himself. 'Yes, I'm starving as a matter of fact.' He tried to make his voice sound as normal as possible. 'What's for dinner?' He took Jude by the hand and led her over to the table.

'Lamb and chickpeas. My mother's recipe. Enjoy.' Alma moved towards the door. 'Call me when you are ready for dessert.'

They sat down.

'And, by the way,' Alma added, turning to look at them, 'may I say, you are both looking quite lovely tonight. Beautiful. Like twins. Only I can't quite work out which of you is the evil one.' She smiled and disappeared through the door.

Nine

'I'll see you at the weekend, then, Michael.' They walked down the stairs. At the bottom Jude buttoned Michael's coat then leaned her face against his chest. He stroked her hair.

'OK. Have a good time in Amsterdam. I'll miss you.'

'Me too. I've got something for you, before you go.' She put her hand in her pocket and pulled out a large silver ring with a single ruby set into the band.

'What is it? A bracelet?'

She shook her head. 'It's a cock ring.' She handed it to him. 'I've had it engraved.'

Michael turned the ring, reading the inscription engraved inside it.

He smiled as he read it. ' "For Michael, from your loving mistress, Jude." Thank you. Whenever did you have it done? You haven't been out of my sight for the last three days.'

'Weeks ago. I've been saving it.'

'That's very forward thinking of you. And rather – I don't know – confident. I mean, how could you be sure I'd give in?'

'I told you, I have an infallible radar for submissive men and I haven't been wrong yet. I'd like you to wear the ring all the time from now on as a symbol of your submission to me.'

'Of course I will, though I hardly need a reminder. It's engraved indelibly on my soul now.' He turned it over in his hands. 'The only thing is, I don't know how to put it on.'

'You'll work it out. You put your balls through first then your dick. But don't do it with a stiffy or you'll never manage it.'

When Jude had found out Alan would also be in Amsterdam on business she had suggested they share a hotel room. They'd each go to their separate meetings during the day and, in the evening, they'd explore the city's seamier side together. He'd checked into the hotel around noon and had spent the afternoon presenting a seminar on knowledge management to an international bankers' convention. He'd left her a note saying that he'd be back by eight and had arranged an outing for after dinner.

Jude sat at the dressing table putting on her make-up. She decided to put up her hair rather than wearing it down, because Alan always found the sight of her bare neck irresistible. She pinned it up, leaving a few loose tendrils around her face. She put on a sheer black body-shaper and self-supporting stockings. Her black dress clung to her figure, flared out from the waist and ended just above her ankles. Her shoes were suede with pointy heels and several strands of chain that fastened round the ankle.

She was sitting on the edge of the bed doing them up when Alan let himself into the room.

'Hello, darling, you're early.' Jude smiled.

Alan put down his briefcase and went over to her. 'I managed to sneak away during cocktails. You look beautiful.' He kissed her neck. 'Did you put your hair up specially for me?'

She nodded.

'Thank you. Are you ready for dinner?'

'Yes, I'm starving.'

'OK. I'll have a quick shower and change. I thought we'd eat downstairs in the restaurant.'

'And afterwards you've got a surprise?'

'Yes, a colleague told me about a place where they have a live sex show. It's vanilla, I think, but might prove inspiring.'

The food in the hotel restaurant was expensive but bland. Soft, inoffensive music and silk flowers on every table seemed to be their only gesture towards ambience. Jude thought they could have been eating in any city in the world. There were no local ingredients or recipes. She was willing to bet that they served up the same fare no matter the location of the hotel. They ate mushroom risotto and shared a bottle of Chablis.

'I've been seeing a former colleague of yours, Alan.'

'Michael Read, you mean? We were hardly colleagues; he worked for our main competitor. But I've met him a few times, conferences and the like. We moved in the same circles.' He topped up her glass.

'What do you think of him?'

'I'm not sure I'm qualified to judge. I only knew him professionally. I'm told he was a tough negotiator with plenty of nerve and a mind like a steel trap. He always seemed to be one step ahead of the opposition. And he was something of a ladies' man, I think. I've seen hard-headed businesswomen go weak at the knees when he walked into the room. I can't say I knew him personally at all. But if I have to give an opinion – which I can see by the look in your eyes I do – I've always found him rather arrogant.'

'I won't argue with you there.'

'Surely he's not submissive? I can't believe that of a man like him.'

'Most people wouldn't believe it of a man like you.'

'I know, but that's not what I meant. It's just that his work, his attitude, everything about the man just screams dominant.'

'Yes, that's what he thought.'

'Until he met you?'

Jude nodded.

In the lift down to the lobby Alan held her hand and bent to kiss her neck.

'My cock's been hard all through the meal.'

'Really? I didn't think the food was that good.'

'I don't think I even tasted it. I couldn't take my eyes off you.' He took her hand and pressed it against his crotch. 'See what you do to me.'

'I hope you aren't stretching my best silk knickers.'

'I'll buy you some new ones. I should have thought of bringing my own, really. Yours are a little tight for me.'

She squeezed his cock through his trousers.

'They're roomy enough when you haven't got a stiffy.'

It was a warm night and they decided to walk to the bar, a few streets away. Jude always thought that Amsterdam only came alive at night. By day, the city was a living museum, its canals and historic buildings an irresistible lure for sightseers. By night, bright lights, dark streets and the open sexuality of its natives gave the city an air of seediness and sin that attracted an altogether different kind of tourist.

Here, Jude's preferences were not only freely expressed, they were celebrated. London had its fetish underbelly, of course, but it was hidden, secret and slightly shameful. Amsterdam embraced its kinkiness, announcing it to the world as proudly and naturally as it marketed its tulips and cheese. Jude couldn't help loving a city that celebrated its sleaze with such enthusiasm.

The bar was down a dingy side street, sandwiched between a café and a baker's shop. Inside the air was thick with smoke. There was a small bar at one side of the room and a raised platform with a double bed on it at the other. In between the two, a hodgepodge of tables and chairs had been arranged facing the stage. Alan led her over to a vacant table at the edge of the platform and they sat down. A white-aproned waitress with dyed red hair and too much make-up walked over and lazily took their drinks order. A jukebox pumped out loud rock and roll.

'There's a show every half-hour, apparently, so we shouldn't have to wait long.' Alan had to shout so that she could hear him above the music.

'Do you think it's the same actors at every show?' asked Jude. 'Doing it every half-hour is beyond most blokes, no matter how horny he is. If "actor" is the right word – you can't "act" getting it up and sticking it in, can you?'

'And you must get thoroughly sick of sex, mustn't you? If you get home from a hard night fucking and your wife's in the mood your heart must sink like a stone.'

'Not to mention your cock.'

The waitress arrived with their drinks on a tray. A naked man and a woman stepped onto the stage. There was a desultory round of applause and the lights dimmed.

The woman's body was silicone pneumatic and had been waxed so ruthlessly that she looked as though she had been skinned. All that remained of her pubic hair was a narrow exclamation mark above her slit. Her hair was poodle-blonde with two inches of black roots. Her eyebrows had been plucked into a thin line, giving her an air of permanent surprise. Heavy mascara gave her eyes a spidery look. A slash of shiny blue eye shadow had been applied to each lid. Her scarlet-painted lips were obscenely pouty and obviously surgically enhanced.

The man's body was enviously muscular and shone slightly in the dim light. Jude suspected he applied baby oil before every performance to achieve the effect. His dark hair was short and spiky and his chin was fashionably stubbly. His pubes had been neatly trimmed and his cock, already half hard, was cut. The woman got to her knees and began sucking him. He held her head and pumped his hips, fucking her mouth.

She sucked energetically, but without enthusiasm. After a few minutes she sat on the edge of the bed, facing the audience, and spread her legs. The man knelt between her parted thighs and began to lick her. The girl writhed and moaned, running her hands up and down her torso. She fingered her own nipples, arching her back and thrusting her chest forward.

The room was silent, all eyes turned to the stage. A girl giggled at a table behind them. The couple stood up and Jude could see that the man was now fully hard. Their hands explored each other's bodies. The man stroked her bottom. They French-kissed noisily, tongues moving frantically. He bent and sucked on a nipple. She threw back her head and began to moan. They lay down on the bed and he climbed on top of her. His cock slid into her with practised ease and they began to fuck.

The girl moaned and wriggled. She wrapped her legs around him and Jude could see that the soles of her feet were dirty. The man fucked her relentlessly, his buttocks clenching on each thrust.

Alan leaned over and whispered in her ear, 'I don't know about you, but this isn't doing anything for me.'

'Me neither. Why don't we go back to the hotel and see if we can do any better?'

'Good idea.'

They wove their way between the tables and out into the street. She grabbed Alan's hand and pulled him into a shop doorway. She got down on her knees and unzipped his fly.

'Jude! Anyone might walk by.'

She looked up at him and smiled. 'So? You've got nothing to be ashamed, of, I assure you.' She took his cock into her mouth. He moaned. She wrapped her hand round the base, steadying it. She slid her mouth up and down along its length. His skin felt silky and hot. He was rigid with excitement. Her nose banged against his belly. The material of his trousers rubbed her face.

She sucked hard, deep-throating him. Alan put one hand on the back of her head and rocked his hips. He was panting. His breath hissed loudly between his teeth as he exhaled. Her mouth slid against his cock. She licked the sweet spot under the helmet; she bathed the head with her tongue.

Jude heard footsteps in the street behind them. They paused for a moment, then walked on.

'They saw us, Jude. You should have seen the look in their eyes.' Alan fucked her mouth, rhythmically. Jude moved in synchrony with his pumping hips. The muscles in his thighs were taut and straining. She knew he was on the edge. He was holding his breath, now, letting it out in a sudden rush just when Jude feared he might suffocate. His balls were tight and hard. Jude stroked them with a finger as she sucked.

'Permission to come, please, Mistress.' Alan's voice was breathy and hoarse.

'Yes.' Jude's mouth was back on him in a second. Alan's hands were on the back of her head. She fingered his balls. He moaned and his legs began to tremble. Spunk flooded onto her tongue. She kept her mouth over his cock, holding onto his hips. Alan was groaning and panting. His cock pumped out sperm.

The hands on the back of her head relaxed. He stroked her hair. His thigh muscles softened.

'Thank you, darling. That was wicked.'

Jude slid her lips along his softening cock and let it plop out of her mouth. Alan helped her to her feet. She pointed at her closed mouth and Alan nodded his understanding. She wrapped her hands round his waist. Alan pulled her close. She pressed her body against his and they kissed. Alan's hungry mouth sucked hers, lapping up the sperm she had saved for him. Breath snorted out of his nostrils as he swallowed. He drank his own semen, licking her face for any dribbles that might have escaped. He sucked on her tongue and lips.

Her nipples tingled. Her cunt, she knew, was moist. There was a little knot of tension in the base of her belly that ached for release.

'Let's go back to the hotel. I think I need to come.'

'I can do it right here, if you're desperate.'

'No chance. If you think I'm going to lie down in a filthy doorway some tramp has used as a toilet you must be mad.' She put Alan's cock back into his trousers and zipped him up. 'You've left a slimy, wet patch on the front of my dress. Look.'

'I'm sorry, Mistress. I'll get it dry-cleaned for you.' He took her hand and they walked towards the hotel. 'Perhaps you should punish me for it, later?' He smiled at her wickedly.

'Perhaps.' She slid their joined hands into his coat pocket. 'But, as I'm sure you know, when a slave asks you to punish him, the best punishment . . .'

'Is no punishment at all.' Alan smiled. 'Beat me, said the masochist.'

'No, said the sadist.'

Jude closed the door of the hotel room behind her. She took off her coat and dropped it onto a chair.

'You'd better get undressed, Alan, and be quick about it.' She opened a drawer. 'Fortunately for you, I had the foresight to pack a few toys this morning. I've brought my favourite crop. The long, swishy one.' She picked up the crop and flexed it. 'If you remember, Alan, last time I used it on you I left bruises that lasted a week.'

'Yes, I remember, Mistress. Do you want me to take off my knickers?'

'You mean *my* knickers, don't you, Alan? Take them off and give them to me.'

Alan slipped them down over his legs and stepped out of them. His cock was already hard. Jude took the knickers and stuffed them into his mouth. She picked up a roll of bondage tape and tore off a piece.

'Close your mouth, please.'

Alan complied and she stuck the piece of tape over his lips, sealing them.

'There,' she said, smoothing the tape, 'now you won't disturb the other guests with your screams. Though there's nothing we can do about the sound of the crop. Still, they do call it "the English vice" don't they? They'll hardly be surprised.' Jude fetched a dining chair and put it in the middle of the room. 'Bend over this, please. Put your head on the seat and stretch your hands down so that I can fasten them to the legs. That's right.'

She got out four sets of handcuffs and used two of them to fasten his wrists to the front legs of the chair. She used the others on his ankles. Alan's upturned arse poked obscenely towards the ceiling. His balls and the underside of his stiff cock were clearly visible. He was panting. Forced to breathe through his nose, his breath snorted noisily as he exhaled. She ran her hands over his buttocks, using the tips of her fingers to tease and arouse him. His legs trembled.

'I'm going to undress now, Alan. It won't take long.' She unzipped her dress and hung it over the back of a chair. She left on her shoes, stockings and body-shaper, knowing how much they'd excite Alan when she finally released him. She picked up her crop and walked slowly around Alan's chair. Jude knew that he'd be listening to the soft brush of her high heels against the carpet. Perhaps he would be able to hear the quiet shushing noise her stockings made when her legs rubbed together. He'd be rigid with anticipation, dreading the first blow, but longing for it. She swished the crop through the air. Alan's body jerked in expectation of pain, then relaxed.

'You want it, don't you? You want to feel that intense burn of pain that turns instantly to pleasure. You want me to whip you until you're sweaty and limp. You'll struggle and fight. You'll thrash your legs and scream. Yet all the time you'll be desperate for another lash.' She ran the leather tip of the crop down the crack of his arse and over his balls. His body stiffened and he moaned through the gag.

'Your whole body is hungry for it, Alan, we both know that. You need it. But, the question is, do you deserve it? I could untie you, if I wanted to. Maybe I'm not in the mood . . .'

Alan thrashed and struggled. He grunted into the gag. He shook his head from side to side, unmistakably indicating 'No'. She stroked his back.

'OK, Alan, you've made your feelings abundantly clear. I won't disappoint you.' She took a step back and brought the crop down across both buttocks. She slashed him again and again, leaving bright welts against his pale skin. Alan's body jerked each time the crop made contact.

Jude whipped each thigh in turn. She started at the top and worked her way downwards. The crop swished through the air. Alan grunted in pain. His cock dribbled pre-come. A neat row of parallel red lines formed across the back of his legs. She whipped his arse again, putting her whole weight behind the crop.

Alan was trembling and moaning. Breath snorted down his nostrils with every blow. A patch of dark bruise was visible at the outer edge of each buttock.

'I'm going to give you six more strokes, Alan, then it's over.'

She raised her arm and brought the crop down across his arse. It swished noisily through the air and landed with a crack. Alan grunted. She hit him again, a few inches higher. His body shook. The cuffs clanked against the chair legs. She whipped him hard on each thigh. Raised, red welts formed instantly. She lashed him across the fattest part of his cheeks.

He was covered in sweat. His rigid cock bobbed about between his legs. Her final stroke landed low down on his buttocks at the top of his thighs. Alan's body jerked violently. The chair wobbled; metal cuffs rattled noisily against the wood.

Jude dropped the crop and stroked his welts. Her trembling fingers explored each mark in turn. She kissed them.

'I've a good mind to leave you there like that and force you to listen while I make myself come.' She removed the tape over his mouth.

'That would be terrible, Mistress, but of course it's up to you.'

She unlocked his cuffs.

'It's a good thing you have such a talented tongue, Alan, otherwise you'd be spending the night bent over that chair.' She ran her hands over his chest, teasing his nipples with her thumbs.

'Then I'd better make sure my performance is up to standard, hadn't I?'

Ten

'You look beautiful, Jude. Red really suits your colouring. You look all sultry and smouldering. And the corset really emphasises your curves.'

Jude sat at the dressing table putting on her make-up as Michael watched her from the bed.

'Thanks.' She turned to look at him. The open admiration in his eyes made her stomach leap. 'You look rather gorgeous yourself, I must say. I love that upper body harness on you. And now we've shaved your chest, it really makes your nipples stand out.' Jude turned back to the mirror.

'I must admit I rather like it myself. And thank you for making me wear the collar. I just love the weight of it against my neck. Do you like my trousers?' Michael stroked his thighs.

'They're OK, but I think we might make a little adjustment when we get to the club.'

'You're making me nervous now. Where are we going again?'

'It's called the Whipping House, it's in Limehouse. It's a friend's birthday – Mistress Venus – she's hired the place for the night. It should be interesting. They've got a very well-equipped dungeon and it's extremely . . .' – she searched for the right word – '. . . atmospheric. You'll like it. In fact, I'm surprised you don't know it.'

Michael shook his head. 'I get out and about occasionally. The Rubber Ball, Torture Garden; we all like to dress up. And it's a good way to meet like-minded people, but I've never been much of a scene player. I can understand how people get off on the exhibitionism, and I certainly don't underestimate the power of public submission. But, for me, it's always been between me and my partner and no one else. It's all about trust and boundaries and shared exploration. I tend to think that doing it in public somehow devalues that. Do you know what I mean?' Michael walked over and stood beside her.

'Yes, I do. That's pretty much how I feel. It's what goes on in private that really matters to me.' She turned and looked up at him. 'But I go out with friends from time to time and it's good to get your face seen, especially if you earn your living like I do. And, there's a lot to be said for public humiliation, as you will find out later.' She smiled at him. Michael began to speak, then thought better of it. His half-open mouth and raised eyebrows managed to convey both surprise and acquiescence.

'I'm putting myself entirely in your hands, Jude.'

'Are you nervous?' She held his hand.

'I'd say I'm excited and unsettled rather than nervous. I know it sounds obvious, but I never realised how uncomfortable and unfamiliar things would feel now I'm not in control of what's happening to me.'

Jude brought his hand to her lips and kissed it. 'But you're not afraid?

'I'm not afraid, exactly. I'm sort of lost. Like I'm adrift in an endless sea with no oars and no compass. I've got all these completely new emotions boiling away inside me. It's strange.' His eyes burned with intensity.

'Strange but pleasurable, I hope?' She shifted along the seat and patted it for Michael to sit down.

'Not just pleasurable, Jude, it's fantastic. It sounds corny, but it's almost like I've been born again. Everything I thought I knew has fallen away and I'm a completely new person – like a phoenix, burned to a cinder then reborn from the ashes. Do you understand?'

Jude nodded. 'Yes, I do. It was like that for me, too. I'd had fantasies about kinky sex all my life but never even told anyone. Then I met a man who saw himself as dominant. I shared my fantasies with him and nothing was ever the same again.'

'You mean you were submissive? I'd never have believed it.' Michael's shock was clearly visible.

'Yes, to begin with. People are often surprised. But, in a strange way, I'm sure it was allowing myself to submit that put me in touch with my inner power. When I let go for the first time it was liberating and empowering. The fear that had held me back just seemed to fall away. I saw myself and my needs clearly for the first time. I knew who I was and I knew what I wanted.'

'Well, you're certainly in touch with your inner power now. The bruises on my arse are proof of that.'

Jude smiled. 'Yes, it just seemed to develop over time. I switched for a while, then found myself being the top more and more often. After a while, it just became natural. Now it's who I am.' As she looked into his eyes she experienced an acceptance and sense of belonging that almost frightened her.

The Whipping House was located in an abandoned warehouse. They walked upstairs past rubbish-strewn landings, broken windows and graffiti-covered walls.

'Is this what you meant when you said it was atmospheric?' Michael held her hand as they climbed.

'Yes. It's great, isn't it? Just the sort of place you'd expect to find a dungeon.'

'You're right about that. I think I saw a couple of rats on the last landing.'

On the top floor a doorway led into a large room. At one side of the entrance an alcove held a coat-rack and a makeshift bar. Loud music pumped out, its heavy bass beat making the floor shudder.

'Good evening, I am slave Eric. May I take your coats?'

They handed over their coats and Eric hung them up with exaggerated care. He was naked except for a leather dog collar, nipple rings and a short barman's apron barely covering his crotch. Jude could just see the tip of a plastic chastity device poking out under its hem.

'Is that a CB2000 you're wearing?' She flicked up the bottom of his apron with the tip of her finger. 'I've been thinking of getting one. How do you find it?'

Eric lowered his head respectfully and lifted his apron. His penis was encased in a plastic cage, held in place by a ring fastened behind his cock and scrotum.

'It's a newer model, madam. It's called the Curve. I find it more comfortable than the 2000.'

'What happens when you get an erection?' Michael's voice left Jude in no doubt he was less than enthusiastic about her intended purchase.

'You can't, sir. At least, it's rather uncomfortable if you do. Can I get you a drink?' He addressed his question to Jude, making it clear he knew which of them was in charge.

'I'll have a glass of red wine, please, and Michael will have mineral water.'

'Yes, madam. Sparkling or still?'

'Sparkling, I think. We're going to sit down, will you bring them over?'

Eric nodded. Jude led Michael over to a seating area at one side of the big room. There was a leopard-print sofa, two armchairs and a red velvet couch. Jude sat down on the couch. Michael began to sit then remembered he hadn't been given permission.

'Sorry. I'm not certain of the etiquette and I don't want to do the wrong thing. Am I allowed to sit down?'

'Of course.' She patted the seat. 'Behave as you normally would. If I want you to do something I'll tell you.'

Michael sat down beside her. 'Thanks. I thought you might want me to kneel at your feet.'

'Later, perhaps . . .' Jude reached into her handbag and retrieved a leather dog lead. She clipped it to the ring on his collar. Eric came over with their drinks and knelt in front of Jude. He handed over her drink, bowing slightly, then gave Michael his mineral water.

'If you need anything else during the evening, madam, just call me.' He bowed and walked away.

'Not that I'm complaining, Jude – I wouldn't dare. But I'd have liked a drink as well.' He looked uncertain.

'Alcohol dulls your senses and alters your pain threshold. If we decide to play a little later you'll be glad you're sober.'

'I didn't realise you intended us to play.' Uncertainty had given way to alarm.

'Relax. I may hurt you, but I'd never harm you. You know that.' She pulled on his lead, bringing his face close to hers. She kissed him.

'Thanks for reminding me.' He cupped her face and kissed her hard on the mouth. 'I'll do whatever you ask.'

'Good boy. I'd like you to go over to Eric and give him your trousers. Your underpants, too – just in case you were in any doubt.' She wound his lead round his neck. The free end hung over his shoulder and dangled against his chest. Michael hesitated, then got up and walked away.

Jude looked around the room. In the dungeon area a woman in a red corset and nothing else was tied to a St Andrew's cross. Her master trailed the tails of a flogger over her buttocks. She arched her back.

A domme in a long rubber dress and a peaked military cap sat on a high-backed mistress chair with a naked, shackled slave at her feet. His back was covered in hardened candle wax and his buttocks were marked from a recent whipping.

Behind her, Jude could hear the whipping bench being used. The crack of leather against skin was followed by a grunt of pain or pleasure. The amplified music reminded her of an excited heartbeat.

On the sofa opposite sat a couple in matching black corsets. The woman wore a thong underneath, but the man was naked. He had been shaved and Jude could see a small tattoo above his penis. Both of them were wearing multi-buckled, thick-soled boots that looked like the outcome of some mad-scientist evil plot to interbreed motorcycle boots with Robocop.

She looked up and saw Michael on his way back. Though he walked with studied nonchalance, his discomfort was obvious. He sat down and laid his hands in his lap, covering his crotch. Jude looked at his hands, making her face deliberately stern. Michael laid them on his thighs.

'How does it feel?' She spoke close to his ear so he could hear her above the music.

'I feel a bit conspicuous.'

'You're not the only man with his willy out, you know. Look at that boy over there.' She pointed to the corseted couple. 'And there's a bloke wandering around totally naked except for a red baseball hat – look, there he is.'

'Oh, yes. And he's delighted with himself, isn't he?'

'Yes, he's enjoying himself all right. If he doesn't stop waving it about he'll have someone's eye out.'

'If he gets too hot in the hat, at least he'll have somewhere to hang it.'

There was a deep, guttural moan behind them and they turned to look. A naked woman lay on her back in a suspension sling hung from the ceiling. A man in leather trousers and combat boots was fisting her arse. As he withdrew, his lubed arm glowed in the light.

'That looks like fun.' Jude smiled at Michael, raising an eyebrow in an imitation of wickedness.

'That's not the word I'd have used.'

'You've experienced it, surely?'

'I've administered it many times but I've never considered reciprocating.'

'Until now.'

He breathed out noisily. 'Especially not now, if I'm honest. But I know better than to disagree with you.'

'You've taken my cock and your eyes didn't even water. I don't have very big hands.' Jude held up her hand and rotated it slowly.

Michael gulped ostentatiously. Jude laughed.

'Just promise me you'll take your watch off . . .'

'Oh, look – it's Venus. I must say hello.' She stood up and wove her way across the room. Michael followed her obediently at the end of his lead.

'Venus. Happy birthday.' They kissed. Venus was tall and slender with hair the colour of a black grape. She wore a long dress with trailing sleeves and a tightly laced corset over the top. Her skin was pale, her eyes outlined in black in the Goth style.

'Lovely to see you, Jude.' She looked Michael up and down with practised disdain. 'And who is your little friend.' She said the word 'little' with malicious emphasis, eyes pointing at his cock. Michael looked at the ground.

'Oh, come on, darling. I'm not taken in by your Cruella deVille act and neither is Michael.'

'So, your little pet is called Michael? Does he sit up and beg? Does he chase sticks in the park? Do you think he'll wag his tail for me if I ask him nicely?'

'He'll do whatever you want if I tell him to. He's extremely obedient.'

'Would you mind if I took him for a little walk, then?'

'Why not? After all, it is your birthday.' She handed over his lead. 'Go with Mistress Venus. Enjoy yourselves. But don't do anything I wouldn't do.'

'Come on, doggie. We're going walkies.' Venus led him away.

Jude watched Venus and Michael weaving their way across the room. As they reached the dungeon, he looked over his shoulder and smiled, nervously. Jude went back to her seat.

Venus led Michael to the St Andrew's cross and secured his hands. She kicked his feet apart and tied each one to the lower legs of the cross. Jude could see Michael's tackle peeking out from under his splayed buttocks. She could see his chest rise and fall, signalling his heightened state. Venus ran the tips of her fingers down his back. His whole body quivered.

Venus teased his back with her fingers, gradually increasing the pressure until her nails were leaving white trails on his skin. Michael struggled. His body banged against the cross. Jude knew that a combination of public humiliation and Venus's fingers had brought him to a pitch of arousal. She felt the hairs on the back of her neck rising.

He was panting and groaning. Jude could hear his hoarse moans above the music. Venus picked up a multi-tailed whip and began to trail it up his back. His thigh muscles were taut and quivering. His cock had stiffened and Jude could see it brushing against the cross, trailing a stand of glistening pre-come. Jude's breathing had become shallow and her cheeks were burning.

Venus began to whisk his buttocks with the whip, barely making contact. There was no force behind the blows but Michael gasped as the leather tails made contact. She whisked the whip up and down his back, alternating sides. She flicked and twirled her wrist, reminding Jude of a drum majorette spinning her baton.

Jude could see that Venus had started to increase the force behind the whip. Michael's back began to redden.

His hands were balled into fists, his muscles taut. Jude's nipples had hardened. She was tingling all over.

Venus brought the whip down on his upper back. His body stiffened and he let out a grunt of pain. He was panting and gasping between blows, head bent back and eyes closed. She whipped his bare buttocks, flicking her wrist and using just the tip of the tails. Michael's legs trembled and he groaned, a long low note of pain and satisfaction.

Venus hung up the whip and selected another. It was a long strip of thick leather with one end folded over and stitched to form a handle. At the working end, the whip's tip had been cut into a triangular point, which looked innocent enough but was capable of providing a vicious sting. Jude was sitting on the edge of her seat.

Mistress Venus put her face close to Michael's and spoke softly. Jude knew her friend was reassuring him and making sure he was coping with the pain. Jude saw Michael nod and smile. Venus held up the whip for him to see and his eyes widened, but he nodded again, indicating his assent.

Jude heard a grunting noise behind her and she turned to see a tall man with a bare chest and leather kilt stroking the upturned arse of a naked man bent over the whipping bench. His buttocks were crisscrossed with angry red stripes and a line of bruises, like fingerprints, at the top of his thigh. His partner lifted the front of his kilt. He stepped up behind the bound man and slid into his arse.

She heard Michael scream and turned her attention back to the play area. Mistress Venus was whipping his buttocks. His body was rigid, straining against the cuffs as the biting tip made contact. Jude could hear his cuffs jangling as he struggled. The whip lashed across his arse time after time and Jude realised she was holding her breath.

'Hello, Jude. That looks like fun.'

Jude looked up and smiled. 'Jo-Jo. I haven't seen you for ages. How are you?'

Jo-Jo shrugged. 'Can't complain. Venus is enjoying herself, isn't she? He seems very responsive.'

'He is. I lent him to Venus as a birthday treat.'

Jo-Jo raised an immaculate eyebrow. 'I can see why you've been keeping him to yourself. Would you mind if I had a little fun? I expect Venus could do with an opportunity to rest her arm.'

'If you like. I'm sure he'd enjoy it.'

Jo-Jo went over and spoke to Venus. Venus sat down in one of the mistress chairs. Jude could see that she was slightly out of breath and her skin was filmed with sweat. Jo-Jo selected a dressage whip from the selection on the wall.

She spent a few moments uncuffing Michael's hands and refastening them lower down. Jude could see his cock was still hard and the surface of the cross was spattered with his pre-come.

Jo-Jo was a short blonde woman whose hair was cut into a sleek bob. She was curvy and voluptuous and dressed in a PVC dress with a zip up the front. The zip had been pulled down almost to her waist, revealing her impressive, braless cleavage. On her feet were shiny leather boots that clung to her shapely calves and terminated in spiteful stiletto heels.

She stepped back and flicked the whip through the air. The tip made contact with Michael's behind and he grunted and hung his head. Jo-Jo delivered a dozen swats with the dressage whip.

Michael's back, thighs and arse were crisscrossed with red weals. An irregular patch of dark bruising was visible on the outer curve of his buttocks. He was covered in sweat. Jude was conscious of moisture and heat between her legs.

Jo-Jo flicked her wrist and the whip cracked through the air, its tip making contact with Michael's arse. His body became rigid and gave a little jerk. She hit him again, bringing the whip down with vicious precision. Michael was moaning constantly. The deep, visceral roar was clearly audible above the pumping music.

Jude watched him receive his beating. Her breathing was thready and irregular. Her chest heaved. Her fingernails dug into the arm of the couch.

Michael's body stiffened and juddered each time the whip made contact. Jo-Jo was breathless and her cheeks had grown pink. Her ample breasts jiggled as she whipped him and the edge of one rosy nipple had become visible. Her sleek hair swung as she wielded the whip.

Jude was mesmerised. Michael's obvious enjoyment of his punishment and the tacit obedience in his surrender to it moved and aroused her almost to tears. Her heart thundered in her chest. Every pore in her body was alive with excitement and pleasure. She could hardly breathe.

She stood up and walked over to Michael. 'Thanks, Jo-Jo. I think he's had enough now. Shall we take him down?'

Jo-Jo unshackled Michael's right hand while Jude did the same on the other side. While Jo-Jo undid his ankles, Jude embraced him. He surrendered into her arms, his head resting on her shoulder. His body was slippery with sweat and he was breathing heavily. She could feel his stiff cock pressing against her hip.

'Are you all right, darling?' Jude stroked his hair.

'I'm fine. I'm better than fine. I'm exhausted but elated. I don't think my cock has ever been so hard.' He lifted his head and looked at her. His eyes were shining.

'You'd like to come, I suppose?'

'I'd like to, but I know it's up to you.'

'We'll save it for later, then. Come and sit down.

She took the handle of his lead and they sat on the couch. Jude ordered him some water and, when Eric brought his drink, he drank as if he were dying of thirst. Jude noticed that his hand was shaking.

'Thank you for bringing me. That was incredible.'

'More incredible than when I whip you at home? I hope not, otherwise I might just let Venus have you.'

'Not a chance. I belong to you now – if there's one thing I know, it's that. And being whipped by someone else seemed to underline it. It made me realise just how completely I'm yours and really brought home to me how much I want that.'

'I'm glad. I was hoping you'd feel that way. And I can't tell you how much it means to me. Submission in private is a wonderful thing, but essentially it's a secret. Yet here, everyone knows you belong to me and that seems to mean so much more.' She wiped sweat off his brow. Michael nuzzled his face against her hand, his eyes closed. She leaned forward and kissed him, a sweet, tender kiss that came from her soul.

Michael and Jude spent half an hour watching the activity in the dungeon. In a room to one side was a medical fetish room where people were receiving enemas and other hospital-related tortures. The naked man in the baseball hat wandered around standing on the edge of the action but never participating. Jude didn't think she had even seen him talking to anyone. He was constantly erect and danced to the music from time to time as if keen to ensure that everyone caught a glimpse of his cock.

Around two in the morning, people began to drift in from Stunners, the drag club downstairs. Jude spotted a tall, slender drag queen in a Marilyn Monroe wig and leopard-skin leggings with huge plastic platform shoes. Though most were convincing and fashionable, some of them had obviously chosen their outfits from the bargain bins at Oxfam. Opposite them sat a huge man with hairy hands and a five-o'clock shadow wearing a powder-blue suit that looked as though it had once belonged to a lady MP.

On her way back from the loo, Jude bumped into Alan. He was dressed in a red leather collar and matching shorts and a pair of high-laced commando boots.

'Alan! What a lovely surprise.' They kissed.

'Hello, darling. Are you having fun?'

'Yes, thanks. Though I was just thinking of calling it a night and going home.'

'You wouldn't consider taking me with you, I suppose? I've got the car outside.'

'I'm with Michael. But now I think of it . . . why not? He's over there.'

She took Alan's arm and led him over to Michael.

'Michael, I'd like you to meet my friend Alan Fox. He's going to come home with us.'

'OK.' Michael deliberately kept his voice even. He stood up and extended his hand. 'Actually, I think I know your name?'

Alan laughed. 'You do. We were in the same line of work before you decided to throw it all up for your art.' The two men shook hands.

'Of course. How do you know Jude?'

Alan looked down at his outfit and raised an eyebrow. 'We met at a basket-weaving evening class.'

'Shall we get our jackets?' Jude picked up Michael's lead. They retrieved their outer clothes and put on their jackets. Michael leaned against the wall and began to put on his trousers. Jude put her hand on his arm.

'No need for that, Michael. We're going in Alan's car. I'm sure he's got a heater.'

'Where are you parked?' Michael's brow furrowed in concern.

'About two hundred yards down the road. You'll be all right; it's two-thirty in the morning, we're not likely to bump into anyone.'

As they went through the alley by Stunners a group of transvestites leaned against the wall sharing a cigarette. Michael lowered his head and picked up speed. Jude pulled on his lead, slowing him down. As they passed the cross-dressers, a tall thin brunette wearing an obscenely short minidress and teetering on platform shoes noticed them.

'Look, girls. Jude's little doggie has got his winkie out.' She pointed. Her voice echoed round the alley.

The rest of the group turned to look and there was a chorus of laughter and wolf whistles.

'Come on, Brittany, knock it off. You've seen a cock before. After all, you used to have one yourself.' Jude smiled sweetly at the transsexual and they walked on.

Back at Jude's, she led them straight to the bedroom. Alan immediately began to undress and Michael stood in front of her, waiting for orders.

'Take off your harness, please, Michael.' She sat back on the bed and watched. When he was naked Alan knelt at her feet. Jude beckoned to Michael, indicating he should do the same.

'Alan, will you get my crop from the drawer, please. You know where it is. Michael, I want you to get the bench from in front of my dressing table and put it in the middle of the room.'

Alan returned with the crop and Michael manoeuvred the bench into the centre of the room. Having completed their tasks, both men knelt at her feet.

'Michael, I'd like you to lay down on the bench lengthways.'

Michael knelt at one end of the bench and lay down along its length. Jude tied his lead around one of the legs. She stroked down his spine with the leather tip of the crop. She trailed it between his buttocks and tickled his balls. Michael's body stiffened and he gasped but remained in place.

'You'd like me to whip you now, wouldn't you? You've spent half the night being whipped by other women. You're lying there, naked, covered in marks and bruises, and none of them were administered by me. Don't you think it's time I left my own mark on you?' She knelt down and stroked his face.

'Yes please, Mistress.'

'Perhaps I will. But to tell you the truth, I'm feeling a little tired.' She got to her feet. 'Alan, will you whip him for me?' She held out the crop. 'Nice and hard, please. And, it goes without saying that if I think you're going easy on him I'll get him to whip you twice as hard.'

Alan got into position and drew back his arm. He brought the crop down on the fattest part of Michael's arse. Michael's body jerked and he let out a long, low moan. Jude stood a few feet away, her hands on her hips. Alan whipped him again a few inches lower and a livid red line appeared. Jude's nipples peaked.

Alan delivered half a dozen more strokes, each one eliciting a deep, animal moan. Michael was filmed with sweat. Jude could see the marks from his earlier beatings crisscrossing his back and buttocks. His hair, usually so artfully styled, was dishevelled and damp.

Michael's hard cock poked out at the end of the bench. Jude noticed that its tip was shiny and wet. Alan's own erection stood out in front of him, signalling his enjoyment of his task. He was sweating and breathing hard from the exertion.

Jude's nipples were sensitive and swollen. They rubbed pleasurably against the interior of her corset. She walked slowly around the bench. Michael's eyes were closed. He was panting. Sweat dripped down his face and dampened his hair. The room was silent except for the sound of the crop and Michael's guttural moans. From time to time, Alan grunted as he wielded the crop.

'I think it's time you changed places.' Jude knelt by Michael and untied his lead. She helped him up and wiped the sweat off his face. Alan handed her the crop and positioned himself on the bench. 'Time for you to get your own back, darling.' She kissed Michael tenderly and handed him the crop.

Unlike Michael, Alan's arse was comparatively unmarked. Jude could just see a trace of bruising remaining from their recent trip to Amsterdam. He laid over the bench, holding onto the legs, his body rigid with suspense, his cock hard. Michael stood with the crop in his hand, looking at Alan's prone body, his face troubled by an emotion Jude couldn't read.

'I . . . I've never actually whipped a man.' His voice was uncharacteristically diffident.

'But you've whipped plenty of women, I imagine?' Jude put her hand on his arm.

'Yes, of course.'

'Then it's the same thing. The only difference is that Alan happens to have a cock and I'm sure he'll thank you for trying to avoid it.'

Michael took up position and raised the crop. It swished through the air and landed in the centre of Alan's buttocks. Alan grunted. The crop cracked down again, making Alan gasp. Jude was conscious of welling moisture between her legs and an excited constriction in her chest.

The crop landed across Alan's arse. Red weals were soon visible against his pale, freckly skin. His cock jiggled and bobbed between his legs as the crop struck.

Despite his initial concerns, Michael whipped Alan with a fervour that Jude found both surprising and arousing. His eyes shone and his cock stood brazenly between his legs. He put his weight behind each blow, drawing his arm back with practised precision.

Jude's nipples ached. Moisture had dampened her panties and made them cling. Alan's body was taut with tension and excitement. He grunted with each sting of the crop. A long, glittering strand of pre-come dangled off the tip of his cock and onto the carpet like a kinky spider's web.

'Enough. Alan, I think it's time you thanked Michael for whipping you. After all, we can both see how much you enjoyed it.' She helped Alan up. He knelt back on his heels in front of Michael and looked up at him.

'Mistress would like me to suck your cock, Michael. Is that OK?' The huskiness of his voice left no doubt as to his state of arousal.

Michael was silent for a long moment. He looked at Jude, then back at Alan. Finally, he nodded.

'I think I'd like that very much.'

'Don't forget, you're not allowed to come without my permission.' Jude sat down on the bench.

Alan took Michael's cock in his hand and gently and expertly rolled back his foreskin. When the shining, dark tip was exposed he lavished it with his tongue. Michael exhaled loudly. Alan swallowed Michael's cock to the root. He fingered his balls and slid his mouth up and down the shaft.

Jude parted her legs and began to finger her clit through the damp crotch of her panties. Her upper lip was filmed with sweat. Her nipples were tender and sensitive.

Michael rested his hands on Alan's shoulders and rocked his hips. He tilted his head back, breathing loudly as Alan sucked him.

Alan's own cock was rigid and purple. He rubbed its tip with the heel of his thumb, eager for release, but Jude toed his hand away with the tip of her boot.

'You've got to wait your turn, Alan.'

Her clit was hard and tingly. She stroked around the perimeter, not quite touching it, knowing that anticipation would make the eventual release all the sweeter. Alan sucked Michael's cock with enthusiasm and expertise. His lips were stretched and taut; his eyes closed. His nose bumped against Michael's pubic bone. From time to time, he gave a little grunt of pleasure. His cock stood proudly to attention, signalling his enthusiasm.

Jude stood up and walked over to her wardrobe. She retrieved her strap-on harness and dildo from the shelf.

'I think the time has come to change places. Alan, will you sit on the bench please. Michael, I'd like you to get on your hands and knees and suck Alan's cock. And please make sure you do a good job. It doesn't matter that you've never done it before. You've got a cock, so you know what feels good. Just do what comes naturally.'

Alan released Michael's cock with obvious reluctance and sat on the edge of the bench. Michael got down on all fours and began to suck him. Jude slipped out of her panties and unhooked her corset, leaving on her stockings and boots. She buckled herself into the harness, inserting the smaller dildo on the inside into her wet pussy. She applied a copious layer of lube and positioned herself behind Michael.

Jude could clearly see Michael loved the taste of cock. His mouth was formed into an obscene O, sliding up and down Alan's cock with obvious relish. His eyes were closed and he breathed noisily through his nose.

She wrapped her hand around her latex cock and positioned it against Michael's arsehole. She let her weight fall forward and the dildo slowly entered him. His body juddered and he grunted appreciatively as it slid home. She held on to his hips and fucked him hard. The textured latex on the inside of her harness rubbed deliciously against her clit. The dildo inside her shifted a little with each jab of her hips.

Alan looked down on Michael as he sucked his cock. He held Michael's head between both hands, thrusting his hips to establish a rhythm. Jude could see the muscles of Alan's flat belly standing out. His face was flushed and his eyes glassy.

Jude held on to Michael's hips and hammered his arse with her fake cock. Her clit rubbed against the bumps inside her strap-on. Her nipples were on fire. She rubbed her thumbs across the swollen nubs.

'Permission to come, please, Mistress.' Alan's voice was throaty and deep.

'Certainly not. I've got plans. You'd better stop sucking him, Michael, since Alan appears to be so short on self-control.'

'I'm sorry, Mistress.' Alan hung his head.

'I want you both to fuck me.' She undid her harness and tossed it aside. She got down on her hands and knees. 'Alan, get some lube from the bedside table and grease up your cock. When you're ready I'm sure you know where I want it.'

Alan hurried over to fetch the lube. He knelt behind her and Jude could hear the squelching sound of him rubbing his cock with KY jelly. She felt its cold, slippery tip at her arsehole and Alan's lube-covered hand on her hip. She gasped as his cock entered her.

Alan held her by the hips and waited. Jude took some deep breaths. When Alan felt her muscles soften, he began to fuck her, sliding his cock in and out tantalisingly slowly.

'Stop a minute now, Alan. Help me to get myself upright, please, Michael.' She held out a hand, and Michael supported her weight, helping her to straighten up. 'Good. Now I want you to put your cock in my cunt.' He knelt in front of her. He moved his knees a little wider, adjusting his height to match hers.

Alan embraced Jude from behind, his hands on her breasts. He kissed her neck and Jude tilted her head back. Michael pressed his body against hers and positioned his cock with one hand.

'It's too tight – I can't get it in.'

173

'It'll go in. There are two holes, but only enough room for one cock. You just have to push a bit harder – Alan's cock is taking up most of the space.'

He tried again, pressing it forward and upward with his hand and putting the weight of his pelvis behind it. Gradually, his cock began to slide into her wet cunt. Jude gasped as it slipped in. With Alan's cock already in her arse, it felt unbelievably tight.

'OK, now we have to co-ordinate our movements. If you both thrust upwards, I'll thrust down, then we do it in reverse . . . that's good.' She moaned as they began to fuck her. Her stretched cunt felt alive. Alan's fingers worked her nipples. His mouth moved against her neck. She could hear his frenzied breathing against her ear.

Michael pressed his body against hers. He wrapped his arms around both her and Alan and pulled them close. He kissed her, his mouth opening to her. His lips were soft and warm.

Jude's pussy was tense with excitement. The evening in the dungeon and then watching the two men punish and suck each other had aroused her beyond endurance. She knew it wouldn't take long for her to come.

Their bodies were slick and slippery against her skin. Their hands roamed over her torso, exciting her nipples and stroking her neck. Mouths kissed her throat. A hot tongue dipped into the hollow of her collarbone. He skin was tingly and sensitive. Her nipples burned. She had lost control of her breathing. She wrapped her arms around Michael and held on to him, gasping.

The tension in her belly burst. Pleasure pumped through her veins. Blood pounded in her head. Her body stiffened. She moaned and sobbed. Her legs trembled and felt weak. Michael held her against his chest and kissed her throat. Behind her, Alan pressed his body against her back, his hands on her breasts.

'You can both come if you want to.' Jude's voice was thick and throaty.

174

Alan came first, ramming his cock hard into her arse. He trembled behind her, his fingers digging into the flesh of her breasts. She gasped and shook, still possessed by an extended orgasm. He groaned and grunted, rocking his hips as he pumped out spunk.

Michael gave a final, deep thrust and exhaled loudly. Jude could see a pulse beating in his throat. His neck was covered in a red rash of arousal. His strong arms embraced her. Jude held him by the shoulders, her trembling body pressed up against his. His mouth was half open, his face filmed with sweat. His eyes were eloquent with such tenderness and lust that Jude felt as though her heart might burst.

Afterwards, the three of them shared a shower and climbed into Jude's king-sized bed. Jude lay on her side with Alan curled around her back. Michael lay facing her, holding her hand. He leaned forward and kissed her tenderly.

'Thank you.' He smiled at her.

'What for?'

'For tonight.' He stroked her cheek. 'And for everything else.'

Eleven

A week later, Jude put the finishing touches to Michael's make-up.

'You don't think I look too tarty?' Michael wasn't sure why he cared, but he wanted to be the best woman he could, for Jude.

'Is there such a thing?'

Jude had selected a PVC skirt and a cerise halter-neck top for Michael. He wore fishnet stockings. They felt strange against his legs, clingy and thick. On his feet were tight, spike-heeled boots that laced up the front. His dark wig was combed into a bouffant and hung to his shoulders.

'There's a fine line between divinely slutty and running the risk of being arrested for soliciting, don't you think?' He peered into the mirror.

'I think you look beautiful.' Jude smoothed his wig. 'Now, we just need to find something for me to wear and we're ready.' Jude took off her robe. Underneath she wore a deep, black suspender belt and seamed stockings. Michael watched her walk across the room and slide back the wardrobe door. She stood with her hands on her hips, looking at the row of outfits. For the thousandth time, the sight of her naked arse made Michael's cock respond.

'Any ideas?'

Michael walked over and laid his hands on her shoulders.

'You look perfect as you are.'

'Thank you. But we really will get arrested if I go out like this.'

'How about that one? Black always makes you look dramatic?'

Jude picked up the dress and held it up. 'Good choice. I always feel slightly dangerous when I wear this one.'

'Then it obviously suits you. You're so dangerous you ought to carry a health warning.'

Jude put on the black leather dress. It clung to her body and ended mid-thigh. Its bodice was boned, emphasising her curves and enhancing her bust. It had a sweetheart neckline that curved around the upper contours of her breasts and terminated in a deep V at her cleavage. Michael's cock tingled inside the rigid embrace of his feminising underwear.

'You look incredible.'

Jude looked at her reflection in the mirror. 'What shoes shall I wear?

'Well, I always like you in boots . . .'

'They are divinely kinky, aren't they?' Jude selected a pair of shiny black ankle boots which fastened with a row of silver buckles up the side. She finished the outfit with a coffin-shaped velvet handbag.

'Are you ready for the evening ahead?'

Michael nodded. 'Whatever it holds . . .'

'Oh, I think you'll find my plans enjoyable. And there's no need for you to worry. They don't involve anything you haven't already done.'

'Well, not quite. I've never been out in public dressed like a King's Cross tart.'

'That's true. How do you feel about it?'

Michael looked into Jude's eyes. The confidence and amusement he saw there aroused him beyond measure. There was no doubt or diffidence in her intelligent eyes.

Inside his underwear, things grew a little more constricted.

'I am a little nervous. I'm concerned I might bump into someone I know.'

'Well, if you do they'll be in drag too, so I doubt your cover is likely to be blown.'

'That's what I keep telling myself, anyway. But my overwhelming feeling is excitement – no that's not true – more than anything else I feel unbelievably horny. Being ordered to go out in a dress somehow seems like the ultimate surrender. I've given up my masculinity to you and the whole world knows it. Do you understand?'

'I do, yes.' She smiled. 'And I want you to know, that no matter how much it arouses you, it arouses me more.'

He stroked her cheek. 'I don't doubt it. You appear to be totally insatiable.'

'Oh, I'm not sure that's true. I'm perfectly willing to be sated, it just hasn't happened yet.'

'Perhaps you haven't met the right man.' He ran his finger down from her throat and between her breasts.

'And you think you are him?' She raised an eyebrow.

'I did rather hope you might find me a suitable candidate, at least.'

She took his hand and kissed his palm. 'Perhaps you are.'

Michael sat in the back of the taxi as quietly as he could. He attempted to look inconspicuous but didn't deceive himself that he was winning the battle. He sat with one hand on his PVC-covered thigh. Jude held his other hand in both of hers and rested it against her crotch. Her fingers stroked his palm.

The taxi drew up outside Stunners and they stepped out. Michael fiddled in his handbag and handed over the fare.

'Are you ready? It isn't too late to go back home if you're not sure.' Jude smiled at him.

'And if I do want to go home?'

Jude shrugged. 'I won't punish you, Michael, if that's what you're thinking.'

'No, that isn't what I meant. If I let you down, if I can't find it in myself to obey you. Where does that leave us?'

'I don't know to be honest. We'd just have to work it out. To tell you the truth, I hadn't really considered that you might refuse.'

He looked at her. Her eyes glistened with sincerity and tenderness. Her dark hair moved in the breeze. One long strand blew onto her mouth and stuck to her lipstick. He put out a hand and pulled it free.

'How can I refuse, Jude? Just looking at you makes me want to get on my knees. It's an old cliché, I know, but I feel as though I'd walk to the end of the earth for you.'

'Thank you. But I doubt if you'd get very far in those heels.'

'You know what I mean. I'll do anything you ask. You are my mistress and I am your devoted slave. I'm standing here in a dress, aren't I? What more proof do you need?'

Jude smiled. 'I'd like you to go into Stunners and chat up a nice TV. Or maybe someone will chat you up. Either way, I can't imagine you'll have much trouble. When you've met someone, I want you to bring him out to me. I'll be in Alice's café having a cup of coffee and a chocolate muffin.'

'That sounds easy enough ... though I suspect that isn't all you have in mind.'

'Let's not try to run before we can walk. But make sure he's a cross-dresser, not transgendered. You understand the difference?'

'Of course I do. Cross-dressers and transvestites are men who like to dress up, for whatever reason. Transsexuals believe they are women and their ultimate goal is to have reassignment surgery.'

179

Jude nodded. 'Just as long as we're clear. I want you to pick up a man in a dress and I want you to make sure he's got a cock.'

'It shall be done, Mistress.' He gave her an exaggerated bow.

She patted his bottom and walked away. Michael watched her open the door to the café. He felt suddenly lonely. With Jude by his side, he felt invincible. Alone, he felt out of his depth and very small. But he couldn't fail her; that was unthinkable. He closed his eyes for a moment and conjured up her face, her smile. He walked inside.

When his eyes grew accustomed to the light, he looked around the room. Everywhere he looked there were men in drag. There were a few men in normal clothes, but they were by far the minority. Michael couldn't help feeling self-conscious even though, in reality, he was far less conspicuous than he'd been all evening.

He walked over to the bar and ordered a double gin and tonic. He thought about asking for a pint of bitter but somehow it didn't seem appropriate. If he kept this up, he'd be plucking his eyebrows and growing his hair before long. He laughed softly. Jude had really got under his skin. Even when she wasn't there, she still had power over him. She had sneaked inside his brain and was somehow corrupting him from within.

He paid for his drink, putting his change carefully back into the pink suede purse Jude had given him. He stood at the edge of the dance floor and adopted a pose he hoped looked friendly without making him seem like a total pushover – a girl had some pride after all.

He looked around the room with deliberate nonchalance, trying very hard not to look as though he was staring. Like at the Whipping House, there was a mix of convincing and less believable cross-dressers. A long-legged feline creature sashayed into the room, dressed in scarlet Capri pants and an angora bolero. He was carrying a small poodle in his arms and had decorated the dog's topknot with a pink silk ribbon. He walked up to a small group of she-males and made a show of air-kissing each one of them and loudly addressing them as 'Dahling'.

A couple who were identically dressed, and so alike they could be twins, perched on barstools, deliberately displaying shapely thighs clad in fishnet stockings. Each of them had an impressive décolletage that looked more like the result of hormones than padding.

The same lady conservative MP wannabe they had seen the previous week was there, her handbag hung over her wrist and a wineglass held delicately in her other hand, pinkie extended.

Michael became aware of someone standing next to him. He turned and found himself gazing into the bluest eyes he had ever seen in real life.

'Hello. I couldn't help noticing that you have the most beautiful eyes. What an extraordinary colour.' He cringed inwardly at the corniness of his chat-up line, but he was trying his best. He remembered to smile.

'Contact lenses, I'm afraid. They're supposed to be the same shade of violet as Elizabeth Taylor's.' The transvestite had deliberately softened his voice, though it still had a masculine pitch.

He wore a dark wig, styled to resemble a 1950s Hollywood star. Not quite Elizabeth Taylor, in spite of the eyes, more Ava Gardner, Michael thought. He had obviously used the same era as an inspiration for his make-up. His lips were a glossy scarlet and his eyebrows were immaculately pencilled. Subtle shading defined his eyes and his cheeks had been enhanced with a hint of rouge.

He wore a long, sage ball gown, of the type Audrey Hepburn would have worn to collect an Oscar. It had a halter neckline and fastened at the neck with a pussycat bow that hung down his back. His shoulders were smooth and shapely and Michael thought they had been powdered. They glistened slightly in the light.

'You look beautiful.' This time, Michael wasn't just spinning a line.

'Thank you. My name is Madeline.' He extended a perfectly manicured hand, allowing his fingers to remain limp, in the feminine fashion. A gold bracelet around his wrist glinted in the light.

'And I'm Michael.' He shook hands.

'That hardly suits you, I must say. Don't you have a feminine name, as well?' Madeline smiled. His head was slightly lowered and he looked at Michael through his mascara-enhanced eyelashes. His lower lip was extended slightly in what could only be described as a pout. In spite of himself, Michael felt his heart quicken a little.

'I'm afraid I don't. My mistress hasn't given me one.'

'Oh, I see, you're one of those.' Madeline spoke with exaggerated significance. Michael couldn't help noticing a little playfulness in his tone.

'One of those what? You make me sound like a freak.' He looked Madeline in the eye. He stuck out his own bottom lip, hoping that the gesture looked charming rather than petulant.

'Submissives. You dress up because your master or mistress wants to symbolically emasculate you.' He smiled and took a sip from his glass.

'I can't see what's wrong with that. After all, plenty of people in this room have been emasculated literally, not just figuratively.'

'But that's their free choice. They're not handing power over their lives to someone else. They lose their penises to become the women they know themselves to be. To make the outside match the inside, if you like. That makes sense to me.'

'Whereas what I do, doesn't?' Michael noticed that Madeline had a splash of freckles across the bridge of his nose. They made him seem somehow girlish and innocent.

'Let's just say it isn't for me. Though, obviously, if we can't embrace diversity in here what hope have we of doing it anywhere? I'm just glad to have a place where I can dress as I want, be who I want. So, if it works for you I'm not going to tell you not to do it.' Madeline rolled the edge of his glass back and forth against his lower lip.

'And what brings you here? Not submission, obviously.'

'No, I'm not the submissive type, I assure you. I just come here to relax. During the day I run my own business. It's a macho world, very competitive and aggressive. Here, I get to relax and express my feminine side.'

'So it's a hobby, not a way of life, for you.' Michael leaned close. Their upper arms brushed and he shivered.

'No, it's strictly recreational. I'm too fond of my cock to want to give it up.' He handled his crotch, for the first time using a masculine gesture that Michael found both shockingly incongruous and arousing.

'I'm not arguing with you there. Listen, Madeline, my mistress is downstairs in the café. She's instructed me to . . . well, to pick up someone and bring them down. I hope you're not offended, but would you be interested?' He smiled in what he hoped was a good imitation of womanly wiles.

'Just to bring someone down? Or does she have something else in mind?'

'She hasn't told me, I'm afraid, but I rather think she probably has something in mind, yes.'

Madeline looked at him, his painted lips smiling enigmatically. He seemed to be appraising Michael. Though his manner was soft and docile, Michael could clearly see the intelligence and determination in his eyes.

'Why not? After all, it is a little dull in here tonight and we girls should stick together, don't you think?' He took Michael's hand and led him to the door.

In the café, Michael introduced him to Jude. Madeline extended his hand regally.

'Pleased to meet you, Madeline,' said Jude. 'Why don't you both sit down?'

Michael sat down opposite Jude and Madeline took the chair beside him. He smoothed down the skirt of his dress with his hand before putting his weight on the chair, then crossed his legs elegantly at the ankle. Michael reflected that he still had a lot to learn. Madeline rested both hands on the table and smiled. Michael could see Jude taking in his performance with admiration in her eyes.

'Michael tells me you asked him to chat up someone in Stunners. Well, here I am, so what now?'

'That depends on you, Madeline. I was hoping you might be prepared to assist us with a little scenario.'

Madeline raised an eyebrow with studied precision.

'Let me guess. You want your little friend to get down and dirty with a tranny boy?'

'You make it sound so sordid . . .'

'Isn't sordid what you were after? A quick fumble in the alley? A little humiliation and a test of his obedience?'

'That's all true, but I was rather hoping you'd both enjoy it as well. After all, as Woody Allen said, sex is only dirty if you're doing it right. But I certainly wouldn't want to coerce you. If you're not interested, I'll just send Michael upstairs to find someone else.'

'I didn't say I wasn't interested; I just want to be clear. So what's on offer? A hand job? A quick suck? I'll fuck him if you like, but I don't do it without a condom.'

'What I'd really like is for Michael to suck you – if that's acceptable to you.' Jude smiled persuasively.

'And you wouldn't want me to reciprocate?'

Jude shook her head. 'No, that won't be necessary.'

Madeline sat back in his chair. He looked at Jude for a long moment. He drummed his fingertips softly against the table. Finally, he shrugged.

'OK. I might look like a woman, but underneath this bodice there beats the heart of a red-blooded male. What man would turn down a free blow job?'

Michael felt the blood rushing to his face. For the first time, it occurred to him just what Jude wanted him to do. It had been one thing sucking Alan in the privacy and safety of Jude's bedroom. Though Alan had been a stranger to him, his association with Jude meant he knew Alan could be trusted.

Though Madeline seemed perfectly open and genuine, and Michael had always considered himself a good judge of character, what did he really know about the man apart from the fact that he had a penchant for ball gowns and was very skilled with the make-up brush?

Yet, Jude wanted him to do it, and so he would. She may hurt him, but she'd never harm him; she had said that to him more than once. If things turned nasty, he could easily take care of himself and Jude had a mobile phone in her bag and could call the police if necessary. And anyway, Michael recognised that his concerns about Madeline were more to do with his own anxiety than any genuine danger.

Underneath the fear, he was conscious of a knot of tension in his diaphragm that was as pleasurable as it was unsettling. Madeline was right: there was something unspeakably sordid and squalid about sucking off a bloke in a dress on the orders of your mistress. He wanted it. He longed for the humiliation and degradation with a hunger that burned so strongly it was almost painful.

'Let's go outside then, girls. I know a quiet spot where we won't be disturbed.' Jude led the way. In the open air, Michael felt a little chilly in his skimpy clothes. His cock was already semi-hard in the constricted grip of his underwear. He could feel his cock ring digging into him. He realised that his breathing was irregular and his skin was goose-pimply and sensitive.

Jude guided them over to an area in the corner of the yard where there were half a dozen industrial dustbins and a pile of empty cardboard boxes. The stink was offensive. Michael could smell food waste. Jude walked behind the bins, expecting them to follow. She kicked aside some boxes and cleared a space.

Michael was breathing through his nose in an effort not to gag from the stench of the bins. He felt filthy and ashamed and, in spite of himself, unbelievably excited.

'Well, I must say, if you wanted squalor, you've definitely got it. Shall we get on with it before my gown is ruined?' Madeline lifted up the front of his dress and bunched it up round his waist. Underneath he was wearing a 50s waspie corset and a pair of black French knickers trimmed with lace. Unlike Michael, he had no cache sex and his cock was clearly visible through the sheer fabric and already hard. 'Might as well get rid of these.' He took off his panties with a speed and efficiency that Michael envied, being careful to hold up his gown so as not to get it dirty. He handed his panties to Jude. 'Why don't you give them to Michael as a souvenir? They're Janet Reger.'

'On your knees, Michael.' Jude put the panties into her handbag. 'You know what to do. You've had some practice now, after all.'

Michael looked at the ground. He was torn between his desire to obey instantly and his repugnance for the filth. The yard was cobbled and covered in mud. Food detritus had spilled out of the bins and spattered on the ground. He looked at Jude for guidance but her eyes were hard and stern. He kicked some newspaper and a banana peel out of the way and got to his knees.

186

The cobbles were cold and wet and hard. They hurt his kneecaps but he knew better than to complain. Without waiting to be told, he took Madeline's erect cock in his hand, making him gasp. The cock was long and purple at the tip. A bead of pre-come shone at the eye and Michael put out his tongue and licked it away.

He opened his mouth and slid his lips slowly down Madeline's cock. His nose bumped against scratchy pubes. He could smell Madeline's perfume. He recognised it as Coco by Chanel. Underneath the expensive scent he could detect the deeper musky aroma of man flesh. He'd smelled the same thing on Alan, partly sweat and partly something he couldn't define but recognised, unmistakably, as masculine.

He began to suck in earnest, sliding his mouth up and down. Madeline's balls banged against his chin when he hit bottom and his nose rammed against his fragrant pubes. Madeline was moaning softly, the timbre of the sound unmistakably masculine.

Michael stroked his balls as he sucked. Madeline's cock was silky against his mouth. He could feel its hardness. It almost felt as though he could feel the blood pumping inside it. He had one hand on Madeline's thigh and could feel the taut muscles quivering under his palm.

His own cock was rigid and uncomfortable in the unforgiving grip of his cache sex. Under his wig, his scalp was hot and uncomfortable. The long, fake hair against his shoulders had made his neck sweaty and clammy.

Madeline was gasping and moaning. He reached down and put his hands on Michael's head. He began to rock his hips, establishing a rhythm dictated by his growing arousal. Michael responded, matching his movements to the other man's thrusts. Madeline's balls had grown tight, the scrotum thickening under Michael's fingers.

The cobbles dug into Michael's knees. The stench of rotting garbage and Madeline's more human aroma filled his nostrils. He looked up at Jude. She was standing with her hands on her hips, a look of rapt concentration on her face and lust shining in her eyes. She was breathing hard. Her exposed décolleté gleamed slightly in the light of a nearby streetlamp.

If she hadn't ordered him to pleasure Madeline, he would have pulled her down onto the filthy cobbles and fucked her senseless. He sucked as if his life depended on it. He closed his eyes and concentrated on sensation; the silky feel of Madeline's erect cock, the scent of his pubes and the feel of his nose and chin bumping on flesh.

He wanted to show Jude that he was not just obedient, he was enjoying it. Her desires had become his. Michael tried to communicate wordlessly his pleasure in making Madeline come. He mouthed the cock with an abandon and sensuality that he hoped conveyed his enjoyment.

Beside him, he heard Jude exhale loudly. When he glanced up at her, he noticed that she had laid one hand on her heaving chest and the other was by her side, clenched into a fist. Madeline was pumping his face hard. His hips pounded like pistons. The hands on the back of Michael's head pressed him ever forward. He softened his throat and surrendered to the sensation of cock filling his mouth.

Madeline's thighs were tense and straining. He was groaning and grunting, the manliness of the sounds belying the artful femininity of his appearance. His fingers gripped handfuls of Michael's wig. His hips hammered. His cock began to pulse in Michael's mouth.

'I'm coming . . .' his voice was loud and booming and unmistakably male. It echoed around the yard.

Hot, salty sperm began to flood onto Michael's

tongue. At first he experienced a moment of blinding panic. Though he had sucked Alan willingly and with pleasure, Alan had not come in Michael's mouth. He hadn't been faced with a choice between spitting or swallowing. He was pretty certain, however, that Jude would expect him to swallow. After all, when his own cock was sucked he expected that. He began to swallow the creamy liquid. It was extremely salty, but if he allowed it to squirt on the back of his tongue, it didn't even taste too bad.

He was panting, he realised, his breath snorting out noisily through his nostrils. His cock was rigid and uncomfortable inside his cache sex. Madeline's hands gripped his wig as his hips pounded, his thigh muscles hard and quivering. Madeline gave one final thrust and stopped moving.

He let go of Michael's wig and smoothed it down with both hands. His cock softened in Michael's mouth.

'Thank you. You might not be an expert, but you did a wonderful job.' Madeline's voice had regained its feminine pitch and composure. Michael couldn't help being proud to receive the praise. 'Are you sure you wouldn't like me to return the compliment, Jude? After all, he did it so beautifully, it seems only fair.'

Michael looked up at Jude, trying not to look too hopeful. Jude shook her head.

'Thank you, Madeline, but I have other plans.'

Madeline held up his gown and walked carefully between the piles of rubbish. He lowered his dress and smoothed it with his hands. He smiled at them both and walked away in the direction of Stunners, his back erect and his hips swaying like a catwalk model.

Back at Jude's she ordered Michael to strip and wash his face. Restored to his masculine self, he felt on more familiar ground, but he had no doubt that Jude had something in mind that would stretch his boundaries.

When he came out of the bathroom Jude had changed out of her clothes and was wearing a silk kimono.

'You look beautiful, Jude.' He walked over to her and stroked her cheek.

Jude laughed. 'I've just changed out of my finery and taken my make-up off.'

'Well, you still look stunning.'

'Thank you. So do you, as it happens. Now, why don't you lie down on the bed for me?'

Michael walked over to the bed, eager to obey. He noticed that Jude had put a tray, covered by a white linen napkin, on the bedside table. He thought he could just see the corner of something silver and shiny glinting in the light. His stomach turned a small somersault of anticipation or fear; he was unable to distinguish between the two. Much to his surprise, he realised he didn't even care.

'On your stomach, please. That's right, now spread your arms and legs, I want to tie them to the corner posts.'

Michael did as he was instructed. He lay on his face, in the centre of Jude's bed. The duvet had been covered by a sheet and beneath that he could feel what he thought was probably rubber. Jude clearly had something messy in mind.

She wrapped a chain around each wrist and fastened it with a padlock. She pulled on the chain, making sure that he couldn't free himself. Then she fastened the other end to the posts at the corners of the bed. She pulled them taut, ensuring that the tension was sufficient to keep Michael's arms extended and limiting his ability to struggle. She repeated the process with his ankles.

Michael felt like a scientific specimen, pinned down for dissection. His rigid cock was trapped uncomfortably underneath him. Although he had just taken a shower, his armpits prickled with sweat. Jude arranged a pillow under his head and turned his face to the side, resting his cheek against the fluffy surface.

'Comfortable?' She stroked his back, making him shiver.

'As comfortable as I can be under the circumstances.'

'And how are you feeling?'

'Scared, elated and unbelievably excited.'

'And you trust me?' She fingered his cheek.

'With my life.' The unfamiliar sensation of not being able to respond to her touch in any way was both frustrating and titillating.

Jude took off her robe. She sat down beside Michael and removed the napkin that was covering the tray. Michael lifted his head, trying to see. Jude picked up the tray and moved it into his field of vision. Michael gasped.

The tray held a number of surgical needles in sterile wrappers. There were sachets of antiseptic wipes, a bottle of antiseptic, cotton wool and, most worrying of all, a small silver-handled knife. Michael recognised it as an expensive Japanese model. He had a similar set in his kitchen.

The knot of pleasurable tension in his diaphragm tightened and a lump developed in his throat. His cock, however, didn't seem to share his ambivalence but remained unapologetically erect.

'I want you to enjoy this experience to the full, Michael, so I'd like to blindfold you. As I'm sure you know, when you can't see your other four senses go into overdrive. The merest touch can seem like ecstasy. Sounds are magnified and your sense of smell becomes more sensitive.' Jude opened the drawer in the bedside cabinet and took out a leather blindfold lined with red velvet.

Jude fitted the blindfold, buckling it firmly at the back of his head. Michael was totally blind. As Jude had promised, his other senses seemed to take over and compensate. He was acutely aware of the sensation of cool air against his skin. The linen sheet underneath him was smooth and the rubber beneath it had begun to feel warm and clammy. He could smell the vanilla scent of the shower gel he had used and a hint of sandalwood from a scented candle Jude had lit. He could hear a distant rumble of traffic and the muffled sound of music from next door. He felt alert and on guard and completely, joyously helpless.

'Now, relax. I know what I'm doing, you can trust me.' Jude's voice was reassuring and soft. Michael could just make out a slight huskiness; the product, he hoped, of her arousal at his vulnerability.

There was a sound that initially confused him, but it soon became obvious to him that it was Jude putting on a pair of latex gloves. He heard ripping paper and felt something intensely cold on his back. His body stiffened involuntarily as he tried to work out what Jude was doing to him. She must have opened an antiseptic wipe and was cleaning his back with it. There was obviously alcohol in the antiseptic. It cooled his skin, like ice, as it evaporated. It was not unpleasant, but he couldn't help feeling nervous about what would follow.

He heard paper rip several times, followed by the sound of metallic objects clattering onto the tray. Jude's finger pinched the skin on his upper back, at one side of his spine. He felt something cold against the compressed flesh between Jude's fingers then a moment's heat and intense pain. When she let go, he could feel something cold and hard and thin, resting against his skin. She had pierced him, he realised, with one of the surgical needles.

He gasped and struggled, fear overwhelming him. For a second, he forgot that Jude was his lover and he was submitting willingly to the pain. He was filled with pure, naked terror that hit him physically like a hot wave. He

192

felt her reassuring hand on the small of his back and heard her voice soothing him.

'Shh, shh, darling. You're OK. Do you want me to stop? I won't think any less of you if you use your safe word.'

'No, I'm fine. It was just a shock. I want you to carry on. I need you to carry on. I'm sorry I was afraid, I should have known I can trust you completely.' He loved the weight of her warm hand on his back. It was as though he could feel her love and tenderness seeping into his pores through hers.

'If you're sure.'

'Yes, I am. Please do whatever you want. Please, hurt me.'

She pinched his skin again. This time he braced himself for the pain. When it came, there was a moment of burning intensity that made him gasp, immediately followed by an endorphin rush that left him feeling light-headed and slightly drunk. She repeated the process four more times.

Michael struggled to make sense of the sensations. She was play-piercing him, he thought. He was pretty sure he now had a horizontal row of needles through his flesh. His skin felt unnaturally tight. It burned where the needles penetrated his skin, and his back felt wet. He assumed he was bleeding, but he couldn't be certain. Jude moved on to the left side, repeating the process.

He felt her pinch a small piece of flesh, compressing it with her latex-covered fingertips. The pressure was unpleasant and bordered on painful but, Michael knew, it was nothing compared to the pain to come. He felt the sharp tip of the needle and pain and pressure as it penetrated his flesh. Instantly, a hot rush of blood seemed to course up his body and into his brain. It crashed over him, like a hot torrent of water in the face. Michael even thought he could hear the whooshing sound it made.

He felt drunk and dizzy. Blood pounded in his brain and thundered inside his ears. Though he recognised pain, somehow his body had transformed the experience into the most intense and desirable pleasure. He longed for more and feared he might die if she didn't give it to him. He felt consumed by his love for Jude and, somehow, the pain seemed to represent that love.

Jude forced the final needle on the left side through his flesh. He gasped and panted into his pillow. His body was rigid, his arms and legs taut. Chains creaked and rattled as his body jerked, responding to the pleasure-pain. He felt a cold antiseptic wipe on his back. Jude cleaned each piercing. The alcohol stung a little, but he loved it.

He was sweaty and exhausted. His cock was so hard he feared it might burst. The sheet underneath him was damp and tangled. His wet hair hung limply in his eyes. He felt Jude wiping down both of his buttocks. He inhaled sharply in surprise. His cheeks grew cold and tingly as the alcohol evaporated. He heard Jude pick up something from the tray and he held his breath.

Something cold and hard and thin dug into the flesh of his arse. It felt like a blade, but he couldn't be sure. It was painful, but not as sharp and unbearable as he had anticipated. Jude crisscrossed his buttocks with the sharp implement. He was panting hard. His hands were balled into fists. Sweat dripped down his face. He could tell that he was leaking pre-come; underneath him there was a patch of sticky wetness on the sheet.

Jude pressed harder with the blade and the pain increased, but it seemed dull and transitory, rather than the focused sharpness he would have expected. Jude paused. He felt the flat of her hand stroking his hot cheeks. Her thumbs pressed into his flesh, kneading and massaging. The touch of her hands, even inside latex, was ecstasy to him. He let out a long, low moan of satisfaction. He felt something, tickly and soft – Jude's hair, he thought – against his bottom. Then her lips made contact. She rubbed her face against him. He could feel her heat and her hunger. She licked him, her tongue wetting his tender flesh.

Michael felt as though his cock might explode. His nipples were sensitive and hard, rubbing against the sheet. Jude's mouth moved away. Her weight shifted a little on the bed and he thought he heard her picking up something from the tray. Suddenly he became conscious of a sharp point against the flesh of his right buttock. It dug into him painfully, making him gasp. This is the tip of the knife, he thought. He held his breath. The blade's tip began to move down his buttock. Jude wasn't pressing hard, he realised, and it seemed to bounce along his flesh, making contact only occasionally. It burned and stung but he could certainly cope with it.

But coping with the maelstrom of sensations and emotions that were boiling inside him was another matter. He was so excited he was trembling. His arms and legs were stiff and painful. His shoulders felt as if they had been dislocated. He could hear blood pounding in his head. His body was acutely sensitive to every stimulation, be it physical or sensory. He could hear the sheet rustling. He could hear the sound of Jude's excited breathing. He could feel the texture of the linen underneath him and smell the fabric softener that had been used to launder the pillowcase. He could feel the air itself, like little hard pinpricks, against his excited skin.

He was overwhelmed with tenderness for Jude. At the same time he was acutely aware of her power and his surrender to it. It seemed to be a tangible presence, hanging in the room like mist, or the hint of a perfume that lingers long after its owner has departed. He experienced his own helplessness and need as a blinding moment of clarity and vision that somehow seemed to put the rest of his life into context. He longed for the pain she gave him; he needed the pain she gave him. And he knew, beyond doubt, that the agony he experienced under her loving hands was the conduit of her own longing and need.

The blade's tip danced across his flesh. His buttocks were stinging and hot. He could no longer identify the individual sources of pain; his whole arse was on fire. He felt Jude alter the angle of the knife and its edge slid across his skin. He bucked and shook. It burned with an intense, focused moment of exquisite pain.

She ran the edge of the knife several times across each of his cheeks. Michael was gasping, practically screaming. Tears formed in the corner of his eyes. Saliva dribbled out of his mouth. Trapped between his sweat-slick abdomen and the bed, his cock ached for release.

Michael felt the tip of the knife again. This time, Jude pressed it hard against his flesh. He felt it move against his buttocks, leaving a trail of fiery pleasure-pain in its wake. Chains creaked as he struggled. Adrenaline pumped through his veins. A hot wave of excitement crashed over him like a flood, knocking the breath out of him. It was so powerful and overwhelming that, for a moment, he honestly felt he might die from pleasure. He considered asking Jude to stop, but instantly decided that he didn't care if he did.

The tip of the blade was moving against his other cheek. Jude seemed to be moving it in some deliberate pattern that he couldn't read. The point dug into his flesh, burning and exciting it. He had lost control of his breathing and he was wet with sweat. He gasped into the damp pillow, helpless and satisfied. He heard the knife clatter against the metal tray. Jude stroked his buttocks, her hand warm and soft. She brought her fingers to her lips, rubbing something wet against his lips. He opened his mouth and sucked her fingers, tasting the coppery tang of blood.

Her fingers disappeared and he assumed it was over, that any moment Jude would release him and take him into her arms, stroking his painful muscles and brushing his wet hair out of his eyes. But he felt her parting his buttocks with her fingers and something cold and wet against his arsehole. She was lubing him up to fuck, he assumed.

He felt her finger enter him and he moaned, a long, deep, soft note of pleasure. The nerve endings in his arse seemed to be as hypersensitive as the rest of him. Every movement of Jude's slender finger inside him brought sensations of intense pleasure. The tip massaged his prostate, providing tantalising moments of joy.

He felt a second finger slide into him, stretching his sphincter and magnifying his pleasure. His shoulders ached and throbbed. The pain didn't matter. Somehow it seemed to intensify his enjoyment of the pleasurable sensations Jude was creating in his arse.

A hard, knot of tension at the base of his belly ached for release. His whole body was trembling. As her fingers slid inside him he began to rock his hips, rubbing his erection against the sheet under him.

Jude's fingers withdrew momentarily and, when they entered him again, there was some resistance. She pressed gently, rotating her fingertips against his hole. As her bunched fingers slid past his sphincter he felt as though every pore and particle of his arse was alive with pleasure. He felt stretched and full. Her invading fingers rubbed against his prostate, teasing and exciting him.

He thrust his cock against the sheet, hips moving rhythmically. He was wet with pre-come. His wet hair rubbed against the pillow as he thrashed. Behind him he could hear Jude's hoarse breathing and he could feel her warm hand on the small of his back. He was conscious of her weight beside him on the mattress, shifting slightly as she fingered him.

Her fingers stretched him; the sensation of taut skin and straining muscle was intensely arousing and unfamiliar. Though he knew the sensations were caused by Jude's fucking, he couldn't quite shake off the feeling that he needed to go to the loo urgently. The feeling was perversely pleasurable and obscenely exciting. Lying passively on his front and allowing Jude to abuse his arse, to enter him via an opening that was designed only for exit, felt wicked and incongruous.

Jude pushed her fingers into him and he felt a momentary resistance before they sank into his willing hole. He guessed that she had added another finger, stretching him so tight that he felt as though his ring might split. Yet there was no real pain, just a sensation of welcome fullness and tightness.

Something about the passivity of the act and Jude's skilled manipulation made him feel like a Christmas turkey being stuffed in readiness for the oven. He wasn't sure why, but this image excited rather than shamed him. Seeing himself as nothing more than meat seemed to symbolise his surrender. Jude could use his helpless body as she saw fit and that was all he wanted and needed. Her audacious invasion of his flesh and his willing submission to it was his only desire.

His cock rubbed against the damp sheet. He felt as though he was breathing in fire. Sweat ran into his eyes. Jude's fingers moved inside him, stroking his sensitive prostate on every thrust. Every so often, Jude gave a little grunt of exertion as she fucked him. She was panting audibly and her hand on his back was warm and damp.

The tension in the base of his belly had spread through his body. He felt as though every cell and tendon was rigid with tension and anticipation. He was close. He felt Jude's fingers withdraw for a second then slide back into him. For a moment, he felt as though they weren't going to fit. Jude gave a little throaty grunt and he felt her putting all her weight behind her shoulder. Her slippery hand slipped slowly past his tight sphincter.

Michael felt a fleeting stab of pain as her knuckles slid past his muscles.

'How many fingers is that? You've got your whole hand inside me, haven't you?' His voice was a throaty whisper, the sentence broken up by gasps.

'Yes I have, darling. I wasn't sure it would go in, but it has. Does it feel good?'

'It feels incredible. I think I'm going to come. Please don't tell me I can't.'

'I wouldn't dream of it. You've earned it this evening.'

Michael thrust his hips, rhythmically rubbing his cock against the bunched sheet. Her fist opened his arse, stuffing and stretching it. Somehow it felt both horrible and exquisite at the same time. The extreme distension of his muscles seemed completely unnatural and was inextricably associated with defecation. Yet, at the same time, Jude's possession of him was completely fulfilling and thoroughly desirable.

His breath caught in his throat. His hips pistoned. Jude's hand moved inside him. The tension in his gut focused and burst. His cock fucked the damp sheet, pumping out spunk. He could feel its warm wetness pooling against his belly. His arse spasmed around Jude's hand. He became aware of the sound of a man screaming and moaning. The sound seemed to express alarm and satisfaction in equal measure and, slowly, he realised that the screams must be his own.

Jude's reassuring hand on the small of his back somehow kept him in contact with reality. Though he knew he was chained naked to her bed with her hand in his arse, he felt as though he were floating in space, blind and weightless, conscious only of his pleasure.

His whole body was shuddering. He was on the edge of tears. The sheet underneath him was clammy and creased with a patch of cooling moisture at his crotch. Jude gently withdrew her hand.

He felt her removing the needles from his back one by one and dropping them into the tray. He gasped in relief as they withdrew. She cleaned the area with an antiseptic wipe. He heard her pulling off her latex glove. She fiddled with the chains at his ankles and released him, lying his aching feet softly on the bed. She released his hands and, finally, unbuckled his blindfold.

Then she lay down beside him and kissed his eyelids. 'You've been crying.'

'Perhaps, I don't know. I'm not even sure I haven't died and gone straight to heaven.'

Jude laughed. 'I take it that means you enjoyed it?' She stroked his hair.

'I did. Though I'm not sure I want a repeat performance any day soon.'

'No need to worry about that. Needles and cutting are a strictly occasional pleasure.'

Michael put his arm around her, wincing with pain as he moved his stiff shoulder.

'Did you actually cut my arse? I couldn't really tell what you were doing.'

She nodded. 'Most of the time, though, I was just using my credit card that had been in the freezer. When it's very cold, the edge feels like the blade of a knife.'

'But you were using a knife, weren't you? I'm sure I felt the blade.'

'I did. But I didn't cut you as such; it's more like scratches. I've written my initials on your arse – you can look in the mirror when you've got your breath back. I expect you could do with a nice soak in the bath before we go to bed.'

'You've carved your initials into my arse? What am I? A prize cow?' He raised his eyebrows in mock surprise.

'No . . .' She kissed him. 'You are the man I love.'

Twelve

A month later, they drove to the south coast. Though Michael knew the general location, Jude had been mysterious about their destination. On the outskirts of Brighton, she stopped the car outside a parade of shops.

'This doesn't look a very promising location for a weekend away.' They were in a quiet residential street outside a row of shops: a newsagent's, a chippie and a bookmaker's. The fourth shop was too far away to read the sign.

'We're just calling in en route. It's something I've been meaning to organise for some time and this seemed like the ideal opportunity.' Jude locked the car. As they grew closer to the last shop, he could see it was a tattoo parlour. Vivid, colourful designs decorated the window between photographs of what Michael assumed were satisfied customers and their inked skin.

He felt a little flutter of anxiety under his diaphragm followed by a hot rush of blood to his head. Whatever Jude had planned, he wanted it. He'd never considered a tattoo, but the thought of having his skin indelibly inscribed at her command suddenly seemed irresistibly attractive.

As they stepped inside a bell sounded and a young man appeared from behind a beaded curtain. His head was partially shaved and his remaining hair was arranged into a tall, red Mohican. His exposed scalp was covered in black tribal tattoos, as were his arms. Michael could see similar designs above the collar of his T-shirt.

'Jude!' The man smiled.

'Hi, Adam, lovely to see you again. Thanks for opening up after hours for me.' Jude embraced the young man. 'And this is Michael.'

They shook hands.

'I've got everything ready if you want to come through.' He parted the bead curtain and they followed him through to a small room with a couch and a chair by its side. Beside the chair was a metal trolley and on its shiny surface were an array of inks and the tattoo gun. It looked big and scary to Michael, even though he knew the needles themselves would be quite fine.

Along the back of the room was a long shelf along which were organised inks, latex gloves, a metal steriliser unit and the various tools of his trade. Adam sat in the chair and reached for a pair of gloves. He patted the couch.

'Hop up, Michael.'

Michael looked at Jude for guidance.

'Um ... Where am I having it? What do I need to take off?' He felt his cheeks burning from a mixture of embarrassment and excitement.

'It's going on your inner thigh; but take everything off. It should make things a little more exciting if you're naked.'

Michael shrugged off his T-shirt and dropped it onto a chair by the door. He toed off his trainers and bent to remove his socks. As he unzipped his fly he remembered he was wearing one of Jude's thongs. He hesitated for a moment, then continued.

He turned his back on Adam and slipped out of his trousers as quickly as he could. He pulled down the thong and put it on the chair, hiding it underneath his clothes. He felt conspicuous and slightly ashamed but, underneath it all, he felt the first stirrings of arousal. He climbed onto the couch. It creaked slightly as he mounted it and the leather covering was cold against his skin.

'Which side do you want it, Jude?' Adam sat with his gun poised.

'The right, I think.'

'Open your legs for me, please, Michael.'

He felt a gloved hand on his thigh. He bent his legs at the knee and pressed the soles of his feet together, exposing his inner thigh for Adam. Jude rummaged in her handbag and took out a pair of handcuffs and his lead. She snapped the lead onto the ring of the thin leather collar she insisted that he wear when they went out together. She cuffed his hands in front of him and fastened the chain to his collar with a double-ended snap clip.

Michael felt vulnerable and exposed. His cock was stirring. He wanted to cover it with his hands, but he couldn't move them. Jude pulled up a chair and sat beside him.

The tattoo gun began to buzz like a dentist's drill and Michael felt a finger on his inner thigh. There was a fierce, localised burning sensation and he flinched.

'Sorry. It hurts most when I'm doing the outline; it shouldn't take long. Why don't you take a few deep breaths?'

'Breathe deeply, darling. Close your eyes. I'm here beside you,' Jude whispered into his ear, her breath hot on his cheek.

The pain was intense and concentrated. The needle dug into his flesh and felt as though it was burning him. Michael tried to lie still, focusing on calm thoughts and waves crashing onto a golden beach. Jude rested one warm hand on his shoulder as the other stroked his face. From time to time she whispered soothing words in his ear or kissed him.

The needle screeched; its droning noise seemed to fill the room and get inside his brain. Michael visualised an azure sky and smooth sand that was hot under his toes. A wave gushed up the beach, wetting him to the ankles.

'I'm changing needles now. Then I'm going to fill in the design. This shouldn't hurt quite as much. Are you doing OK?' The buzzing gun became quiet and Michael opened his eyes.

'I'm fine, thank you.'

Adam changed needles and dipped the tip into a pot of colour. Michael gazed up at the ceiling. He noticed a dark crack in the centre, running from the light fitting to the wall, bisecting the white expanse like a scar. Adam switched on the gun and began to ink in the design.

The needle didn't burn with quite the same intensity but it was still so painful that it made Michael inhale sharply. He closed his eyes again and conjured up his beach, allowing the warm paradise of his imagination to take the edge off his pain. He was conscious of endorphins coursing round his body, cushioning his pain and filling him with wellbeing.

He felt slightly drunk. He knew his face was flushed. His cock was half hard, lying flat against his belly. His nipples were erect and excited. Jude's fingers brushing his cheek made him shiver; he nuzzled his face against her hand.

The buzzing needle droned on, barely reaching Michael's consciousness. He could feel the leather beneath him growing slightly clammy. Adam's fingers pressed against his flesh, his other hand using a tissue to wipe away what Michael could only assume was blood.

Michael was panting slightly, breathing through parted lips. His stiffening cock tingled pleasurably, enjoying his helplessness and the burning of the buzzing needle. Jude's hand on his shoulder reassured him and made him feel safe.

The needle stopped and Michael heard Adam putting the gun down. He felt something wet and cold against his sore inner thigh and opened his eyes to see Adam spraying it from a bottle of what he assumed to be antiseptic. Adam tore off some paper towel and carefully wiped the area clean.

'Do you want to look, Jude?' Adam dropped the towel into the bin.

Jude stood up and bent over the couch to inspect the tattoo.

'Do you like it? I copied the design you sent me, I think it works beautifully.'

Jude was silent for a long moment. When she spoke, her voice was husky and soft. 'It's beautiful, Adam, thank you. Let me undo Michael, so he can have a look.'

She unclipped his cuffs from his collar and he sat up. Adam picked up a hand mirror from the shelf and passed it to him. Michael held it between his legs and tilted it to see the tattoo.

His skin was red and angry, but the design was beautiful. Inside a circular border of Celtic knotwork, the letters J and M were intertwined. The letters were stylised and elaborate, but they were still readable. The border was coloured in red and the letters were black.

'It's lovely. I will treasure it always.'

Adam laughed. 'Well, you've not got much option, mate. It's with you for life now.'

At lunchtime they stopped at a pub and ate in the garden. It was a warm spring day and a light breeze was blowing. The sun seemed to pick up the fine hairs on Jude's arms and make them gleam. Her hair moved in the breeze.

'Would you like to know where we're going?' She smiled at him.

'Of course, though if you want it to be a surprise, that's fine as well.'

'We're going to a cottage on the North Devon coast, near Bideford. They have a very well-equipped dungeon. It's called –'

'The Edge.'

'You know it?'

Michael shook his head. 'I know of it. I've always wanted to go.'

'Well, your dream is about to come true. We've made a bit of a detour because I wanted to take you to Adam. But there was something I wanted to talk to you about before we get there.' Jude looked suddenly serious.

'Nothing bad, I hope?'

Jude laid her hand on top of his. 'Oh, I doubt it you'll find it a problem. Though you may find it something of a surprise.'

'I'm intrigued.'

'You remember when I told you I started out as submissive?'

'How can I forget? You could have knocked me down with the proverbial feather.'

'Well, as I said, I don't have those feelings any more and I certainly don't get off on humiliation.' She took a breath. 'But I do like receiving pain. For example, you might have noticed I get you to bite my nipples really hard.'

'Of course I have. And I love doing it.'

'Well, I also love to be whipped. And I like breast bondage and nipple torture.'

Michael's eyes widened. He looked at Jude and, for the first time he could remember, saw uncertainty in her eyes.

'You look ... I don't even have a word for it ... You're maybe a little nervous about telling me this, aren't you, and worried about my reaction?'

'Yes, I am. It's not something I can usually talk about with my lovers. Somehow they seem to feel differently

206

about me when they find out. As if I'm diminished in their eyes. Do you understand?'

He nodded. 'Of course I do. But I don't feel any differently about you, I promise. If anything, I love you more, knowing that you trust me enough to share this with me.'

She squeezed his hand. 'I was hoping you'd feel that way. I did try to get Alan to whip me once, but it was hopeless. He just doesn't have it in him. It didn't fit with how he feels about me.'

'But I couldn't imagine it making him feel any differently about you. He doesn't seem the type.'

'No, it didn't. He understood. He just couldn't give me what I wanted. What I need.'

'But you think I can?'

'You were dominant before you met me. I *know* you can. The only thing that worries me is . . .' She looked at her hands. Her diffidence moved him almost to tears.

'Whether I'll still respect you in the morning?'

She laughed. 'Something like that. Whether you'll still be able to see me as your mistress, I suppose. You do understand? I'm not submissive at all – I'm just turned on by pain.'

'Yes, I understand the distinction. I may be new to this, Jude, and I have a lot to learn, but there's one thing I'm certain of. You will be my mistress until the day I die. Nothing can change that. It will be an honour and a privilege to hurt you and very much a pleasure. And, now I've been on the receiving end, it will mean even more to me because I understand what courage and trust it takes. If anything, I'll think more of you, not less.'

'Thank you, Michael. You have no idea what that means to me. I've never had a relationship that gave me everything I wanted before. There was always something missing, or some part of myself I had to hold back. Do you know what I mean?'

He picked up her hand in both of his. 'Of course I do. It's the same for me, though I didn't know it. And I can't thank you enough for being able to see it. This is all I ever wanted. You are all I ever wanted.'

Jude smiled and Michael thought he could see tears shining in the corner of her eyes.

They arrived at the Edge late in the afternoon. They put their luggage in the cottage and went to explore. They walked along the beach then Jude led him down a lane and through a small wood. In a clearing they came upon a ruined Gothic church. It had lost its roof and the pointed arched windows lacked glass, but its stone walls had lost none of their grandeur.

'It's beautiful, Jude. How did you know it was here?'

'The land is owned by a friend of mine. It's not really a church. It's a folly, built a hundred years ago to look like a ruin. Shall we go inside?'

The building had an imposing oak door.

Michael whistled. 'It must be at least eight feet tall.'

Jude turned the handle and leaned against the door. It gave a suitably authentic creak and opened slowly. Inside, there were rows of pews and a stone floor. At the front there was an impressively carved pulpit. Behind the altar, a massive wooden cross bearing a figure of Christ in torment hung on the wall.

'Don't you think it's wonderful? It's so atmospheric.' Jude walked down the aisle and stepped over the altar rail. Michael followed her. Dry leaves and twigs crackled underfoot. It smelled of earth and damp stone. It had all the mystery and magic of a consecrated place of worship. Michael felt as though he ought to whisper and put a coin in the collection plate on his way out.

The altar was a block of intricately carved grey stone – Michael thought it might be a type of marble. He put out a hand and stroked its chilly surface. Jude caught his wrist and brought her face close to his ear. She whispered and he knew that she shared his reverence for the holy place.

'Take your clothes off. Hurry.'

Michael experienced a shiver of shock and outrage, and then quickly saw the appeal of her suggestion. He stripped off his clothes, laying them on the altar. Jude pulled the belt from his trousers and wrapped the buckle end around her hand several times.

'Bend over the altar.' Her eyes shone with lust and wickedness.

Michael lay down over the altar, leaning his upper body flat against the marble. He extended his arms, forming his upper body into the shape of a cross. It reminded him of a medieval painting he had once seen of a monk presenting himself for punishment; his body flat against the stone floor, his arms outstretched. Michael's cock was growing hard. Its tip brushed against the cold marble.

Behind him, he could hear Jude's feet on the stone floor and leaves rustling as she walked. He could hear her excited breathing, an echo of his own. His nipples tingled as they made contact with the icy altar stone.

The belt slapped down across his arse. The sudden pain knocked the breath out of him. His buttocks were on fire. She struck him again, bringing the leather strap down hard across the top of his thigh. He grunted.

Michael's breathing was loud and rasping. He could hear birds twittering and the distant sigh of the sea. The belt cracked loudly. The sound echoed around the church, as shocking and out of place as a gunshot in a library.

His arse burned with pleasure and pain. His skin tingled. His nipples rubbed against the cold stone. The belt lashed across both buttocks and he moaned: a long, low note of agony and appreciation.

Behind him, he could hear Jude panting. He could imagine her upper lip filmed with sweat and her hair loose and messy around her shoulders. He knew her pussy would be moist, leaving a dark stain on the crotch of her panties.

She began to whip him hard, bringing the belt down again and again. The sound echoed, filling the air like thunder. Michael's body jolted and juddered. His cock bounced underneath him. Heat warmed his whipped arse and spread through his veins. He knew his cock was wet with pre-come, lubricating the marble.

Jude brought the belt down with such force that the sound disturbed a bird nesting in the church and sent it fluttering away, wings beating furiously. Jude's breathing was loud and rasping behind him. He felt her hands on his reddened arse; they felt cool next to his inflamed skin. She stroked his raised welts, running the tips of her fingers delicately along their length. He moaned and rubbed his aching cock against the marble.

She got down on her knees and began to kiss his weals. Her lips were warm and moist, her face soft. He could feel the roughness of her hair as she pressed her cheek against his tender flesh.

'Put your clothes on, darling, and we'll head back to the cottage. I think we need a bit more privacy for what I have in mind next.'

On the short walk back to the cottage, Jude seemed excited and quiet. Her hand in his was clammy and damp. He glanced at her as they walked. Her lips were red and puffy and her eyes seemed to be shining. She kept her head down and walked briskly.

She led him straight to the dungeon. Inside she stripped off her clothes. There was no tease or sensuality in the way she undressed. Michael could tell she just wanted to be naked as quickly as possible. He stood watching her, knowing that she would tell him what she expected of him soon enough.

She went over to the whips hanging on the wall and selected a long, swishy riding crop. She handed it to

Michael, silently went over to the spanking horse and bent over it. Instead of lying across its length, she bent her body at the waist and rested her forearms on the leather surface. Her arse poked lasciviously into the air, her slit just visible beneath her buttocks.

She turned her head and spoke over her shoulder.

'I want you to whip my arse. I'm going to finger myself while you do it. The more aroused I become, the harder I'll want it. If I tell you I want it harder then do it. And, whatever you do, don't stop. Do you understand?' Her voice was deep and throaty.

'Yes, I understand. I won't let you down.'

Jude smiled and turned away. She put her right hand between her legs and began to finger her clit. Michael could clearly hear the squelching moisture. He raised his arm and brought the crop down. It swished through the air and landed with a crack. Jude gasped. Her body jerked forward on the horse but her fingers continued to move. He struck her again, slightly harder. She let out a deep moan of pleasure.

Her fingers moved frantically between her legs. Her body was rigid. Her hair fell over her face. Michael whipped her hard. The air was filled with the sound of the swishing crop and Jude's excited moans.

Michael was panting from the effort. His shirt was damp at the armpits and clung uncomfortably to his back. He'd have liked to strip off, but he'd promised Jude he wouldn't stop and he intended to live up to his promise. Inside his jeans, his erection was compressed uncomfortably.

Jude was panting, her chest heaving as she fingered herself. A damp tendril of hair clung to her back. Her skin glowed in the dim light. Her shapely arse was decorated with angry red stripes. It was the most beautiful sight Michael had ever seen.

Her slit was glistening, her lips swollen. Michael cut across both buttocks with the crop. Her body juddered and she grunted. Michael noticed that she had begun to rub her nipples against the leather horse. The knuckles of her left hand were white as her fingers dug into the edge of the bench. Her breathing was clearly audible in the quiet room, reminding Michael of a heartbeat.

His face was damp with sweat and his hair hung in his eyes. The handle of the crop had grown slippery. He changed hands for a moment and wiped his sweaty palm on his thigh.

He began to increase the force behind the crop, leaving vivid red marks on her white arse. Jude was thrashing around on the bench, rocking her hips in rhythm with her moving fingers. She was covered in sweat, her hair clinging to her damp shoulders. She was breathing in great, loud snatches that reflected the heat of her arousal.

Michael whipped her rhythmically. New scarlet stripes formed on top of the old ones. Her upturned buttocks were one mass of red. He could see the skin growing inflamed and becoming raised. Bruises were beginning to form, turning some parts of her arse from crimson to a regal purple.

'Harder, Michael.' Her voice was a hoarse whisper, urgent and needy.

He obeyed her, bringing the crop down with a force that hurt his shoulder and made him grunt with effort. His shirt was damp and clinging to his body. His erect cock ached for release.

Jude's body was rigid with excitement. He could see her thigh muscles taut and trembling. Her excited fingers moved against her clit. Moisture had wet her whole hand and run down over her thighs, making her spread pussy glisten. Her back was slick with sweat. She had begun to wail; a constant, high note of pleasure and pain that seemed to get inside Michael's head, infecting him like a virus with her excitement.

Michael knew she was close. He whipped her hard. The crop cracked through the air. The sound hung in the air and echoed around the room, harmonising with Jude's excited keening. Michael found it intoxicating. Jude rubbed her nipples against the leather. Her fingers gripped the edge of the horse, steadying her. Her hips rocked, rubbing her crotch against her ever-moving fingers.

Michael could smell her arousal. He rained blows down on her arse, watching almost mesmerised as weals and bruises formed. Jude's wailing became more urgent and higher in pitch. Her fingers moved frantically, she rocked her hips slowly several times then stopped moving, her body rigid.

Michael brought down the crop across her arse again and again. She was coming, that was obvious, and she'd instructed him not to stop until she was ready. His desire to obey her possessed him. Her orgasm and the pain he was giving her were the only things that made sense to him. He whipped her as if his life depended on it. He was panting and sweaty, his shoulder hurt and his hand holding the crop was slick and slippery.

Jude was practically screaming, her body twitching and writhing as she came. Her arse was dark and discoloured. Red, blue and purple marks and raised welts obscured the pale skin. Her swollen cunt gleamed in the light; her moving fingers were shiny with moisture. Her cunt lips were the same livid colour as her whipped arse. She was gasping, screaming and almost laughing. Though her hair obscured her face, Michael was certain she was crying as well.

'Stop.' Her voice was so weak that Michael almost didn't hear it.

He dropped the crop and it clattered to the floor. He got to his knees and kissed her beaten arse. He cooled it with his tongue, explored each angry weal with the tips of his fingers. Her skin was clammy and hot. He could smell her excitement. Her body seemed to be gripped by some involuntary quiver that, though he didn't understand why, filled Michael with overwhelming tenderness.

'Fuck me.' Jude's voice was hoarse and urgent. She stood up and lay back along the length of the spanking horse. Michael pulled down his trousers. He moved her legs over his shoulder and positioned his cock. He thrust his hips forward and entered her. Her cunt was hot and tight and hungry. She moaned as he slid into her, a long low note of satisfaction and pleasure.

'I want you to hurt my tits while you fuck me. Pinch them, bite them, anything.'

Michael moved her legs to his waist and reached for her nipples. He raked his fingernails across their reddened tips. Jude gasped and arched her back. He scratched her stiff nipples, making her moan. He caught them between thumb and forefinger and pulled on them, stretching out her small breasts. His cock moved inside her. His thighs banged the edge of the bench as he fucked her.

'Pinch them hard.' Jude spoke through clenched teeth, her voice deep and urgent.

'You want me to hurt you, Jude? Is that what you want?' He squeezed her nipples.

'Yes, yes. Hurt me, please.' Her eyes shone with entreaty.

'I can't tell you how exciting it is for me hearing you say that.' Michael increased the pressure on his fingers, pinching her hard.

Jude wrapped her legs around his waist, pulling him close. She rocked her hips, rubbing her clit against his crotch. Strands of wild hair clung to her face and neck.

Michael pinched her nipples. He twisted them. Jude moaned constantly, the tone of the sound rising each time he hurt her. A red flush of arousal darkened her throat. Her cheeks were flushed. Her lips were moist and rosy. Michael's body was tingling and sensitive. His cock was rigid.

Jude was panting and gasping. She slid up and down the leather-covered horse. Her legs gripped his waist, pulling him deeper. Sweat ran down Michael's face and into his eyes. He was breathing hard, sucking in great gouts of air as he pounded her cunt.

He pinched her nipples hard, pulling and twisting them, distorting her breasts. His fingertips were white. His hands hurt, but he squeezed her swollen nipples with all his might. Jude gasped and moaned. Her back was arched, her body stiff. Her legs held him in a tight embrace, ankles locked behind his back.

His balls banged against her arse. His groin burned with delicious tension. His skin felt alive and tingly. He was close. He could come any second if he wanted to, but he held himself back, waiting for Jude. Her body began to buck. She wailed, the note increasing in pitch as her orgasm approached. Her legs clutched him. Her cunt swallowed all of him.

He pulled on her nipples, squeezing the flesh between his fingers. Jude rocked her hips, rubbing her clit against him. She was coming; he knew the signs. Her eyes were closed, her cheeks flushed. Her teeth were gritted and her lips drawn back. She trembled all over and her cunt squeezed his cock relentlessly.

'Permission to come, please, Mistress.' Michael gasped out the words between breaths.

'Yes!' Jude elongated the syllable like the hiss of a serpent.

Michael thrust his hips. The tension in his groin built towards its zenith and exploded. His cock pumped out spunk inside her. His crotch ground against hers. Her legs around his waist were slippery and wet. Her feet dug into his back. She put her hands on his and moved them away from her nipples. He leaned forward, bending his body over hers.

He circled his hips, wringing out the last shreds of orgasm. Jude held on to his hands, watching him as he came.

Back in the cottage's bathroom, they shared the tub. As Jude dried herself she sat on the edge of the bath, watching him.

'Did you enjoy us switching, darling?' She towelled her hair.

He smiled. 'It was incredible. Thank you for trusting me.'

'And your orgasm – was that good, too?'

'At the risk of repeating myself, it was incredible. I won't forget it in a hurry.'

'I'm glad, because it's the last you will be having for a while . . .' She walked out of the bathroom.

'What do you mean?' Michael shouted after her. She came back into the room with a small box.

'Do you remember Eric, at the Whipping House?'

He nodded. 'Of course. How could I forget? The helpful little slave with the nipple rings and the apron.'

'That wasn't all he was wearing, if you remember.'

'No, of course, there was the chastity thingy. I didn't much like the look of that.' Michael's eyes widened as realisation dawned.

Jude nodded. She opened the box. 'I did say I was thinking of buying one.'

'Yes, you did. But somehow I never quite imagined that would mean I'd end up wearing it.' He bent his head and looked into the box.

'Let's put it on, then we can find somewhere nice to have dinner.' Jude put the various plastic components down on the vanity unit.

'It looks a bit complicated.' Michael couldn't help sounding dubious.

'It's quite simple, really. This bit,' – she held it up – 'fits around your cock and balls like your cock ring.

You'll have to take that off for the time being, unfortunately. Then your cock goes in the cage and the ring snaps into place and locks to the one round your balls. And, just in case you get any ideas, we fit a padlock. There are two locking padlocks, as you can see. And several of these little plastic ones.'

Michael looked at the array of plastic parts. He poked the cock cage with the tip of his finger. 'Surely I could just cut off the plastic padlocks and put on another. You'd never know.'

Jude shook her head. She picked up one of the small plastic locks. 'They've thought of that. If you look, you will see that each one is individually numbered.'

'I see. Fiendish. How long are you thinking of making me wear it?'

'Oh, I don't know. I haven't really decided. I rather think that we'll both know when it's the right time to take it off.'

'How do I ...' In spite of himself he felt panic beginning to rise. 'Can I go to the loo? What about washing?'

'You can piss with it on perfectly normally, though it might be better to go into a cubicle rather than doing it at the urinal if you don't want to get stared at. And you can wash using a sponge or flannel. You just can't get a good enough grip on it to make yourself come. Now; let's put it on.'

Thirteen

Michael wore his chastity device constantly at the Edge. Jude frequently demanded that he pleasure her, seemingly oblivious to his discomfort. The plastic cage bit into his flesh when he got an erection and created pressure on his balls and, for the first time in his life, he began to dread becoming aroused. By the end of the weekend he was frustrated beyond measure and possessed by an inner restlessness that exhausted and dispirited him.

The journey home seemed interminable. At the halfway point Michael had taken over the driving. The activity eased his agitation a little but did nothing to assuage his stifled desire.

Though he'd used orgasm denial to control his partners, he'd never limited his own relief. Like most men, he enjoyed delaying his orgasm and he had always ridden the edge of frustration to increase his creativity, but going without altogether was incomprehensible. He'd been coming at least daily since early adolescence.

Self-denial wasn't really in Michael's vocabulary. He was a creature of excess. He loved his food and wine and, like Jude, considered himself a sensualist. Moderation didn't come naturally.

The sudden withdrawal of a means of expression he had never sought to limit left him feeling incomplete and distorted. He was no longer himself but some abbreviated and diminished version he no longer recognised.

His desire to obey made him determined to be stoical. And yet obedience was proving far more challenging than he'd bargained for. He'd known she would torture him and subject him to all manner of humiliation, and he'd known he could bear it all. But deliberately curtailing the sexual appetite that his submission to her created seemed perverse and unreasonable.

They pulled up outside Michael's flat around eleven. He turned off the engine and handed her the key.

'Will you come up? I know you said you didn't want to stay, but perhaps a drink before bed?'

'I don't think so. I've got an early start; I just want to get to bed.'

'OK.' He was struck by a sudden, overwhelming terror that she was losing interest. 'Will I see you soon?' The words were simple, but the sentiment behind them was so painful he could hardly make them come out of his mouth.

Jude undid her seatbelt and slid over to him. 'You sounded like a little boy then. All nervous and vulnerable.'

'That's ... that's how I feel.' He couldn't meet her gaze.

'Why? After all we've been through together, surely you can talk to me?' She held his hand.

'I'm probably being stupid, but I feel as though the rug has been pulled out from under me. We've spent every spare moment together for weeks. We've just shared the most intense weekend of my life, yet you don't want to come upstairs with me. I don't know what I've done wrong.'

'You haven't done anything wrong. In fact, you couldn't have pleased me more.' She smiled.

'Then why are you punishing me?'

'Is that how it feels?'

He nodded.

'I didn't put you in the CB2000 to punish you. It's . . . a lesson, if you like.'

'So you're teaching me a lesson? That's another way of saying you're punishing me, isn't it?'

'No. I'm not punishing you and I'm not displeased. I'm not coming upstairs because I'm tired, nothing more. There are some things you have to learn for yourself and this is one of them.'

'And I have to learn that on my own? You can't help me? That seems harsh.'

'I've given you all the help I can by making you wear it. What happens next is your journey to make alone. But I'm not abandoning you. We'll talk often. And it will pass soon enough.' She brought his hand to her lips and kissed it.

'Not soon enough for me, I assure you.'

'You're finding it difficult?'

'It's hell. I don't even feel like me any more. I feel as though I've lost part of myself.'

'That's good. It sounds as if you're beginning to understand.'

As the days passed, Michael began to feel he was living in a nightmare. He'd never realised quite how often he got hard in the course of a normal day. Several times in the night he was woken by an erection being strangled by the plastic cage. He had to concentrate hard on something else to get it to subside, bringing to mind the unwanted erections of adolescence and his desperate attempts to curb them. Every morning, his piss-proud cock strained against its prison, jolting him out of sleep and sending him off to the loo bent double and hobbling like an old man.

But if the night-time was miserable, the daytime was unbearable. The subject of his work seemed inappropriate and tormenting. It titillated and shamed him, and

Michael came to see it as the symbol of his dilemma; condemned to spend his days working himself into a frenzy of lust he was never permitted to relieve.

He'd got through the first weekend after their return by spending hours at the cinema and accepting a dinner invitation from one of his banking colleagues. At the end of the second week, the prospect of another weekend alone deprived of the one outlet he craved seemed like a vision of hell. He sat down at his desk, dazed and distracted.

At the Edge, his situation hadn't bothered him so much because he was still allowed the fulfilment of giving Jude pleasure. Sure, he was frustrated, but at least there had been some point to it while he was with her.

Now, he just felt frustrated, restless and abandoned. It was the last of these he found hardest to take. Though she'd assured him she loved him more than ever, he didn't understand why she was doing this to him. Her refusal to explain and her insistence that he'd work it out for himself was infuriating and disheartening. He'd been in the thing for a fortnight now and he still hadn't a clue what he was supposed to understand. He picked up the phone and dialled her number.

'Jude Ryan.'

He felt better just hearing her voice.

'Hi Jude, it's Michael.'

'Hello, darling. How are you doing?'

'I've been better, I must admit. I'd feel a lot better if I could see you, though. I've been really lonely.' He held the phone with both hands and spoke into it with his eyes closed.

'Lonely? Or perhaps you mean horny?' She laughed.

'Both. Of course, I'm horny, but I miss you desperately. If only I could see you, I know I wouldn't find it so difficult. Please.' The desperation he could hear in his own voice made Michael feel ashamed.

'I never said it would be easy.' Her voice was like a tender caress and Michael drew strength from it, even though it was perfectly clear she couldn't be swayed.

'I don't know how much more of this I can take, Jude.'

'You're stronger than you think. You'll work it out. I think you're already beginning to understand.'

'All I understand is that I miss you and I'm so horny I can hardly think. I want you, Jude . . . I need you.'

'And I need you. This is just as hard for me, you know. You're nearly there. You just need to put all the pieces together. I promise you, it will be worth waiting for.'

When he put the phone down, Michael was overcome with humiliation and rejection. What did she mean, he was nearly there? He was no closer to understanding than when she'd first locked him into the thing.

Yet, she'd been kind and loving and her voice had soothed him. He tried to cling on to that. She clearly wasn't doing this out of malice, though he was completely mystified as to her real motives. It was so unfair. It was easy for her to say she found it difficult. She wasn't the one with her crotch locked away. He could hardly think straight any more.

He wished he could hate her; it would make things so much easier. Yet most of him still wanted to please her. If only it weren't so difficult. He just needed to come once. He'd get his sense of perspective back and he might even get a good night's sleep.

Perhaps there was some way to get out of the thing. If she'd used the metal padlock he might have been able to pick it, but the plastic lock seemed foolproof. If he cut it off, even if he ordered some new locks from the manufacturer, they'd have different serial numbers and she'd know.

Perhaps there was some way to get out of the thing without taking the lock off. Or, if not, maybe it was possible to make himself come with it on? He could just about get the tip of one finger inside the cage to touch his cock; perhaps there was a way to give himself an orgasm. After all, he wasn't the first man to find himself in this position. He was willing to bet someone had come up with a solution.

He turned on his computer and opened Internet Explorer and, within minutes, he had discovered that some men were able to work their balls between the interlocking rings, freeing themselves. He unzipped his trousers and pulled them down to his ankles. He tried to manipulate his balls through the ring, pulling the skin of his scrotum through first as the website described, but he just couldn't do it. It hurt his testicles and they were just too big to squeeze through the gap. When he finally gave up, his scrotum was red and sore.

According to the article, some men could work the cage part down and pull their penis out at the top. He tried that too, but it was obvious immediately it wasn't going to work. The cage was held in place firmly by the plastic ring around his scrotum and wouldn't budge.

He wasn't going to be able to get it off, but it might still be possible to make himself come. He did a new Internet search and soon found a website that claimed orgasm could be achieved by holding a vibrator against the plastic cage. Another site suggested using the tip of the vibrator directly against the end of the penis.

He had a selection of vibrators in his filing cabinet for use in his work, so he opened the drawer and retrieved one that had latex sleeves that could be slipped over the vibe, providing different-shaped tips. A long, thin protuberance about as thick as a pencil might do the trick.

He tried pressing a vibrator against the plastic cage but it was merely unpleasant. It didn't resonate in the right places, it just made his balls feel as though they were being subjected to a mild electric shock. It was never going to get him off. But the pencil-fine sleeve was more promising. By lifting up the cage as far as he could, he managed to press its tip against the sensitive underside of his helmet. When he turned on the power, his cock began to tingle pleasurably.

He felt goose pimples rising and his nipples instantly became erect. He slid a hand under his T-shirt and stroked them with his thumb. Inside the cage, his cock began to stiffen. The vibrator's slender tip buzzed away against his sensitive spot. It was divine yet tantalising at the same time. He longed for more direct stimulation; to be gripped in an experienced fist and wanked to a glorious orgasm. But it would do. It was the best thing that had happened to him in a fortnight and he was determined to make it work.

His lengthening cock was uncomfortably restricted. The plastic bit into his skin and he felt as though his balls were being compressed. It was a sensation he had grown familiar with over the last fortnight but he'd never got used to it. The CB2000 locked his penis in the downward position. Deprived of the room it needed to expand or change angle, his genitals were squeezed and squashed.

He'd known that he'd have to endure the discomfort if he was to make himself come, but he hadn't anticipated it would be so intense. This was the first time he'd allowed himself to become fully aroused. Until today, at the first sign of erection he'd found some way of making it go down.

Michael was sweating. Damp hair clung to his face. The vibrator's flexible tip buzzed away against his sweet spot. The sensation was delicious but the pain in his balls was getting hard to ignore. He closed his eyes and focused all his attention on the pleasure. The vibrator's electric hum seemed to fill the room.

His whole pelvis was alive now, tingling and tight. He fingered his stiff nipples, raking them with his nails. His burning nipples seemed to be directly connected to his cock, cranking his arousal up a notch. Better still, it distracted him from the pain in his balls.

He leaned over to the filing cabinet and found a pair of nipple clamps. He gasped as they bit into his flesh. The pain was intense and pure and powerful. He felt a warm rush of excitement in his brain. His heart was beating like a drum.

He pressed the vibrator's tip hard against his cock. It buzzed against his sensitive flesh, creating exquisite sensations. His cock was filling the cage now, pressing uncomfortably up against the plastic. His balls were compressed and painful, but the nipple clamps hurt so much he was almost able to ignore it. He concentrated on the pleasure, going deep inside himself and focusing his entire being on the buzz at the tip of his cock.

He yanked on the chain connecting the nipple clamps. The pain made him moan, a long, deep, animal note that burned his throat. Sweat dripped down his face. His T-shirt was damp at the armpits. His hand hurt from holding the vibe in place; his knuckles were white.

He wiped the sweat out of his eyes with his T-shirt. His chest was heaving. His nipples burned. Michael was getting desperate. He was exhausted and in pain. The vibrator buzzed away but the pleasure remained at the same level; tantalising rather than fulfilling. He knew that if he was going to come, the pleasure would have to build. But he'd been at it for ages and it just wasn't happening. It felt good, all right, but it was going nowhere.

His balls were going numb and they throbbed with an ache that was increasingly harder to ignore. It only really became bearable when he tugged on his nipple chain and gave himself so much pain that it blotted out everything else. The pleasure in his cock seemed a little stronger when he did that too, but he knew he couldn't sustain that level of discomfort long enough to come. He wasn't even close.

In frustration he turned up the speed on the vibe to maximum and tugged hard on the chain, stretching out his nipples. The metal teeth bit painfully into his flesh. His cock tingled where the vibrator touched it and he felt as though he might be getting close. He gave the chain another tug and his nipples burned with pleasure-pain. It was intense. It was incredible. Almost unbearable, but fantastic at the same time.

He was breathing hard through clenched teeth and, as he kept up the tension on the chain, he began to moan. The moan became a roar as pain filled his consciousness. His cock tingled with pleasure, but the tension that presaged orgasm eluded him.

His nipples were pulled out from his chest by the chain, their tips white. He could see the metal cutting into his flesh. The clamp on his right nipple began to slip off, scratching his skin. He let go of the chain and released his nipples, crying out in pain as sensation returned. He switched off the vibrator and threw it across the room. It was never going to work. He was wasting his time and all he'd done was get himself even more worked up.

If only there was some way to come that didn't involve touching himself. For the first time in his life, he envied his adolescent self. Like most boys his over-charged teenage libido had occasionally got the better of him and he'd come with no physical stimulation at all. He'd come in his trousers the first time a girl had let him touch her naked pussy, though he'd quickly got hard again and satisfied them both. He'd always put it down to extreme arousal and lack of experience.

His adolescent years had been characterised by unbearable frustration and very little opportunity for relief. He laughed softly, as he realised that was exactly the position he now found himself in. The ability to come without being touched would certainly come in handy now.

226

Michael looked down at his trapped cock, now returned to its non-aroused state. Maybe he could? It hadn't happened for twenty years or more, but who was to say he still couldn't do it? If it had happened once, it must mean that his body had the capacity to do it, mustn't it? He just had to find the way. As a teenager it had always been the result of extreme arousal denied an outlet. What was different now? It might work.

But it would take some extreme stimulation to work, he was sure of that. He thought about the Internet and its limitless supply of porn, but instantly realised he needed more. A real-life woman as horny as he was and eager to please him. Carrie, of course. Why hadn't he thought of her before? If he saw Carrie and subjected her to the most perverted and extreme stimulation his frustrated brain could come up with, maybe he'd get turned on enough to come. And, if he used the vibrator at the same time, maybe that would help. It was worth a try, anyway. What did he have to lose?

Carrie had been delighted to hear from him and had readily agreed to come over that evening. Michael had taken the Tube home, showered and shaved and changed into jeans and a T-shirt. He'd eaten a meal of pasta and salad with a glass of wine and was feeling much more relaxed.

Carrie was inevitably on time and Michael led her straight to his playroom.

'Let's start by taking your clothes off, shall we?' He watched as Carrie slipped out of her dress. Underneath she was wearing a white corset with two scooped cutouts under her breasts. Its lower edge terminated just above her naked pussy. Her stockings were white fishnet and her shoes were black platforms.

Her chest rose and fell visibly as she breathed. Her cheeks were red and her lips were plump and dark. He leaned forward and ran the tip of one finger along her slit. He held it up for her to see, glistening with her moisture.

'You're already aroused, aren't you?'

'Yes, Master, I am.' Carrie's cheeks burned with arousal and shame.

'I like the white undies, you look like a slutty bride.'

'Thank you, sir.' Carrie looked at the floor, knowing that a good submissive doesn't meet her master's gaze without permission.

'Let's get you restrained, then we can get down to business.' Michael went over to a drawer and took out a leather arm binder. It looked like a chaotic tangle of leather straps, but Michael's experienced fingers quickly made sense of them. A leather band fit around her neck, like a collar, and a long, stiffened strap passed down the centre of her back. Other straps were fitted to this horizontally and were buckled around both arms, binding them together. Her hands fitted into a leather pocket, like an oversized single mitten, and were fastened in place with the final strap.

With both arms bound behind her, Carrie's breasts were thrust unnaturally forward. Michael couldn't resist gripping both nipples and squeezing until she began to moan.

'Does that feel good?' He squeezed harder and Carrie let out a long, slow breath. 'I think I'll blindfold you. That way, you'll have no idea whether a touch will bring pleasure or pain. I find that uncertainty always makes things just a little more exciting, don't you?'

He chose a blindfold, then arranged a selection of implements and toys on a small trolley and covered it with a cloth. He wheeled the trolley over to Carrie and fitted the blindfold. Her body was taut with expectation and her arousal was palpable.

Michael took her arm and led her over to the spanking horse. He sat her down on its edge. She looked beautiful, blindfold and bound. A pink flush of arousal was visible on her throat and upper chest. Her nipples stood out hard and dark. He picked up a neurologist's wheel from the trolley and began to roll it over Carrie's breasts.

Designed to test the reactions of patients with nerve damage, it looked like a medical version of a pizza cutter except that the steel disk had a row of sharp teeth around its edge. It could be rolled gently, to provide stimulation, or hard, to provide pain.

Her breathing grew ragged and fast as the wheel made contact with her skin. She began to whimper softly as the wheel moved over her breasts. As he increased the pressure, she began to moan.

Michael felt his cock begin to stiffen inside its cage, pressing the plastic against his trapped balls. He had anticipated this by putting a pair of nipple clamps on the tray for his own use. He took off his T-shirt and fitted the metal clamps to his already abused nipples. He gasped as they bit into his flesh, but it did the trick. The discomfort in his confined genitals faded into a background awareness.

He picked up the wheel and ran it back and forth across Carrie's excited nipples. She let out a series of short yelps and her body trembled all over. He rolled the wheel down the centre of her chest and over her belly. Her chest heaved as the points made contact with her skin. Trailing it across her thigh, Michael watched her face respond. Her lips were parted and rosy. Sweat was beginning to film her brow. Her cheeks had darkened and seemed to glow in the overhead light.

She seemed to be possessed by a manic quiver. She was trembling all over. Her breathing was ragged and fast. A bead of sweat trickled down between her breasts and was lost in the thumbprint of her belly button. Michael laid the wheel quietly back on the tray, careful not to provide her with any auditory clues. He bent his head and, holding his breath in case the feel of it on her skin alerted her to his intentions, sucked a nipple into his mouth.

Carrie's body shuddered so violently he had to catch her by the arms to steady her. He bathed the swollen nub with his tongue and drew it into his mouth. Her skin was silky against his face. He began to bite and nibble, drawing his teeth along its length. His cock was tingling. The rigid grip of the cage was difficult to ignore but the constant pain from the clamps took the edge off it.

Carrie was moaning and panting. He treated her other nipple to the same loving attention, nipping and biting it.

'Oh my God. I think I'm going to die.' Carrie's voice was a husky whisper.

'No, you're not. Not yet, anyway.' He stood up and embraced her, leaning her head against his chest. He winced as her face touched his nipple clamps and he immediately changed position. Her skin was moist and clammy. Her long hair was damp at the hairline. He brushed it away from her face. He bent his head and kissed the top of her head.

When she was calmer he sat her up again and selected a pair of nipple clamps similar to the pair he was wearing but larger. Carrie had exceptionally large nipples. When she was aroused they stood out as fat as the tip of his thumb. The clamps he had chosen were broad enough to grip the entire width of her nipple. He knew that this was not only more painful, but more arousing; mimicking as it did the grip of a lover's fingers.

Carrie let out a long, whistling breath between clenched teeth as the first clamp bit into her flesh. When he fitted the second she gave a high-pitched cry, tilting back her head and wailing at the ceiling.

'Does that hurt, darling?' He pulled on the chain, making her moan.

'Yes, it does.' Carrie spoke between gasps.

'Shall I take them off, then?' He yanked the chain again. Carrie began to pant.

'No,' she finally managed to whisper.

Michael put his face next to her ear. He kissed her neck. Brushing a strand of her abundant hair out of the way, he whispered, 'Ask me nicely, then. Otherwise I'll take them off and send you home.'

Carrie turned her head and laid her cheek against his. Her skin was hot and damp against his face.

'Please, master. Leave the clamps on me.' Though her voice was soft, it was full of pleading and need.

Michael's cock was rigid now, straining against the plastic confinement of his device. His balls were trapped unpleasantly between the two rings. He took a step back and pulled on the chain attached to his clamps. They bit into his tender flesh. He let out an involuntary gasp and Carrie instantly responded. He could see her body become alert. She held herself still and listened.

He knew he was moaning and panting, but he couldn't help himself. He didn't want Carrie to know he was hurting himself; that would be too humiliating. And he certainly didn't want her to know about his CB2000. That was one of the reasons he had blindfolded her. She would know from the sounds he was making that he was aroused, but she'd have no idea of their cause and, most importantly of all, she wouldn't know that he had been denied access to his own cock. If things worked out, he'd achieve orgasm while she was still blind, then he'd let her come and send her home none the wiser.

So far, it seemed to be going well. He was far more aroused than his session with the vibrator had managed to achieve. A familiar knot of tension had settled in the base of his belly and the tip of his cock was tingling. So far, he'd managed to keep the distracting discomfort of the device at bay by using the nipple clamps. All he needed to do now was crank things up to the next level.

He helped Carrie to stand and led her over to the corner of the room where a leather suspension sling hung from chains attached to the ceiling.

'I'm going to put you in the suspension sling. You've done it before, so you know what to expect. I'm going to lift you up so that your bottom's sitting on the edge, then I want you to lie back and I'll lift up your legs and fasten them. Is that OK?'

Carrie nodded her agreement and Michael knew that she was so excited that she didn't trust her voice to work. He put a hand on each of her buttocks and lifted her. Carrie co-operated by parting her legs and wrapping them around his body. He hoisted her up until her bottom was on the edge of the leather sling, then manoeuvred her until she was sitting on it fully, her weight supported. She lay back slowly until she was flat on her back. Michael could see that her bound arms made it difficult, but with a little wriggling and repositioning she managed to get herself comfortable.

Michael lifted her left leg and attached her ankle to the cuff set into the chain support for the sling. He did the same to her right and stepped back to look at her. She lay flat in the sling, her legs parted obscenely.

Just looking at her and how vulnerable and exposed she seemed made his cock prickle with excitement. The pain between his legs was beginning to intrude so he yanked viciously on his chain. His nipples burned. He was sweaty and breathless. His body was a coiled spring, wound up by arousal and hunger, ready to explode.

He brought over the trolley and looked at the array of toys. He selected four medical clamps with long handles like scissors and laid them on the trolley's metal surface ready for use. He stood between Carrie's spread legs and pinched her right pussy lip near the top. She moaned and wriggled, making the sling swing. He

232

applied one of the clamps to her labia and locked the mechanism to the closed position. He fitted another clamp lower down then repeated the operation on the other side.

The clamps dangled down, stretching her lips apart. He pulled the clamps apart, pulling her cunt open, exposing its glistening, rosy, moist interior. His trapped cock gave a throb of protest and he released the clamps and fiddled with his nipple chain, causing the teeth to dig into his flesh. It did the trick; he soon forgot about the pain in his balls and was able to concentrate on his growing arousal.

Michael tore off some bondage tape and used it to stick the handles of the clamps on Carrie's pussy lips to her thighs, thus holding her cunt open for him. She looked like the victim of a bizarre medical experiment and her helplessness and acquiescence excited and moved him.

'Are you OK?' He stroked her belly and covered the mound of her pussy with his open hand. Her skin was warm and soft and he could just feel a hint of her moisture at the base of his palm.

'Yes, I'm fine. I'm a bit uncomfortable but it's incredible. Just promise me you'll let me come at the end of it!'

Michael laughed softly at the irony of her request. He swivelled his thumb without moving his hand and rubbed her clit. Her pussy was wet and hot and her clit was hard and swollen. She shivered as his thumb made contact.

'I'm going to find a few more toys. I'll leave you alone for a moment, but I promise I won't be long.' Michael trotted round the flat and began gathering up household objects that he could use to penetrate her. He soon had an armful of phallic-shaped implements, and in the kitchen he put them all into a carrier bag, along with a selection of suitable fruit and vegetables. He carried them back to the playroom and tipped the lot out on the trolley.

Michael's cock was filling its cage and was so rigid he could almost believe it might shatter the plastic. His balls were squashed and painful between the two rings but he was so highly aroused that the pain was overridden by the pleasure. His cock was tingling. He unzipped his jeans and pushed them down to his ankles. He stroked the tip with a fingernail.

He found an identical vibe to the one he had used earlier and positioned its tip. He used the roll of bondage tape to fix it into position, rolling it right around his body in case its weight dragged it away from his cock at the decisive moment. It felt so good that the pain in his balls faded to the back of his consciousness.

He picked an item from the trolley at random. It was a fat bottle of glue from his office desk with a rounded lid like a deodorant can. It was at least as fat as his cock, but Michael knew that the hard metal body would make it feel bigger. He slid the tip up against her wet hole and pushed it home in one movement. Carrie gasped as she felt it touch her, then shuddered as it filled her. The leather hammock rocked as she moved and Michael almost lost his hold on the glue bottle.

He fucked her slowly with the bottle, watching fascinated as it came out covered in her moisture. Carrie was panting and moaning and, from time to time, her body gave an involuntary jerk. He slid the bottle out and positioned it at her arsehole. Lubricated by her juices, he knew it would easily slip into her. He pushed it against her tight bud, wiggling it slightly, until it slid home.

Carrie's thighs were trembling. He could see her chest heaving as she gasped for breath. The sling wobbled. The vibrator buzzed away against his cock, making it tingle. His nipples were on fire and he longed to take off the clamps, but he knew he needed their stimulus to distract him from the discomfort in his balls.

Michael fucked her cunt with the handle of a wooden spoon, a small jar of mixed herbs, then a narrow marble rolling pin he used when making his own pasta. The rolling pin made her gasp from the cold as it entered her, but she clearly appreciated the intrusion. She writhed and wriggled, pressing her crotch against it. He rubbed her clit with his thumb, making her moan and squirm.

He slid out the rolling pin and laid it on the trolley. He picked up a banana and peeled it. He pushed the fruit's soft tip against her cunt and tried to enter her with it, but it was too soft and broke up immediately. He put the remains of the banana on the trolley and bent his head to lick her.

Carrie moaned as he lapped at her cunt. She rocked her hips, trying to build up a rhythm. But he ignored her movements and ate the remains of the banana. He opened a Mars bar he had found in the fridge and slid it into her. He began to fuck her with it. Within a couple of thrusts it had begun to melt inside her. When it withdrew it was covered in a thick film of melted chocolate and, very soon, began to wear away.

Michael's cock was alive with pleasure, tingling and sensitive. The vibrator's insistent buzzing seemed to reflect the urgency of his need. He fucked her with the chocolate until her body heat had turned it into a soggy mess. He put the remains down on the trolley and slid three fingers inside her.

She wailed as his fingers fucked her. The sling swung and rocked, making the chains creak. He drew out his chocolate-covered fingers and began to lick them. He brought them to her lips and smeared her face with the melted mess. She opened her mouth and licked at his fingertips, moving her head forward in an attempt to capture them in her mouth. He wiped his dirty fingers over her lips one more time then returned them to her cunt. He rubbed her clit hard with the flat of his fingers as he pushed his thumb into her hole.

Michael found a fat cucumber and pushed it inside her. It filled and stretched her and he was fascinated by the round shape her cunt made as it accommodated the vegetable. Carrie's thighs were trembling. Her chest was heaving. She was moaning and gasping, making incomprehensible sounds of delight. He slid the glue bottle out of her arse and chose an enormous courgette from the trolley. He squirted a generous dollop of lube on its tip and spread it over one end of the courgette. When he slid it into her arse, she began to wail, her legs thrashing against the chains, making the sling rock wildly.

She looked obscene and beautiful with her cunt lips clamped open and vegetables sticking out of her holes. Her face was smeared with melted chocolate and her body was filmed with sweat. Her breasts were thrust forward, her nipples hard and swollen where the clamps bit into them. He reached forward and removed both clamps at once. Carrie gasped and wriggled as pain hit her. The chains creaked and rattled as her cuffed legs flailed.

Michael gripped both her nipples and squeezed hard. She screamed and thrashed. His own nipples were on fire, throbbing and painful. His trapped balls ached and his cock chafed against the plastic. The vibrator buzzed away on its highest setting. It felt good, but it was going nowhere. He sighed in frustration. He pulled hard on his nipple chain and put his hand against the vibrator, pressing it harder against his sensitive spot.

Nothing. In fact, the vibe was beginning to feel painful rather than pleasurable. He switched it off and unwound the tape that held it in place. He dropped it all onto the trolley with a thud and pulled his trousers back up. Gingerly, he removed the clamps and moaned in pain as blood rushed back into his abused nipples. He slid the vegetables out of Carrie's cunt and dropped them onto the trolley. He released the clamps holding her lips apart and got on his knees between her legs.

He covered her cunt with his mouth and began to lick. She tasted of chocolate and banana and was so wet that his mouth slid easily over her engorged flesh. He spread her lips with his fingers, and concentrated on her clit. He knew it wouldn't take long. Her thighs were tense and quivering. Her clit danced in his mouth. She was moaning and sobbing. Chains creaked; the sling rocked.

His tongue moved against her taut clit. He drew it into his mouth and sucked on it, making her gasp. She was trembling all over. She was screaming and sobbing. The sound echoed around the room and filled Michael's brain. He wanted her to come more than anything. Denied an outlet himself, he was determined to give her the reward she deserved. She had to come for both of them and he had to make sure it was good.

Carrie let out a long, high wail. Her whole body became rigid. He thrust three fingers into her hole and instantly her cunt gripped them like a fist. She was coming. Her clit quivered in his mouth and he felt her muscles contract in wave after wave of pleasure. She was screaming and panting. Michael held on tight, keeping his moving mouth pressed against her clit. He could feel her coming around his fingers and on his tongue and it seemed so powerful he felt as though he could almost taste it.

He rode it out with her, holding on to her thighs when they started to tremble uncontrollably and moving round the sling to hold her when she began to cry. He unshackled her and lovingly removed the arm binder and took her to his bedroom to lie down.

When she'd recovered she showered; then Michael sent her home in a taxi. He'd have loved to sleep with her cradled in his arms as they usually did, but he couldn't risk her discovering his chastity device.

As he lay in his bed alone, sleep wouldn't come. He felt frustrated and ashamed. Jude had wanted him to endure his enforced celibacy, not to try to cheat. He felt as though he'd let her down and the failure burned. It was his first disobedience, but it was certainly spectacular. He'd never done things by halves, of course, but he had never expected to fail Jude – and himself – quite so thoroughly.

He wanted to obey her completely, he realised. Her approval meant everything to him. Without it, his life seemed meaningless. He needed her. The realisation thundered through his brain like a narcotic rush. A few short months ago, such an admission would have been impossible. He didn't need anyone. Women needed him, craved his company and the sexual outlet he could provide, but he had never known the hunger that they felt for him. The hunger that can only be satisfied by complete surrender.

But now, his hunger for Jude was endless. He had to be with her, to please her, to receive her punishment and her love. And it didn't really matter if she chose to give him pain or pleasure, because both were the symbols of her love. His need for her was as simple and natural as his need for air.

Suddenly he knew with a blinding clarity what it was she had wanted him to learn. It was so simple and obvious he couldn't understand why he hadn't worked it out before. He sat up in bed and looked at the clock. It was just before midnight. Jude would still be awake. And, even if she wasn't, surely it would be all right to wake her with his news. He dialled her number.

'Hi, Jude, I hope I didn't wake you?'

'Hello, Michael. No, you didn't. I've just got back from Dee's. Sadie's back from New York and they had a dinner party to celebrate. It's good to hear your voice, actually. I've been missing you. I should have told you that earlier.'

'I'm glad to hear that. I've felt as though I was on my own the last couple of weeks.' He lay down in bed and curled his body around the phone.

'I explained that, Michael. You've got to work it out on your own, I can't help you, I'm afraid. I'm sure it won't take much longer.'

'That's why I'm calling. I think I've worked it out at last. At least, I hope I have. It seems so obvious now I don't know why it took me so long.'

'Some things are like that. You have to go through the experience to truly understand. But do tell me what you've learned, I can hardly wait.' Jude's voice was tender and warm and Michael thought he could hear her need for him.

'I belong to you, Jude. Body and soul. You are in control of my body and my orgasm and that's just the way I want it to be.'

Jude didn't answer at once. Michael began to wonder if he'd got it wrong and a little flutter of anxiety began under his ribs.

'Are you still wearing the device?' she finally asked.

Michael realised he had been holding his breath. 'Yes – though I have to tell you I tried very hard to get out of it without actually breaking the lock and when that didn't work I tried to use a vibrator to make myself come.' He was ashamed, but he needed to confess. There could be no secrets, he knew that now.

'I expected you would.'

'And tonight I saw Carrie and did all sorts of wicked things to her and strapped the vibrator to my cock, but it still didn't work.'

Jude laughed. 'I'm glad to hear it. So you haven't come since you fucked me two weeks ago?'

'I haven't.'

'I'll drive straight over. There shouldn't be much traffic on the roads at this time of night. I'll be with you in a quarter of an hour.'

Fourteen

A few weeks later Jude and Michael drove to the Edge for the weekend. It was a baking hot day, but the car's air conditioning kept them cool. The sun shone into the car, warming Jude and making her feel alive. On the outskirts of Bristol, they stopped for lunch.

The pub was a timber-framed Tudor building with whitewashed walls and a crisscross pattern of dark wood. In the centre of the building there was an enormous arch leading to a courtyard where, in days gone by, the stagecoaches had passed through on the way to the stables.

Jude sat outside waiting for Michael to come back from the bar. Nearby, children laughed as they played on a climbing frame. A pigeon pecked crumbs at her feet. A small aircraft buzzed overhead. The sun warmed her back. It gave a cosy glow to the scarred wood of the table and made the grass gleam. Everything was bathed in light. Colours were altered and seemed to glow from within. It was the kind of light that painters always tried to capture on canvas. Jude couldn't help wondering how she'd achieve the effect with paint.

She was looking at the building, its white walls contrasting starkly with the black wood, when she spotted Michael coming through the door with their drinks on a tray. His dark hair shone in the light, the colour of a polished conker. His skin was tanned and, if Jude hadn't known him, she might have taken him for a Greek or Italian. There was something exotic and mysterious about him.

He walked with a sort of loping grace that Jude found extremely masculine. The muscles in his arms were standing out as he carried the tray and she could just see a glimpse of his belly over the top of his jeans. As he neared the table he noticed her looking at him and he stuck out his tongue. Jude laughed.

'They'll bring our lunch when it's ready.' Michael passed Jude her drink. He put both elbows on the table and leaned forward, his face close to hers. 'You were looking at me pretty hard when I brought out the drinks. You had this funny expression on your face I couldn't read.'

Jude laughed. 'You're a very beautiful man.' She smiled at him.

'You told me a long time ago that I was completely aware of the effect I have on women and you were right. But I'm really glad you think me beautiful. It makes me feel all tingly.'

'It's a funny thing, but I find you much more handsome now than when we first met. I was aware that you were attractive, of course, but somehow I felt as if there was something missing.'

Michael leaned closer. 'Of course there was. It might sound strange but I've only really felt complete since I gave myself to you. I'm a changed man on the inside. Why shouldn't it show on the outside?'

'Maybe you're right. I certainly think you're more open and relaxed now – more yourself. You've stopped hiding, perhaps.'

'How can I hide from you, Jude, when you've seen into my very soul?'

'It works both ways, you know. Absolute, total surrender.' She gazed at Michael. His dark eyes were gleaming with intensity. She put out a hand and stroked his cheek.

The waitress arrived with a tray of food. She was young and pretty, though her chin was speckled with acne. She was wearing a pair of high platform shoes completely unsuitable for someone who was on her feet all day. Jude thought she was probably a sixth-former earning a bit of extra cash.

'Enjoy your food.' She spoke with a strong West Country twang that Jude found charming.

'Thank you.'

The waitress wobbled away on her high heels.

'Have you anything in particular planned for the weekend or are we just going to enjoy ourselves in the dungeon?' Michael buttered a piece of French bread.

'I have. Tomorrow we're both going to get our nipples pierced.'

Michael raised an eyebrow. He let out a long, low whistle.

'With this nipple ring I thee wed?'

Jude laughed out loud. 'Something like that. And I've got something special lined up for this afternoon, but I'm keeping it as a surprise.'

'I can hardly wait. I've got something for you, Jude. I was going to wait until we got to the Edge, but I'd like you to have it now.'

He produced a flat, jeweller's box from his back pocket and laid it on the table. Jude wiped her fingers on her napkin and picked it up.

'Thank you.' She opened it. Inside was a silver bangle with a single ruby set into the band. 'It's the same as the cock ring I gave you, isn't it?' She lifted it out of the box and held it up to the light. 'And it's engraved.'

'Of course. Can you read it?'

' "For Jude, from your willing slave, Michael". Thank you, it's beautiful.' She put it on and held out her wrist, admiring it.

* * *

242

Later that afternoon at the cottage Jude went into the bedroom, ordering Michael to wait for her in the living room. She laid out an outfit she had brought from home for him on the bed and put some toys into a bag.

She stripped off her clothes and changed into some sexy underwear, knowing that the sight of it would arouse Michael. She put on self-supporting stockings, high heels, a red velvet corset with a frothy feather trim, and a red silk thong. Her breasts were bare and she darkened her nipples with a little rouge. She put her long, cotton summer dress back on over the top.

When she opened the door from the bedroom, Michael was leaning against the arm of the sofa, waiting.

'I thought you'd never come out again.' He smiled.

'I was just getting things ready. I've laid out some clothes in there for you. I want you to put them on and then we're going to walk to the folly.'

'The ruined church? I loved it there, so atmospheric.'

Jude nodded. 'That's why I thought of it. Go in and put the clothes on. I'll wait out here.'

Michael walked over to the bedroom door and opened it. Jude heard a soft gasp as he saw the clothes. He turned his head and smiled at her, his eyes communicating his excitement more eloquently than any words. He closed the door.

The wait was interminable. What was taking him so long? Jude had to remind herself that he wasn't used to putting on feminine clothes and the dress had buttons all the way up the back that were bound to provide a challenge. Her stomach was fluttering with excitement and her cheeks were hot. Finally, he opened the door and stepped into the room.

Michael was wearing an ivory satin wedding dress in the Victorian style. Its bodice was fitted and the skirt was draped into soft folds across the stomach and had a bustle at the back. The neckline was off-the-shoulder and the long sleeves terminated in a point at the back of each hand. On his feet were satin pumps made of the same silk. He lifted his skirt, to show her his white stockings. He pulled it up to his thigh to show her the frilly white garter he was wearing.

The look on his face left Jude in no doubt that he was delighted by his outfit. In his hand were his wig and the veil. He held them out to her.

'I think I need a bit of a hand with these.'

Jude sat him at the dressing table and fitted the wig and the headdress. When she had finished he looked beautiful. He looked at himself in the mirror and smiled.

'Well, I'd marry me. Shouldn't you have on a top hat and a tail coat?'

Jude shook her head. 'You should know by now I'm not the traditional type. I think you'll find I'm suitably dressed for the occasion. Shall we go?' She held out her hand.

Within ten minutes they were at the folly church. Michael opened the creaking door and they walked inside. She took his hand and led him up to the altar. It was dark and still. Above the roofless building they were sheltered by the green canopy of the trees. The sun shone through the branches, making the stone gleam like gold.

Jude stripped off her dress and Michael gasped when he saw her underwear.

'I take it you approve?' She twirled for him.

'You said you were suitably dressed for the occasion and, I must say, I've got to agree with you.'

'There's one thing missing, though. Jude opened the bag and took out her strap-on harness. She removed her thong and buckled it in place, sliding the small dildo inside it into her eager pussy. Her fake cock stood out brazenly in front of her. She reached into the bag for a riding crop and handed it to Michael. Silently, she went over to the altar and laid herself across the icy stone. Jude looked at him over her shoulder in wordless entreaty. Michael held up the crop and she nodded. She laid her cheek on the cold stone and closed her eyes.

She heard Michael's feet moving through the dried leaves as he got into position. She could hear his dress rustling. Birds were twittering. The crop swished through the air and cut her across both cheeks. She gasped.

'Again. Hard. Don't stop until I tell you.' Jude's voice was throaty and hoarse.

Michael whipped her again and again. The sound of the crop echoed around the building. Her arse was on fire. Her body jolted each time it made contact with her burning flesh, rubbing her nipples against the cold stone. She had begun to sweat. Her hair clung to her face. Endorphins rushed around her body. Blood thundered in her brain.

She could hear Michael grunting from the effort and, between strokes, his excited breathing. The silk of his dress swished from time to time and leaves crackled under his shoes. Her nipples were on fire. She could feel the moisture between her legs. She wriggled her hips, moving her pussy against the plastic dildo inside her.

The crop lashed against her arse and she felt the flash of agony that turned instantly to pleasure. Her buttocks tingled and burned with delicious pain. Her body jolted, mashing her nipples against the rough stone. Jude gripped the edge of the altar and lifted her chest away from the surface, until just her nipples were in contact.

Michael whipped her again and, this time, the jolt rubbed her excited nipples against the stone. She gasped.

'Harder and faster. Keep hitting me until I tell you to stop.' She was panting hard, making her voice sound breathy and broken.

He began to whip her rhythmically, bringing the crop down over and over again. Her arse burned all over. Each cut of the crop hurt more than the last, yet her body transformed it immediately into the most exquisite pleasure. She juddered with each blow and her nipples were being rubbed raw against the rough altar stone.

She was moaning and screaming. Sweat ran into her eyes. Her long hair clung to her back. Her whole body was trembling. Her cunt tingled. She tensed her muscles around the plastic cock and rocked her hips to rub her clit against the textured interior of the harness.

Jude could hear the sounds of the forest and the distant growl of the ocean. She could smell earth and wood and stone. The sound of the whip ricocheted around the church.

Michael was grunting and panting as he wielded the crop. His fractured breathing left her in no doubt that his arousal was as profound as her own. He brought the crop down repeatedly on her sore buttocks, delivering the punishment she had ordered. Jude wanted to come. The whipping and the dildo inside her had brought her to the edge. But she had plans and she didn't want to come before she had seen them through.

'Enough.'

Michael dropped the crop with a thud. He began to stroke her sore buttocks with both hands. She felt his mouth against her cheeks, kissing and licking her weals. She could feel his panting breath against her skin.

'You're all red.' He kissed her tender flesh as if his mouth might heal her.

'It's time to switch, I think.' Jude sat up. Michael helped her to climb down the steps that led up to the altar stone. She picked up the crop. 'I want you to lift up the back of your dress and bend over the altar.'

Michael instantly complied. Jude pulled his white frilly knickers down to his ankles. His body was taut with expectation; his buttocks were clenched. Jude could see the muscles in his thighs quivering. She drew back her arm and brought the crop down as hard as she could across the meat of both buttocks. Michael moaned and she could see his body jerk.

Jude whipped him repeatedly, slashing him across the arse and thighs until they were marked with livid red stripes. He was groaning and trembling. She was out of breath and hot. Her hair had become wild, damp tendrils about her face. She pushed them off her face with the back of her hand. A warm knot of pleasure and tension had settled in the base of her belly. Her nipples were sensitive and tingly.

Michael was panting. His arms held his bunched skirts out of the way. Jude could see his stiff cock between his parted thighs. It swung from side to side as the crop lashed him. He was groaning constantly, a long, single note of pain that changed in pitch when the crop struck. Across his buttocks, raised, scarlet weals formed. The scarlet was interspersed with areas of darkening purple bruises. Jude thought it looked beautiful.

Jude brought the crop down over and over again, breathing out through gritted teeth as it made contact. She could see a strand of glistening pre-come dangling from the end of his cock. His whole body was trembling. His fingers were white, where he gripped his skirts. As the crop landed he let out a sharp grunt. He hung his head and Jude could see he was exhausted and aroused to bursting point. She also knew that he would never ask for mercy, but would submit to her punishment until she decided to stop. She dropped the crop.

Jude stepped up behind him and, putting her hand between his legs, took his cock into her hand. Michael gasped. She smeared her fingers in the moisture drooling from its tip then worked her sticky fingers against his arsehole. She slid her hand under her harness and coated her fingers with her own juice, then used it to

247

grease the tip of her fake cock. She pressed it up against his dark hole then pushed forward, using her weight to enter him.

He let out a long, low moan as it slid home.

'Play with your cock. I want us to both come. I know I'm not going to take long.' She thrust the dildo inside him, circling her hips. Inside her, the smaller dildo swivelled pleasurably against her G-spot. Her clit rubbed against the knobbles inside the harness. Her nipples tingled. She bent over Michael's body and rubbed them against his back. She held on to his hips and began to fuck him hard and deep.

Michael lay bent over the altar, his face on one side, his cheek resting against the stone. His wig was damp around the hairline and clinging to his face. His bridal veil spread out against the stone like angel's wings. His left hand worked his cock. His eyes were closed and his lips were slightly parted. Jude knew that he was close, lost in his own imminent climax and her possession of him.

Sweat dripped down Jude's neck. Her corset clung, damply, to her body. Her aching nipples rubbed against the silk of Michael's bodice. Her clit tingled. Her heart was pounding. She was panting. Every nerve ending in her body was alive and working overtime. Her skin was hypersensitive. She was goose-pimply all over. Her skin prickled deliciously as it brushed against Michael's gown.

The warm glow in her belly was spreading through her body. Excitement pumped through her veins. Blood pounded in her ears. She was close; just a few more strokes and she'd be there. She gripped Michael's waist and fucked him hard, her hips moving like pistons. Her clit rubbed against the harness, the dildo filled her. One, two, three, she counted the thrusts. She was coming. She screamed. Her voice echoed around the church, sending birds flapping. Waves of pleasure crashed over her like a flood.

Underneath her, Michael's body began to tremble. He let out a deep, throaty moan and circled his hips, pressing his arse against her fake cock. Jude held on to him, riding out the waves of orgasm as he began to come. He quivered in her arms, moaning and grunting as his own orgasm overwhelmed him. Jude felt shivery and sensitive. Her nipples were rigid; she rubbed them against the fabric of his dress as she continued to come.

Michael's body began to relax and his eyes opened. He held up his spunk-covered hand for her to see, then licked it clean. When he was finished he smiled at her. Jude slid her latex cock out of him and took off her harness. Michael stood up, readjusted his dress, pulled up his knickers and sat down on the altar. From her bag, Jude retrieved a bottle of champagne and two crystal flutes. She held up the bottle for Michael to see.

'It might have got a bit warm since I took it out of the fridge at the cottage, I'm afraid.'

Michael smiled. 'I can't think of a better way to quench my thirst.'

Jude opened the bottle with a pop and set it down on the altar. She sat down on the stone beside Michael. She poured the champagne and handed him a glass.

'I know it isn't customary to consummate the marriage on the altar, but since we have, we ought to drink a toast, don't you think?' Jude picked up her glass and clinked it against his.

'I couldn't agree more. What should we drink to, do you think?' Michael took a sip.

Jude watched him drink. His wig was dishevelled and wonky and his face was damp with sweat, yet he still looked beautiful to her.

'We've come a long way together, haven't we?'

Michael nodded. 'You bet. And it's a journey I never thought I would even begin, I must admit.'

'But you're glad you did?'

'More than I can possibly say. When we first met – it seems like ages ago now – you reminded me what William Blake had said about the road of excess leading to the palace of wisdom. Do you remember?'

Jude nodded. 'Yes, it's always been a favourite quote of mine.'

'Well, I feel as though I've been walking down that road with you at my side.'

'That's lovely, thank you. Shall we drink to that, then?'

'Yes; why not?' Michael raised his glass. 'To the road of excess . . .'

They drank their champagne.

The leading publisher of fetish and adult fiction

TELL US WHAT YOU THINK!

Readers' ideas and opinions matter to us. Take a few minutes to fill in the questionnaire below and you'll be entered into a prize draw to win a year's worth of Nexus books (36 titles)

Terms and conditions apply – see end of questionnaire.

1. Sex: Are you male ☐ female ☐   a couple ☐?

2. Age: Under 21 ☐ 21–30 ☐ 31–40 ☐ 41–50 ☐ 51–60 ☐ over 60 ☐

3. Where do you buy your Nexus books from?

☐ A chain book shop. If so, which one(s)?

_____

☐ An independent book shop. If so, which one(s)?

_____

☐ A used book shop/charity shop
☐ Online book store. If so, which one(s)?

_____

4. How did you find out about Nexus Books?

☐ Browsing in a book shop
☐ A review in a magazine
☐ Online
☐ Recommendation
☐ Other _____

5. In terms of settings which do you prefer? (Tick as many as you like)

☐ Down to earth and as realistic as possible
☐ Historical settings. If so, which period do you prefer?

_____

☐ Fantasy settings – barbarian worlds

- ☐ Completely escapist/surreal fantasy
- ☐ Institutional or secret academy
- ☐ Futuristic/sci fi
- ☐ Escapist but still believable
- ☐ Any settings you dislike?

_____

- ☐ Where would you like to see an adult novel set?

_____

6. In terms of storylines, would you prefer:

- ☐ Simple stories that concentrate on adult interests?
- ☐ More plot and character-driven stories with less explicit adult activity?
- ☐ We value your ideas, so give us your opinion of this book:

_____

_____

_____

7. In terms of your adult interests, what do you like to read about? (Tick as many as you like)

- ☐ Traditional corporal punishment (CP)
- ☐ Modern corporal punishment
- ☐ Spanking
- ☐ Restraint/bondage
- ☐ Rope bondage
- ☐ Latex/rubber
- ☐ Leather
- ☐ Female domination and male submission
- ☐ Female domination and female submission
- ☐ Male domination and female submission
- ☐ Willing captivity
- ☐ Uniforms
- ☐ Lingerie/underwear/hosiery/footwear (boots and high heels)
- ☐ Sex rituals
- ☐ Vanilla sex
- ☐ Swinging

☐ Cross-dressing/TV
☐ Enforced feminisation
☐ Others – tell us what you don't see enough of in adult fiction:

_____

_____

_____

8. Would you prefer books with a more specialised approach to your interests, i.e. a novel specifically about uniforms? If so, which subject(s) would you like to read a Nexus novel about?

_____

_____

_____

9. Would you like to read true stories in Nexus books? For instance, the true story of a submissive woman, or a male slave? Tell us which true revelations you would most like to read about:

_____

_____

_____

10. What do you like best about Nexus books?

_____

_____

11. What do you like least about Nexus books?

_____

_____

12. Which are your favourite titles?

_____

_____

13. Who are your favourite authors?

_____

_____

14. Which covers do you prefer? Those featuring:
(tick as many as you like)

☐ Fetish outfits
☐ More nudity
☐ Two models
☐ Unusual models or settings
☐ Classic erotic photography
☐ More contemporary images and poses
☐ A blank/non-erotic cover
☐ What would your ideal cover look like?

_____

15. Describe your ideal Nexus novel in the space provided:

_____

_____

_____

_____

16. Which celebrity would feature in one of your Nexus-style fantasies? We'll post the best suggestions on our website – anonymously!

_____

THANKS FOR YOUR TIME

Now simply write the title of this book in the space below and cut out the questionnaire pages. Post to: Nexus, Marketing Dept., Thames Wharf Studios, Rainville Rd, London W6 9HA

Book title: _____

TERMS AND CONDITIONS

1. The competition is open to UK residents only, excluding employees of Nexus and Virgin, their families, agents and anyone connected with the promotion of the competition. 2. Entrants must be aged 18 years or over. 3. Closing date for receipt of entries is 31 December 2006. 4. The first entry drawn on 7 January 2007 will be declared the winner and notified by Nexus. 5. The decision of the judges is final. No correspondence will be entered into. 6. No purchase necessary. Entries restricted to one per household. 7. The prize is non-transferable and non-refundable and no alternatives can be substituted. 8. Nexus reserves the right to amend or terminate any part of the promotion without prior notice. 9. No responsibility is accepted for fraudulent, damaged, illegible or incomplete entries. Proof of sending is not proof of receipt. 10. The winner's name will be available from the above address from 9 January 2007.

Promoter: Nexus, Thames Wharf Studios, Rainville Road, London, W6 9HA

NEXUS NEW BOOKS

To be published in February 2006

AQUA DOMINATION
William Doughty

Just why would Mary go back to David and his bizarre bathroom? What could be crazier than designing and equipping a luxurious bathroom for the soapy, slippery domination of women? Yet she has returned to submit to watery domination, while dressed in fetish garments of plastic and rubber. And having seen the bathroom, can her friends – Jack, Carol and Faye – resist plunging into such slippery submission?

£6.99 ISBN 0 352 34020 7

TOKYO BOUND
Sachi

James Burke's mastery of the Tao of sex made him a prince of the Excalibur, a Tokyo host club that catered to wealthy women with particular tastes. He brought intense pleasure through the universal force of chi. His world was sublime until a secret society learned of his skill and sought the dark side of his Tao, the power to inflict pain. They would have it or destroy him.

£6.99 ISBN 0 352 34019 3

PLEASING THEM
William Doughty

Robert Shawnescrosse introduces his young and beautiful wife to the peculiar delights he shares with his carefully selected servants at the most peculiar house in Victorian England. Yet he has an even darker secret which requires everyone at the manor to work harder to satisfy the strange desires of three men of dubious integrity.

Why does the puritanical Mt Blanking send young ladies into a muddy pond wearing only their hats? Can the wicked Sir Horace ever obtain the satisfaction he craves through cruelty? And why is David making such strange demands? How can Robert, Jane and their servants offer pleasures extreme enough to please them?

£6.99 ISBN 0 352 34015 0

If you would like more information about Nexus titles, please visit our website at www.nexus-books.co.uk, or send a stamped addressed envelope to:
  Nexus, Thames Wharf Studios,
  Rainville Road, London W6 9HA

NEXUS BACKLIST

This information is correct at time of printing. For up-to-date information, please visit our website at www.nexus-books.co.uk

All books are priced at £6.99 unless another price is given.

ABANDONED ALICE	Adriana Arden 0 352 33969 1	☐
ALICE IN CHAINS	Adriana Arden 0 352 33908 X	☐
AMAZON SLAVE	Lisette Ashton 0 352 33916 0	☐
ANGEL	Lindsay Gordon 0 352 34009 6	☐
THE ANIMAL HOUSE	Cat Scarlett 0 352 33877 6	☐
THE ART OF CORRECTION	Tara Black 0 352 33895 4	☐
AT THE END OF HER TETHER	G.C. Scott 0 352 33857 1	☐
BARE BEHIND	Penny Birch 0 352 33721 4	☐
BELINDA BARES UP	Yolanda Celbridge 0 352 33926 8	☐
BENCH MARKS	Tara Black 0 352 33797 4	☐
BINDING PROMISES	G.C. Scott 0 352 34014 2	☐
THE BLACK GARTER	Lisette Ashton 0 352 33919 5	☐
THE BLACK MASQUE	Lisette Ashton 0 352 33977 2	☐
THE BLACK ROOM	Lisette Ashton 0 352 33914 4	☐
THE BLACK WIDOW	Lisette Ashton 0 352 33973 X	☐

----- ✂ --------------------------

Please send me the books I have ticked above.

Name ....

Address ....

....

....

.... Post code ....

Send to: **Virgin Books Cash Sales, Thames Wharf Studios, Rainville Road, London W6 9HA**

US customers: for prices and details of how to order books for delivery by mail, call 1-800-343-4499.

Please enclose a cheque or postal order, made payable to **Nexus Books Ltd**, to the value of the books you have ordered plus postage and packing costs as follows:

UK and BFPO – £1.00 for the first book, 50p for each subsequent book.

Overseas (including Republic of Ireland) – £2.00 for the first book, £1.00 for each subsequent book.

If you would prefer to pay by VISA, ACCESS/MASTERCARD, AMEX, DINERS CLUB or SWITCH, please write your card number and expiry date here:

....

Please allow up to 28 days for delivery.

Signature ....

Our privacy policy

We will not disclose information you supply us to any other parties. We will not disclose any information which identifies you personally to any person without your express consent.

From time to time we may send out information about Nexus books and special offers. Please tick here if you do *not* wish to receive Nexus information.   ☐

----- ✂ --------------------------